FLAGS
ON THE
BAYOU

Also by James Lee Burke

James Lee Burke is the author of many novels, and the critically-acclaimed, bestselling Detective Dave Robicheaux series. He won the Edgar Award for both *Cimarron Rose* and *Black Cherry Blues and Sunset Limited* was awarded the CWA Gold Dagger. *Two for Texas* was adapted for television, and *Heaven's Prisoners* and *In the Electric Mist* for film. Burke has been a Breadloaf Fellow and Guggenheim Fellow, has been awarded the Grand Master Award by the Mystery Writers of America and has been nominated for a Pulitzer award. He lives with his wife, Pearl, in Missoula, Montana.

www.JamesLeeBurke.com

FLAGS
ON THE
BAYOU

JAMES
LEE BURKE

ORION

First published in Great Britain in 2023 by Orion Fiction,
an imprint of The Orion Publishing Group Ltd,
Carmelite House, 50 Victoria Embankment
London EC4Y 0DZ

An Hachette UK Company

1 3 5 7 9 10 8 6 4 2

A CIP catalogue record for this book is
available from the British Library.

ISBN (Hardback) 978 1 3987 1550 9
ISBN (Export Trade Paperback) 978 1 3987 1551 6
ISBN (eBook) 978 1 3987 1553 0

Printed in Great Britain by Clays Ltd, Elcograf, S.p.A.

MIX
Paper from
responsible sources
FSC
www.fsc.org
FSC® C104740

www.orionbooks.co.uk

To Toby Thompson,
a musician, singer, poet, and a stand-up journalist of
the old school whose work has not only captured the heart
of the New West but of America itself.
Stay on that old-time rock and roll, partner.

1

WADE LUFKIN

Morning on the Lady of the Lake Plantation can be a grand experience, particularly in the late fall when the sky is a clear blue and the wind is blowing in the swamp, Spanish moss lifting in the trees, and thousands of ducks quacking as they end their long journey to the South. However, in this era of trouble and woe it is difficult to hold on to these poignant moments, as was the case last evening when our Christian invaders from the North lit up the sky with airbursts that disintegrated into curds of yellow smoke and descended on the grass and swamp in configurations that resembled spider legs.

A twisted piece of hot metal landed no more than ten feet from the chair in which I sat and the artist's easel on which I painted, but I did not go inside the house. I would like to tell you that I am brave and inured to the damage cannon fire can wreak on the bodies of both human beings and animals. But that is not the case. There's a Minie still parked in my left leg, and I need no convincing about the damage Billy Yank can do when he gets up his quills. The truth is I both fear the wrath of our enemies, as I fear the wrath of God, and at the same time wish that I could burn inside its flame and be cleansed of the guilt that I never thought would be mine.

I went to Virginia in '61, with the Eighth Louisiana Infantry and a promise from our officers that I would serve as a surgeon's assistant and never shed the blood of my fellow man.

Oh yes, in my innocence I was certain I would never bear the mark of Cain. Even if my superiors broke their pledge and ordered me to arm myself and fire into the ranks of boys against whom I bore no animus. I sawed limbs and stacked them in piles at First and Second Manassas and especially at Sharpsburg, where the Eighth Louisiana was mowed down in a cornfield near Dunker Church. Through a window I saw these poor fellows fall, and I went into the fray and dragged them inside, North and South, the living and the dead, and prayed for all of us.

Sharpsburg told us you do not have to die in order to go to Hell.

Then winter came and we began to tire of the mud and the cold and the gray shortness of the days and the fact that the Yanks were not going to give it up and go home, as our leaders had told us. Unfortunately, an army that is not marching or fighting becomes restless and troublesome. I took a stroll along a stream in a snow-covered forest of bare trees, and saw a fellow my age sitting on top of a boulder, reading a book, a black felt hat tied down on his head, a gray blanket stiff with frost on his shoulders. A few feet away a rifle was propped against a tree, a bayonet mounted on the tip of its barrel.

The soldier on the rock was glued to his book, a collection of Robert Browning's poems. I had coffee beans in a tobacco pouch in my shirt pocket and two tin cups and a half loaf of bread and a chunk of ham in my haversack. I also carried my Bible there. It was one week from Christmas. In the dreariness of this particular day

I thought how fine it would be to share my food and my Scripture with a fellow solider, one who loved the same poems as I, one probably aching to see his family, just as I was.

"If you want to gather some twigs and get a fire started, I have the makings of a holiday treat," I said.

He didn't reply. His book was opened in front of his face, hiding his features, as though he were masked. "I hope I didn't disturb you," I said.

He lowered his book slowly. Then my gaze drifted to his rifle. It was a Springfield. In '62 Springfields were seldom seen among the boys in butternut.

"I'm unarmed, sir," I said.

He closed his book without putting a marker between the pages, and set it beside him on the boulder, his face shadowed under the brim of his hat. He let the blanket slide from his shoulders and reached inside his coat. It was navy blue, with gold epaulets sewn on the shoulders. He pulled a small revolver from his waist and leveled it at me.

"I mean you no harm," I said.

He cocked the hammer with his thumb.

"Please, sir," I said, my voice breaking.

There was no anger in his eyes. But there was no mercy, either. Or anything, for that matter.

"Sir, I'll leave. I'm a surgeon's assistant. I'm not a combatant."

I don't know if his hand was shaking or if the revolver slipped, but it fired nonetheless, and I felt the ball rip through the side of my coat. The Yankee officer seemed as startled as I, but that did not stop him from continuing the accidental or wanton choice that would change both our lives forever. He aimed with both hands and pulled the trigger. The hammer snapped dryly on a dead cap.

He looked dumbfounded, or frightened, and I wondered if he had ever fired a shot in anger. I had no time, however, for analytical thoughts. My heart was thundering so loud I thought my head would come off.

Then a creature inside me I didn't recognize took hold of both my body and my mind. "You bloody bastard," I said, running for the rifle. "You'll pay for that."

He tried to cock the revolver with both thumbs. But I had his Springfield now, and I drove the bayonet into his chest, working it upward through bone and muscle and into a lung. I felt his weight curl over the blade, even as he tried to push himself off the blood groove with his bare hands, even as he slid to his knees, his eyes bulging as big and brown as polished acorns, his hands trying to clasp the rifle's barrel.

But I wasn't finished. I pulled the bayonet from the initial wound and aimed at his heart and plunged it into him a second time and leaned hard on the stock until the tip of the bayonet exited his back and pinned him to the snow. His mouth opened slowly and formed a cone, as though he were resting, then his arms flopped away from his body, like a crucified Christ. In his dying he never uttered a word.

I try not to revisit my war experiences and to pretend that the fighting will stay in the East and eventually go away. But I know better. And so do the Africans. In all the parishes, they have been told not to sing in the fields, because singing is the Africans' telegraph, and often their hymns are not what they seem. But how ironic. We claim to be the superior race, yet we fear people who cannot sign their names or count past ten.

In June of 1861 the citizens of St. Martin Parish hanged six slaves and one white man who were charged with planning an insurrection. Others were "corrected." That was the word the local paper used. The article did not use the word "slave," either. We have manufactured a lexicon of hypocrisy that allows us to call slaves "servants." I feel shame when I shake hands with men who I'm sure participated in the hangings and flee their presence when I see them at my church.

I get no peace, though. I voted for Mr. Lincoln, but I do not agree with his policies. After the occupation of New Orleans, the American flag was immediately hung from the Mint, and a mob immediately ripped it down. A riverboat gambler was caught wearing a tiny piece of the flag as a boutonniere, and General Butler, a malignant pile of whale sperm if there ever was one, was allowed to hang this poor fellow from the Mint's flagstaff.

I'm afraid changing my geography will not alleviate my problem, though. I think the real enemy is the simian that still lives inside our skin. Voltaire had no answer for mankind other than the suggestion that we tend our own gardens and let the lunatics go about their way. The same with Charles Dickens. Remember Mr. Dick? He says to David Copperfield, "It's a mad world. Mad as Bedlam, boy!" Mr. Dick had been in Bedlam and wore ink quills stuck in his hair in case he needed to write down a thought or two. Read what he has to say about the mobs who attend public executions. I have the feeling Mr. Dickens was a lonely man.

Enough of this. I am a man with no country and no cause, a sojourner at my uncle's plantation, a painter of birds. But I have become intrigued by a young Creole woman named Hannah Laveau. She was purchased by my uncle one year ago at the slave market in New Orleans, just before the city surrendered, then rented out as what is called a wage slave to an acquaintance on Spanish Lake.

The rental lasted less than a month. My uncle drove his own carriage to Spanish Lake and fetched her to his home in St. Martin Parish and would say nothing about the matter. There were many rumors about his friend, all of them bad. But my uncle would not discuss them, and he gave the young woman a cabin to herself on the edge of the swamp. My uncle is a somber, silent man I have never understood, although he has been very kind to me.

Until last evening I had only a few encounters with the young slave woman, all in passing. Supposedly she spoke Spanish and French and had been a slave in the West Indies, where every kind of cruelty and hardship seemed to have been visited upon the Africans who were brought there. Some of my uncle's Africans say she has magical powers. However, they tend to witness magical events with regularity in order to survive the world the Middle Passage has fashioned for them. Yesterday evening, when the Yankees started bursting cannonballs above our heads, I learned that she was of a strange mix, the kind an authoritarian society does not countenance for very long.

When the first shell exploded, my uncle and his family went into the cellar, and the Africans huddled in their cabins by the swamp's edge. The sun was red, the shadows of the slash pines as sharp as razor cuts. But one shadow that fell across me and my easel was certainly not that of a tree.

"Ain't Master afraid of cannon?" a voice with a French accent said.

I twisted my head around and looked up at her face. She had a shawl over her head, like a cowl. But I could see her features. Her skin was a dark, golden color, her eyes the greenish blue you see in coral pools in the Caribbean.

"I am not a 'master,'" I said.

"Then what are you?"

A slave, or a "servant," in our culture does not speak in the second person to white people. A shell burst above the swamp, and a second later shrapnel struck the water and made a sound like a child throwing gravel. "I'm an unemployed soldier," I said. "Can you read?"

"Yes, suh."

"I've misplaced my eyeglasses and my leg hurts. Can you fetch Mr. Audubon's book *Birds of America* from the table behind the front door? Please bring a chair for yourself."

"I need to start the fires in the hearths, suh. That's part of my job."

"We don't need to notify the Yankees of our presence, Miss Hannah."

"You should not call me 'Miss,' suh."

"I can call people what I wish."

The light was drawing down in the sky, but I could see her eyes inside the cowl she had made of her shawl. They were looking straight into mine.

"Your uncle can sometimes be strict," she said.

"Do I have to yell at you, Miss Hannah?" I replied. But I smiled when I said it. "Bring a lamp with the book and the chair. Make two trips if you have to."

"No, suh, I cain't do that."

She began to walk away. Her dress was to her ankles, her dark overcoat belted tightly around her waist, her leather shoes old and probably as hard as iron. The sun had set the western sky aflame. I thought I heard the ripple of small-arms fire, like the popping of Chinese firecrackers. She stopped and turned around, as though finally aware that the weapons of liberators kill the innocent as well as those who serve the Prince of Darkness. But I was wrong.

"Your uncle took me away from the bad man on Spanish Lake," she said. "I was a cook with Southern soldiers at Shiloh Church. My li'l boy was with me there." Her voice was cracking.

"Pardon?"

"I lost him in the smoke and the shooting and the tents burning." Her eyes were wet. The booming of cannon and the explosion of shells had increased, and someone was moaning in one of the cabins. "I don't know where my li'l Samuel is, suh."

"I'm sorry, Hannah."

She walked toward me, as though I were the source of her unhappiness, the redness in the sky mirrored in her eyes. "I'll get him back. My life is not important. I'm not afraid of Yankees or Rebels. I'll die for my li'l Samuel."

"Don't say these things to others. You understand me?"

"I'll get your book, suh."

"Please answer me, Hannah. I'm your friend."

She walked away. The cannon had stopped, and the mallards resumed their quacking in the shelter of the swamp. The sun was an ember on the horizon, the air damp and as dark as a bruise. I blinked and rubbed my eyes. She seemed to have vanished into the gloom.

2

PIERRE CAUCHON

I mposing the law on both the paddy rollers and the darkies in three parishes isn't easy. The former sometimes get carried away and the latter just don't seem to learn, *unless*—

Don't know what "unless" means? It's better you don't.

It's not quite sunrise, the fog rolling out of the swamp, glistening like a rainbow, but up ahead I can hear the darkies already in the cane at Lady of the Lake Plantation, chopping and stacking, with no singing in the background, which means Mr. Lufkin's darkies have got the word and will not be confusing themselves with jackrabbits itching to get a lot of gone between here and the Atchafalaya Basin.

Last week three of them in New Iberia stole a jug of syrup and a bag of corn and a cane knife and took off, but the dogs and paddy rollers pulled them down from a tree deep in the swamp and subjugated them to a correctional understanding or two. I don't like working through the right words on this subject. The kind that are acceptable. Put it this way. The correctional understanding changed the runaways' perspective.

I'm here about only one darky. Hannah Laveau is her name. I had trouble with her two or three times, particularly when she got rented out for wages to Mr. Minos Suarez on Spanish Lake outside New Iberia. He told me she was crazy and stirring up the other darkies and would I have a talk with her. The truth be known, Old Man Suarez can't keep his member buttoned up and everybody knows it. I was just about to hint that to him and probably get myself in trouble, when he told me she was an insurrectionist. If you want to light a fire around here, that word will do it. Ask the ones who got dropped from a rope in St. Martinville two years back.

It pains me to be used like this. Truth be known, I'm fond of her. She cooked for our boys at Shiloh. That's right. Louisiana units took colored servants with them when they got blown apart at Owl Creek. She's pretty, too. No question about that.

I get off my horse and lead it into the cane. Not one darky looks up from his work. The overseer, known as Biscuits-and-Gravy Comeaux, is a man who never missed a meal. He always has tobacco in his mouth and spits a stream every sixty seconds. I've timed it. Scattered on the ground with the cane leaves are half-moon slivers of iron that look like the parings from a horse's hoof. They are the remnants of exploded cannonballs.

"Good morning, Biscuits," I say.

"Good morning to you, sir," he answers.

I glance at the slivers of metal on the ground. "It looks like the blue-bellies kept y'all occupied last night."

Biscuits beams. "I ain't sure they're blue-bellies. I hear Jayhawkers or Red Legs or whatever they call themselves captured a cannon or two. What brings you out?"

"Is Mr. Lufkin up?"

"Better question is did he ever go to bed," he says, then laughs at his own joke.

Mr. Lufkin is known for his long work hours. Both for him and everybody on his plantation. Supposedly, at age nineteen he came to Louisiana from Pennsylvania and fought at the side of Andrew Jackson at the Battle of New Orleans. He also started buying everything he could get his hands on, particularly slaves, no matter the gender or the age, as long as they were capable of reproduction. As an investment, they're a sure bet, unless they get themselves killed or commit suicide. An adult sells for anywhere between eight hundred and twelve hundred dollars. That's in gold.

"Know a darky named Hannah Laveau?"

"Oh, yes," Biscuits says.

"Has she been any trouble to you?"

"No, not with me," he replies, then lets his eyes wander. There are rings of fat on his neck; his skin is pink, his whiskers white under his chin.

"But the story is a little larger?" I say.

He spits a stream of tobacco juice on the ground. "She's a gris-gris woman."

"So?"

"The other niggers listen to her."

A wind begins blowing out of the swamp, and I can see the moss straightening on hundreds of tupelo trees all the way to the Gulf and the southern horizon.

"It looks like it might be whipping up a storm, huh?" Biscuits says.

"Could be," I reply.

He spits again, this time hitting the ankle of a big-breasted black woman hefting a bundle of cane onto the wagon. Her face turns to stone; her eyes are already dead. I wouldn't try to guess what's in her head.

I swing up on my mare and ride up the lane to the main house of Lady of the Lake Plantation. My horse is a Missouri Fox Trotter; they were bred for planters that spend long days in the saddle and need a horse that knows how to step through the rows without wearing out the planter's butt. Mine is a sorrel, fifteen hands high, and a mighty handsome horse who I admit I dearly love. I named her Varina. That's the name of Jefferson Davis's wife.

The main house is on a knoll, with a fine view of the wetlands and the electric storms over the Gulf. The house is exceptional in another way, too. It's the kind you see in the West Indies, with a wrap-around verandah and ceiling-high windows and ventilated shutters on the second story and chimneys on each side, smoke stringing from both of them. It's a house that was made to breathe.

I get down and tether my horse to an iron hitching post and go to the front door and knock. The porch and the columns that support the verandah are brick, not concrete, and in deep shadow, even though the sun is above the trees now. No one comes to the door. I take out my watch and wait one minute, then knock again.

Mr. Lufkin opens the door slowly, as though it's an unpleasant task. He's dressed in a black suit and a gray vest and slippers without socks and a gold watch that hangs from his neck. His face could have been carved from balsa wood; his hair is uncut and dirty blond, the color of rope, and hangs in his face; the irritability in his eyes is daunting. "What is it?" he says.

I remove my hat. "I'm Constable Pierre Cauchon, Mr. Lufkin. I have a report from Mr. Suarez of New Iberia. He owns a plantation on Spanish Lake."

"I know who Mr. Suarez is and where he lives. What do you want?"

"To discuss any knowledge you may have about a servant named Hannah Laveau. The issue is talk about insurrection."

"I see. Go around to the back."

"Sir?"

"Are you deaf?"

He closes the door in my face. I put on my hat and walk around the side of the house. Two black women are washing clothes in a tub. They're both giggling. I give them one look and their faces drain. Mr. Lufkin opens the back door. I want him to explain what has just happened, to say, *You'll have to pardon me, Mr. Cauchon, we're cleaning the house right now*, or *We're repairing some damage done by Yankee cannon*, or *Mrs. Lufkin is ill and not dressed now*, anything that would undo the insult that he has just delivered me.

"Are you going to come in or not?" he says from the open door.

"Thank you," I say as I remove my hat again and step into the kitchen. I pull the door shut behind me.

"What's this about insurrection?" he asks.

"It's simply a charge that has been made, Mr. Lufkin. Maybe it's not valid. I know the servant involved. She seems like a good—"

I don't get to finish my sentence. "Come in here, Hannah," he calls out, his eyes on me.

Hannah appears in the doorway, holding a broom, a yellow kerchief with red dots on it tied around her head.

"Have you been talking about rebellion and such?" Mr. Lufkin says.

"No, suh, I ain't."

"You've got your answer," Mr. Lufkin says. "Now be on your way."

My face is hot, my mouth dry. I grew up in a shack with a dirt floor by a turpentine mill, and we ate greens and fatback when we could get them. My daddy died of yellow fever and my mother was blind, but she taught me how to read, by God. I know if I leave this room without making this old man take back his contempt, I'll never be the same, like an arm or leg was sawed off me and I was left to flop around on the side of the road.

Here goes, I tell myself. "Mr. Suarez gave me information I am quoting to you. I would hate to return to his home and call him a liar."

"I said no such thing."

"He's either telling the truth or he's not."

"You listen. Mr. Suarez is a business acquaintance, not a friend. Regardless, I do not discuss acquaintances or friends with strangers. This discussion is over."

"I am giving you my word, sir," I say. "I don't like to see it treated in such a casual way."

"Sir, you do not have a *word*. You are white trash. Please leave."

Hannah Laveau's eyes are lowered, her shoulders rounded, her hands resting on the staff of the broom. Then, for just a few seconds, she looks at me. I do not know what she's thinking. Does she want me to sass him? Or is she enjoying my humiliation? Why are her hands curved tight on the broom? Why do the light in her greenish-blue eyes and the shine on the tops of her breasts make me ashamed and aching inside in a way I have never experienced? Why should I care about a darky?

I stare at Mr. Lufkin. It's obvious I disgust him. For no reason. Just because I am who I am.

"I didn't mean to offend you, Mr. Lufkin," I say.

He opens the door for me, breathing through his mouth, a cloth in his hand, protecting himself from the place where I touched the door.

I feel small and my head is dizzy, as though I'm walking on the deck of a boat, as I descend the back steps, even though I am six feet one in height. I would prefer to be disemboweled and have my entrails set afire, as was done to felons in ancient times, rather than re-live the last ten minutes of my life. Fool that I am, I still hope Old Man Lufkin will call me back and say he was in a bad mood and smile and wave goodbye. But when I turn around he looks straight at me, his eyes as hard as marbles, then pulls the curtain across the glass, like a headsman done for the day.

I mount Varina and jerk the bit in her mouth, and needlessly hit her with the quirt, shameful and cruel man that I am.

3

HANNAH LAVEAU

Master Lufkin wasn't fair to Mr. Cauchon, no, but that's because he cain't forgive himself for renting me out to Master Suarez. On my second night on his plantation, Master Suarez gave me the best cabin in the quarters and said I could have anything else I wanted if maybe in a couple of days he could visit with me after the field workers were done and the sun was down on the lake and the wind had blown away the mosquitoes and the workers had washed themselves and eaten their supper and gone to bed, the way the servants do, and then him and me would talk about the West Indies. Then maybe I could see my way to lie with him, and after we were done he would give me any job I wanted and buy me nice things, and if I was afraid I would have a child, I should remember it would be sired by him and always cared for.

I told him I already have a husband. His name is Elkanah. We were bound by a preacher, but Elkanah jumped the broomstick with other slave women and then was sold away, and I was left barren and alone, and then I prayed and prayed, and the Lord give me Li'l

Samuel, and I loved him more than anyone could know and then lost him at Shiloh Church when the Yankees were firing their cannon down the hillside into the tents.

Master Suarez got mad and went back to his house and put me in the cane field for three days. Then at night he came to the cabin with a jug of whiskey and wanted me to drink with him, and I told him I don't drink liquor and I don't chew tobacco, either, and he gave me a cake and said he was a lonely man and his wife was in dementia and man was not meant to be alone. He said all that information was in the Bible, and Eve was made to comfort and console man, so we wouldn't be doing anything wrong if he could lie with me, and I told him no and then no again, and he took off my underthings and hurt me bad and kept on hurting me, and when I told him how much he was hurting me he did it ever harder, his mouth all over my face so I couldn't breathe, until I was weak and crying and knew I was going to die.

Then I did something I have never done. I made pictures in my mind about things that would happen to Master Suarez. Things that would make sure he never attacks a black woman again. Right after I saw those pictures behind my eyes, I didn't feel anything at all, like my insides had been emptied, leaving nothing but a cavity full of light. In my mind I saw my li'l boy Samuel, and I knew that one day he would find me, and we would go where coconut trees and pineapple plants grow and the rain falls when the sun is out and the fish fly over the waves, a place where evil men will never find us again.

I have a lamp at my cabin in the quarters. I also have a stylus and sheets of paper, which slaves are forbidden to own. On a Sunday morning two weeks after Mr. Cauchon visited Lady of the Lake and was shamed by Master Lufkin, I see Mr. Wade walking down the slope to the quarters. I believe he is a good white man, but he makes me afraid. He's got a haint. It's in his eyes. He has done something he cain't get rid of, that twists and turns in him wherever he goes. So he has appointed himself the savior of other people. Mr. Wade is also the kind who doesn't listen and will burn down the house because he thinks there is a hole in the roof.

He's dressed in his Sunday clothes and takes off his hat when I open the door. "How are you this morning, Miss Hannah?"

"Just fine, suh," I reply. "Do you need me for something?"

"I'm beginning a book of paintings. Also a journal. I understand you're writing one yourself."

I stare past him at a place in the middle of the swamp. There is a cut on his chin from shaving. He makes me think of a boy who doesn't know how to turn into a man. He follows my eyes to the swamp. "Is there something out there I don't see?" he asks.

"Suh, I don't know what to say."

"I'm not going to report you because you can read and write. Neither would my uncle. May I come in?"

"Yes, suh."

I have a floor and a table and two chairs and a bed against one wall, and dried food on a shelf and a wood bucket of rainwater I get from the cistern that's for the quarters. My journal and my stylus are on a table, my li'l bottle of ink beside my paper. Punishment for slaves who break plantation rules comes in all kinds of ways, mostly with the whip. I know of a cruel white lady in New Iberia who branded and blinded a slave girl over nothing, just because she felt like doing it.

"Would you like to sit down, suh?"

"Thank you," he says. "Would you object to my painting you? I don't want to impose."

"I don't think that's going to look good, Mr. Wade."

"I understand," he says. He looks at my table. "You use a bone for a stylus?"

"Yes, suh."

"I'll give you a decent one."

"Thank you, but I use animal bones to give them back their life. That's in the Old Testament. We ain't supposed to hurt the animals."

He smiles at me. "You're an unusual lady, Miss Hannah."

"Suh, I ain't supposed to be called a lady."

"I know that, and I know the bind you are in. I carry a Minie ball that I acquired in the service of an odious cause. Would you grant me a degree of respect, please?"

I drop my eyes and say nothing back to him.

"Would you sit down?" he says.

"Yes, suh."

"I came here for another reason. It's about Mr. Suarez. A couple of constables want to question you."

I feel like a cold hand has reached inside my chest and squeezed my heart. I have to breathe heavily to keep air in my lungs. "Something happen to Master Suarez, Mr. Wade?"

"Two nights ago someone cut his throat. And his eyes and other places. With *x*'s. That's the sign of the hex, isn't it?"

"Yes, suh. The gris-gris. I don't have anything to do with the gris-gris."

"I've already told these constables you were here two nights ago and nowhere near Spanish Lake."

I make him look me straight in the face. "How come they think I did it?"

"Because they know Mr. Suarez's history with his slaves."

"Is one of the constables Pierre Cauchon, Mr. Wade?"

He takes a deep breath. "Yes," he says.

"And he's coming back here? After Master Lufkin threw him out?"

"Miss Hannah, get rid of any red cloth or graveyard dirt or pieces of bone in your cabin. That includes your stylus."

"I ain't cast spells on people, Mr. Wade."

"I know," he says. He takes a breath again. But he's white and he *doesn't* know. Not at all. Not at any time in his life. He folds his arms, then puts his hands in his lap, then hits his fists on his knees.

"What else got done to Master Suarez?" I ask.

"He was mutilated on another part of his body. Probably when he was still alive."

"I'm glad."

"Don't say that, Hannah."

"I hope it hurt. Like he did me."

He gets up, his hat in his hand, his back straight. He's handsome in the light shining through the window. "Don't talk to the constables unless I'm there."

"What's going to happen to me, Mr. Wade?"

"I don't know, Hannah. I really don't."

Then he leaves and doesn't put on his hat until he is outside. I want Li'l Samuel in my arms. I want to hold him against my chest and bury my face in his li'l-boy smell and feel his arms around my neck, and I want the two of us to go outside and dance in the sunshine and the wind and see God's glory spread all over the world. But in my world that will not happen. Bad people are going to get me. For some reason it seems that's supposed to happen, like good people don't have a chance. And I don't understand why.

4

PIERRE CAUCHON

You may wonder why I am not in uniform. Well, I was. Past tense. In '62, at Shiloh and later at Corinth, where I was accused of shooting my own toes off. No such thing happened. I was sleeping in my tent and this clod from Mississippi started splitting wood right next to my tent and couldn't tell the difference between my naked foot and a chunk of pine.

This is probably why we will lose the war. What do I mean by that? Three-fourths of our army is made up of troops who don't own slaves, yet they are dumb enough, like me, to get themselves blown into sausage links in order to enrich men who are already rich. How did they get so dumb, you ask? The answer is simple. Most of them are illiterate. There are no newspapers or telegraphs where they live; some of them don't even know a war is taking place. Then they wake up one morning and look out the window and see a regiment of blue-bellies burning their barn, shooting their livestock, and taking a shit in their yard. These kinds of experiences tend to make people resentful.

Look, this is how plantation society works. They create identities for themselves and put on airs and screw down and marry up. The little people do the work; it doesn't matter if you are white or black. We all pick the white man's cotton. Maybe it is not like that in the North. I have never been there, although I have read the Irish in New York broke the water mains and drowned three hundred darkies in their basements. Herman Melville wrote about this.

It's Sunday, and I'm between New Iberia and St. Martinville, and on my way to Lady of the Lake. The road is winding because it follows Bayou Teche. "Teche" is an Indian word for snake. Live oaks grow on each side of the road and form a canopy that makes me think of a church when the sun shines through the leaves. But the fields are not cultivated here and the grass is five feet high and the woods are thick in the distance and often hide an enemy more dangerous than the blue-bellies.

Just as I have these thoughts, my mare's nostrils swell and her skin twitches, as though bottle flies have settled on her rump. At the edge of a clearing I can see sunlight shining on metal, moving through the trees, the wind revealing a mounted column of bearded men seeking purpose or destination or whatever murderous intention pleases them at the moment.

Oh, Lord, were men such as these ever your children? I have never been able to settle this question.

There's nine of them, slouched in their saddles, heads on their chests—the marks, I suspect, of late-night Saturday activities or of burning down a settlement. They are dressed in a mixture of sun-faded blue-belly and Reb uniforms and red-and-white checkered shirts and gray britches with a red stripe down the leg, in the same fashion as the irregulars prowling Kansas and Missouri.

The leader in the column is a man I've heard a lot about but have never seen up close. He wears a deep-red beard that is as fat as a pillow and stained with tobacco juice, and a permanent grin that looks like rictus; he's also cross-eyed. Because there cannot be two like him in five hundred miles, I assume him to be Colonel Carleton Hayes, who has hanged every abolitionist he could find and forbidden the families to cut them down lest the elements and the birds be denied God's purpose. Those were his exact words in a newspaper interview.

With a flick of his reins he turns his column so it will intersect my path, unless I want to see if I can outrun a Spencer repeater they stole off a blue-belly's corpse. They are about forty yards away now and one volley would probably leave Varina and me flopping in the grass.

Right now she's seizing up on me, her ears pinned back, tossing against the reins, probably mad at me for getting us into another mess.

"Howdy do, pilgrim?" the colonel says, tipping his hat. He's wearing boots that look like swashbucklers. His face is blighted with either a pox or a disease that has its origins in the lower regions. His eyes are lit up like lanterns, crossed as they are. "Who might you be?" he asks, his mouth twisted into a corkscrew.

"I am the Reverend Pierre Cauchon, on my way to Lady of the Lake Plantation," I reply, hoping the Creator will not blast me out of the saddle with a lightning bolt.

"That is indeed a grand vocation, sir," he says. "I notice you have two navy revolvers slung from your pommel, but I see no signs of a Bible or saddle bags in which one could reside."

"I carry the Bible in my heart, sir."

"I declare. You are obviously divinely gifted. Tell me, why is it you have not asked my name?"

"Your reputation precedes you, Colonel Hayes. You are well known as a friend of the working man and woman of Christian conscience."

"Thank you for your laudatory comment, Reverend. We were just fixing to eat. I would like for you to join us for some victuals."

"I am honored, sir, but Mr. Lufkin is waiting on me. Mrs. Lufkin is ailing and cannot go into town, so I am bringing our church service to their house."

The sun is hot and white directly overhead, and insects are coming out of the grass and settling on Varina's legs and belly. The colonel leans sideways and spits a mean mouthful. "Before you leave, I'd like a favor from you. For my horse, actually. I want you to get down and lift his tail and kiss his colon."

In the distance a team of mules is struggling to pull a wheeled cannon out of the woods. The cannon is probably a six-pounder. One wheel is stuck to the hub. Two darkies stripped to the waist are pulling on the mules.

"I didn't hear you," the colonel says.

"That's because I didn't say anything."

His men are all grinning now. He wipes at his cheek with a handkerchief. It leaves a white, dry place inside the infection on his skin. "Let me ask you another question," he says. "Have you always been a yellow-belly and a liar, or are you just getting the hang of it during these contentious times?"

I hear someone in the column cock a weapon, and I thud my heels into Varina's sides and we're off and running, with me as low in the saddle as I can get and Varina flying, barely touching the ground, quail bursting out of the grass.

The colonel and his men are all popping at once, their horses swirling on one another, which is probably the only thing that saves my life and Varina's. Minie and Spencer balls are making thropping sounds and toppling and whirring past our ears. But I'm not afraid anymore. Instead I feel like I'm drunk, back on the line at Corinth, the Cross of St. Andrew flapping, running at the Yankee line, yelling *Woo! Woo! Woo!* which is what we call the Rebel yell.

I free one of my Colts from its holster and cock and point it backwards without aiming and fire two or maybe even three rounds at the Red Legs, then gallop across a narrow wood bridge on the Teche and get inside the shadows of the trees on the far bank and swing down, both hands filled, and pour it on Colonel Hayes and his boys, who have got themselves into a bottleneck at the bridge and do not seem anxious to ingest a chunk of lead to go along with their hangovers.

I get back on Varina and go out of the trees in a trot, feeling a whole lot better about myself. I even think about being an ordinary man, heeled with his weapons, loyal to his conscience and his own concept of the Creator, not a Lilliputian working for the planters and other rich people who wouldn't take the time to piss on me if I was burning to death.

In fact, the whole day seems to be opening up to me; the sky is blue, the wind cool, the herons pecking on themselves along the bayou, and hundreds of robins clattering in the live oaks. There are even people going into a church house at a shady crossroads, which means Hayes and his bunch won't be dogging me, at least for now.

Then I start thinking about Hannah Laveau again. And the way Mr. Lufkin debased me in front of her. I can't get it out of my head. The same with her. She's a voodoo woman, a darky white men can't get their eyes off of, maybe an insurrectionist. I know better than to mess with that kind; they're looking for a tree and they usually find it. The lynching in St. Martinville in '61 included a white man. That could have been me. Many a white man hates me because I enforce the law to his detriment.

But I don't care about that. What tangles my mind most is the image of Hannah Laveau holding the staff of the broom when Mr. Lufkin was insulting me, like she wanted to give me power, like we were on the same side.

Another thing bothers me, too. When I took the pose of a preacher, I thought it was to outsmart a murderous man, Colonel Hayes. That was not the real reason. I have never figured out why the stars are in the sky or what's on the other side of eternity or why good people suffer. I have yet to meet a preacher who could answer those questions. Was I wanting to be the one?

I have five more miles to go before I arrive at Lady of the Lake, and my head is fixing to fall off. Frankly I would like to shoot Old Man Lufkin and be done with it. But that's not going to happen. There is only one way I can bring him down for treating me like a bag of garbage. I have found out that Mr. Lufkin owed a sizable amount of money to Mr. Suarez. If I can prove that Hannah Laveau was sent to kill Mr. Suarez, I can hang that old man on a meat hook.

These are not healthy thoughts.

5

WADE LUFKIN

My uncle Charles has been very kind to me because I am an only child whose parents died of yellow fever with no warning, leaving an estate drowning in lawsuits and fraudulent claims, while I was in Virginia, where I caught a Minie ball that came through the surgeon's tent on the banks of the Rappahannock. So perhaps I seem hypocritical when I say that my uncle is strict with his slaves and his animals and the poor whites who come to his door and work for wages, such as Biscuits-and-Gravy Comeaux. But unfortunately it's the truth. My uncle was reared a Christian, just as I, and has always known you cannot own another human being and call yourself a follower of Our Lord.

I believe my uncle fights constantly with his conscience and lays his anger on others. For Uncle Charles, the war is not about the division of a nation; it's about the division of Uncle Charles.

He is not a happy man. At age thirty-three he married a sixteen-year-old girl from the Booth family in Wilkes County, Georgia. She gave him seven children, but God took back four of them. That is why I can hardly bare what I am about to witness. The three boys he thought would be his legacy had written him and their mother often. Then the letters stopped. My uncle went regularly to the telegraph office in New Iberia, but none of the boys' names appeared on the growing lists of captured, missing, wounded, and killed.

Then, weeks after the fighting at Chickamauga, the sheriff and a physician and a Catholic nun from Grand Cote came to the house when Uncle Charles was in the fields. My aunt listened quietly to the message they bore, then shuffled into her bedroom without saying a word and put on a black dress and white bonnet and went into the kitchen and started a fire in the stove and commenced to boil cabbage and ham in a big pot of water, her eyes like oysters behind her glasses. Then she slung the pot on the floor and collapsed, weeping, in a chair, breaking her glasses, her hands pressed to her face.

A slave fetched Uncle Charles in the field and must have told him what he had overheard in the front room, because Uncle Charles came white-faced through the back door and immediately began cursing Jefferson Davis for his conduct of the war and the telegraphic and transportation difficulties he would face bringing his boys back home.

But home they came, on the Great Northern to New Orleans and by boat from New Orleans to the inlet at the foot of the Lufkin property. Through my window I can see the boat, one with a small steam engine and a tin stack and cotton bales piled by the wheelhouse and gunwales to protect the personnel from blue-coat or Red Leg sniper fire.

Until now I kept hoping a mistake had been made about the three boys, all of whom had volunteered. It happens. The Yankees are capturing more ground every day—Vicksburg, Port Hudson,

Baton Rouge, Gettysburg, the Mississippi River itself—and have destroyed any chance of clarity about casualties on the battlefield. There is another problem at work, also, an embarrassment for Confederate idealists. Yes, our volunteers have brave hearts, but many have deserted in order to feed their families and protect their farms from marauders. I suspect the South may become a necropolis or a fresh-air asylum, one we have brought upon ourselves. If the North has wanted to sow chaos, they have succeeded. In my view William Sherman is a detestable man whose methods are no different than Attila's; ash heaps are his hallmark, and ruination and simple-mindedness his weapons of choice.

The coffins are carried off the boat by stout fellows who drop them roughly on the dock and then smell themselves. The day is unusually warm, and I forgive them for their lack of breeding and their disrespect for the sensibilities of others. But I am afraid the origins of the problem do not lie with the weather.

According to a letter from a mortician in Chickamauga, the boys died when a single shell from a siege mortar exploded in their trench. Death was immediate, but the mortician advised that the coffins be kept sealed and the burial take place in a cemetery close by the battlefield. Uncle Charles would have none of it. He railed about the mortician, the incompetence of Jefferson Davis, and the lack of trains in Louisiana.

I join him and his wife and a half dozen slaves and walk toward the dock. The wind is blowing, a dirty froth scudding on the surface of the bay, the sunlight's reflection like a bronze shield. In the distance I can see a solitary rider on a sorrel horse riding toward us. I rub my eyes and look again, hoping my eyesight is playing a joke on me, because I cannot think of a worse time for the reappearance of that dolt Pierre Cauchon.

The men who unloaded the coffins are about to climb onto their boat.

"Get back here!" Uncle Charles calls out.

They do not try to mask their hostility. I suspect all of them are Irish. New Orleans is full of them. A man scrolled with tattoos leans over the rail and blows his nose in the water, then wipes his hand on his pants.

"What would you have us do?" asks a big fellow, a black-haired Celtic pagan if I have ever seen one.

"Open the coffins," Uncle Charles says.

"The fuck, you say," the big fellow replies.

"Don't you dare use that language to me."

"In your ear," the big man says. "If you weren't such an old shite, I'd stuff you up your darky's ass."

"Give me your name, you Irish filth!"

The captain of the boat, dressed in a navy-blue suit and a cap with gold braid, a bearded, jolly man I know well, comes out of the wheelhouse and throws a prizing bar on the dock. "Stop all that nonsense down there!" he says. "That includes you, Mr. Lufkin."

"You'll hear more from me," Uncle Charles says.

"Oh, I'm sure," the captain replies.

Uncle Charles picks up the prizing bar. He has now put himself in a trap, but I think that is what he has been doing most of his life. He stares at his wife, Aunt Ezemily, his knuckles ridged on the steel bar, obviously wondering what he should do next.

"Let these men alone," she says. "They have done their job. Now we must greet our sons."

6

PIERRE CAUCHON

I wasn't figuring on this. A boat that probably has a steam engine the size of a piss pot is leaving the Lufkin property, and a deckhand has just dropped his britches and is bent over with his skinny white ass aimed at Mr. Lufkin and his wife. In the meantime, three elongated crates are lying on the dock, water seeping out of the bottoms.

I lift my hat in a gallant way, even rising in the stirrups to show my respect. Nobody pays a lick. Except Hannah Laveau, who is walking down the slope to the inlet with a pile of folded tarpaulins stacked on her arms.

"I hope I have not interrupted y'all," I say. "If I have, may I offer a helping hand in some way?"

I might as well be a dog turd floating in a punch bowl.

Old Man Lufkin sticks a prizing bar in one of the planks and cracks a board loose. Then backs off and clears his throat and has another try. His wife walks down and helps, and the two of them bend the nails back and tear the boards loose and lay them down carefully one by one.

I have to hand it to them. I don't think I could have done it. From my horse I can smell it; I can also see inside the box. I saw a lot of woe at Shiloh and Corinth, but this is the worst. The body was probably submerged in sawdust and chopped-up ice weeks ago, but some other kind of preservative was probably poured into the soup as well, chemicals that had the opposite consequence. The skin has shrunken and looks webbed on the bones and painted with a yellowish-tan shellac, the bones sticking through, like a pterodactyl that has fallen out of the sky.

I put my handkerchief to my mouth because I'm fixing to throw up. Hannah walks down to the dock and spreads a tarpaulin over the box. Goddamn, if that girl doesn't outthink us every time.

I should turn Varina around and head back to New Iberia, but both of us are mighty tired after the gunfight with the Red Legs. Plus I have an obligation. No matter what private motivations are stewing in the back of my mind, Mr. Minos Suarez had his reproductive equipment lopped off with a butcher knife, and I have to round up whoever did it. It's the law.

So I swing down from Varina and step onto the dock. Thank God the wind has shifted. "Sorry for your loss, Mrs. Lufkin," I say. "And you, too, Mr. Lufkin. I'd like to return on another day, but my job doesn't allow me much latitude."

Mr. Lufkin looks at me as though he's awakening from a dream. "Latitude?" he says. "Who do you think you are?"

"A simple man of the people," I reply.

"This is hallowed ground. You have no right to be here."

"I will tell you something I was not planning to talk about, Mr. Lufkin. This morning I may have stopped an attack on your home. The would-be attacker is Colonel Carleton Hayes."

"You did *what*?" he says.

"I perhaps stopped an infamous Red Leg lunatic from setting fire to your property and carrying off your slaves and silverware and even your thunder mugs—that is, if you have thunder mugs. I will not mention what this man has done to his female captives."

"You're a goddamn liar. Carleton Hayes knows better than to harm me or mine. I know your kind, Mr. Cauchon. You're craven to the core. It's not your fault. It was in your parents' seed. You mutilated yourself to avoid serving your country."

I feel my eyes go out of focus. I never took pride in killing an enemy. Not even when Billy Yank had worked us over. But right now I could do it with pleasure.

There is one lesson and one lesson only I have learned from war. When you have destructive thoughts, you don't share them with your enemy. That's why I carry a corncob pipe, one I never smoke. Instead, I just remove it from my shirt pocket and stick it in my mouth during moments like these, and let silence and composure be my sword and shield.

"Are you just going to stand there?" he says.

"In my research I have discovered you are heavily indebted to the Suarez family, Mr. Lufkin, in large part because you lost your gold buying out the New Orleans slave market after General Butler had already confiscated it. Now Mr. Suarez is dead. One of your slaves had the opportunity to do a great favor for you. That slave is Hannah Laveau. I am now placing her under arrest."

"You can't do that," he says.

"I already have the warrant. The next warrant I obtain will be for you."

His wife goes to Hannah and puts her arm around her. "Don't be afraid, Hannah," she says. "We will do whatever it takes to bring you back home."

"Thank you, Miss Ezemily," Hannah says. "But my home is with my li'l boy. Sometimes he comes all the way from Shiloh to see me. Maybe I'm fixing to be with him forever."

"Oh, child, don't lend yourself to superstition," Mrs. Lufkin replies.

Then Wade Lufkin steps between me and everyone else on the dock, his wounded leg trembling, a catch in his throat. "You will not get away with this, sir. I will call you out. With pistols. Under the live oaks."

"I look forward to it, sir," I say, puffing out my chest.

But I don't look forward to it at all. I feel like the most solitary man on earth.

7

HANNAH LAVEAU

In New Iberia people call this squat, dark building behind the courthouse the "Negro jail." It has iron bars on the windows, but the rest is made of logs that are notched but not debarked, as though this ugly building is unnecessary, as though the plantation owners can handle their own problems, they don't need the sheriff, they got everything in hand.

I have one room and a floor of smooth clay and a wood bed with a wood block for a pillow. I also have a water bucket made of wood, and clean water inside it, and another bucket to use for private things I have to do in the corner, where the jailer cain't watch me. Through the window I can see the moon and Main Street and the live oaks and Bayou Teche and the columned houses that are hung with carriage lamps and at night look like wedding cakes all lit up.

I have been here four days now, and each night, just as I am falling asleep, I see my li'l Samuel smiling at me, inside a gold light, then I fall asleep and he stays with me on the edge of my dreams and keeps me safe from evil men who break in and steal, the ones the Bible talks about.

If I can, I am going back to Shiloh to find the people who may know where Samuel has gone. The Confederates were spread out at the bottom of a hill, near a place called Owl Creek. It was evening and the soldiers were happy because the Yankee cannons on the hilltop were silent and the Yankees on our right were beat, and beat bad, and pulling back for the night. Then Colonel Mouton and General Beauregard had an argument in the tent by the ambulance wagons. Colonel Mouton came through the flap and flung it back against the tent pole and rode out in front of us on his big horse, a purple plume in his hat, his face as flat and empty as a roof shingle, and said everything had changed and that he and his men were going up the hill.

Their faces turned gray, like they ate something dead in the soup, and they couldn't hardly force themselves to move. Then they began dropping their haversacks and canteens and fixing their bayonets on their rifles and pinning their names on their shirts. The drummer boys had already started rolling the "Assembly" with their drumsticks. That sound still brings chills to me. Colonel Mouton dropped his plumed hat on the tip of his sword and held it in the air and turned around in the saddle and yelled, "Damn it to hell, our cause is just, boys! Long live the Southland! Form on me!"

And that's what they did, like they didn't have minds of their own. They followed him up the slope, like men bent against the wind, their shadows rippling along on the grass like they wanted to hide. The trees on the hilltop were dark green inside the shade, the clouds aflame, like God had set Heaven ablaze. Then the cannons commenced to belch smoke and fire, the wheels leaving the ground, a black thunderhead of burnt power and grit and the smell of sulfur rolling down the slope.

A shell exploded twenty feet from me, and I felt something hard hit my head, and for some reason I saw a flowerpot bursting apart and pieces of it flying at me, like azalea petals rather than shards of iron. Then I was on all fours, my ears ringing, not knowing where I was or what had hit me, my li'l boy trying to waddle away from the explosions and the screams and the blood flying in the air, wearing just his napkin, his whole life dependent on his li'l legs, not knowing why any of this had to happen.

I got run down by a horse that was stepping on its own entrails and had the breath knocked out of my lungs by a soldier whose eyes were burned and as sightless as poached eggs.

I searched and searched all night for Li'l Samuel. In the dark I heard the wounded begging for water, but I paid them no mind. I just wanted my li'l boy back in my arms. For a while I was mad at God, then I figured out there was a reason He saved me. I became more and more sure of that, because in the morning everyone around me was dead, and I mean dead, because hogs were grunting all over the battlefield and there weren't any complaints from the bodies on the ground; in fact, the soldiers' pockets were always pulled inside out, and in the middle of all this I was still walking around, with not a speck of blood on me, and the reason was Samuel, my li'l boy, my man-child, who is going to bring God's grace to us all.

In the late afternoon of my fifth day under arrest, the jailer unlocks the door and lets in Pierre Cauchon. The jailer looks like a gnome and has only one eye and a back rounded like a turtle and a mean way of looking at black people. Cauchon puts a coin in his palm. The jailer's hand folds on it, his grin full of teeth that could have been dug up from my vegetable garden.

Cauchon has brought a wood stool he can sit on. He's wearing the tight-fitting white pants of a gentleman, and a split-tail coat and a vest with the shine and coloration of a bleeding pomegranate. I do not know if he realizes his name is pronounced the same as "pig" in French. His face is swollen and lopsided like soft fruit, or maybe he has been bitten by blowflies. He coughs on his hand, but he cain't hide the smell of his breath. He must have slept all night with his head in a beer bucket.

"You finally came to see me, you?" I say.

"I have investigated this murder with all my waking hours, Hannah. You were sent to New Iberia in Mrs. Lufkin's buggy to obtain medicines for her the night he was killed. This does not bode well for you."

"You have julep on your breath," I say.

"Did you hear me?"

"Yes. I smell you, too."

"You should not take my civility for granted. There is a voodoo woman in New Orleans named Marie Laveau. Is she your relative?"

"I ain't sure."

"Even though you could be her twin?"

"I thought you were different, Mr. Cauchon."

He looks like he is about to fall off his stool. "Different in what way?" he asks. His eyes are hooded and make me think of a frog.

"I thought you were capable of kindness. That's the way I wanted you to be. But you ain't."

"I'm just carrying out the law, girl. I took an oath."

"I ain't a girl. You listen, suh. I prayed for you when Master Lufkin called you trash. I wanted you to stand up for yourself. But you weren't able to do that. I feel sorry for you."

He lifts his face into a shaft of tea-colored light shining through the bars in the outside window. He looks like his seat is hurting on the stool. "Marie Laveau is your second cousin. She's a witch. Some people think you're an insurrectionist. Witches and insurrectionists get the same treatment in Louisiana. Know what that can be?"

I can hear rain falling on the banana fronds outside the jail window. I try to think about the rain and nothing else.

"Would you like to be trussed up and soaked in lamp oil and set on fire? Is that what you want? It happened. During the insurrection of 1811."

"Burn me and I will die and go to Heaven. When you burn, you're going to stay burned. And burned and burned. How do you like that?"

"Hannah, there are three slave women who swear you were on the Suarez property when he was murdered."

"I ain't interested," I say.

"You weren't there?"

"No."

"Then if you didn't kill Master Suarez, one of his slaves did. Testify for me. Swear they told you Mr. Lufkin had a bounty on that nasty old man's head."

"Because Mr. Lufkin ain't like that. He's grouchy, but he ain't a murderer."

He removes a flat bottle from his coat pocket and twists out the cork and takes a sip, then screws the cork back in place. "He'p me and I'll buy your freedom. With your intelligence, you could set up a number of businesses in New Orleans."

"You cain't buy what cain't be owned. The Yankees are all over Louisiana. We're going to be free any day now. All I got to do is wait."

"You have it backwards, Hannah. Louisiana has not surrendered, even though it is occupied. Lincoln is emancipating only the
states that have surrendered. Louisiana is never going to surrender."

I have heard nothing about this. I search his face. He keeps his
eyes on mine and doesn't blink. This time I know he is not lying.
I feel sick all over.

"I know about your little boy at Shiloh," he says. "If he is alive,
I will find him and bring him back to you."

I try to swallow but cannot do it.

"Do we have an agreement?"

"I don't know, suh. I'm not sure about anything now. Can I
have a drink from your bottle?"

He looks at the door. It is built of oak and has rusty spikes
driven in the planks and rusty bars in the viewing slot and rust on
the padlock.

"Sharing alcohol with prisoners is not allowed," he says.

"That's not what's bothering you, though, is it?"

He puts one hand on top of the other, weighing his answer, a
man who has the importance of a snowflake on a woodstove. I get
a tin cup from the windowsill. "I ain't going to put my mouth on
your bottle."

"It's brandy, not julep," he says. "That's why I took pause.
Brandy is hard to come by. Here."

I take the bottle from his hand and go to the corner of the room
and drop it in the bucket that contains my waste. "I have decided
I don't want any."

After Pierre Cauchon is gone, I sit on my wood bed in the dark.
There was a tick mattress on the bed, but on the second day after

my arrival the jailer took it away. The rain is still pattering outside and the moon has burned into a shining white hole in the clouds over Bayou Teche and the ducks are floating and bobbing under the drawbridge. I have a bad problem with my conscience. It's not my lie about the voodoo woman in New Orleans, either. It's about the slave women on the Suarez plantation. I don't know if I was there or not.

I sometimes go to a place in my mind that is safe from the rest of the world and stay there for a long time. I did that as a li'l girl in the French West Indies, and I did it at Devil's Island. These were places that had thorns and centipedes and poisonous secretions in the jungles, where everybody smelled of sweat and couldn't wash, where your eyes were always stinging and the sun would eat a hole in the back of your head, where flies were swarming on the excrement the Master gave us to squat on.

My father was part white and worked as an overseer for a Dutch plantation owner and used a whip on his own people. I think my mother killed him. But I will never know. She was taken away one morning and the slaves were ordered out of the field and made to watch her kneel and put her neck in a stock. There was a big blade over her head and a basket below her face. She could not see the blade, but she must have known it was there. The executioner wore no shirt and was muscular and tanned and had white teeth and black hair and a red kerchief tied around his head. He looked at the sea, his nose tilted up, maybe smelling the wind. He never looked at my mother. When he dropped the blade, my mother's body shivered all over and her head fell into the basket.

That's how I learned to go to my private place. I was put on a boat that went to Havana, then to Florida, then to New Orleans, and all that time I stayed below decks and slept in a bunk just above the bilge and did not pay the bilge any mind. Instead, I listened to the water whispering messages to me on the other side of the hull, messages from the porpoises and seagulls, or maybe from God.

I was real close to Him then. When the sailors were drunk and talking about what they had done to the black girls under the forecastle, God told me not to listen, that these were evil men and would pay a price for their deeds, and He also told me the fish of the sea and the birds of the air would always be there for me. That's why animals and birds were the first creatures loaded onto Noah's ark. They were first in importance.

But maybe I have done something very bad. I did not go into my private place when Minos Suarez attacked me. The pain was greater than me, greater than willpower or the ability to push his breath and his mouth and his saliva off my face, so I had hateful thoughts about him and what I would do when I was untangled from his limbs and able to make him hurt the way I was hurting. Even then I knew the kind of injury I would have to inflict upon him in order to make his pain the equal of mine. As he got off me, his naked body silhouetted against the moon, his chest heaving, I could feel my hand curling around an imaginary knife that one day would be real. When that day came, I would strike at the places I knew would hurt, and not simply seek an eye for eye, but instead probe deep into places even he did know existed, twisting my wrist, my fingers entering the wound with the knife's hilt.

You ask me if I killed Minos Suarez? I cain't answer that. I just hope God ain't mad at me.

8

PIERRE CAUCHON

That's what I get. I offer to share my brandy with a darky, and she dumps it in a bucket she uses for the contents of a thunder mug. Thank you very much.

I went from the jail down to the saloon and tied one on, then went to the house I rent on the edge of The Shadows Plantation and fell down the steps going to the privy and knocked myself out.

I woke up in the morning as sick as a gut-shot dog and was refused service in the café at the end of Main Street because, according to the owner, I was "not washed."

I don't have a cistern at my place. Where am I supposed to wash? In the goddamn bayou? If the leaches don't suck you bloodless, the mosquitoes will carry you off.

So I go down by the courthouse and buy a breakfast from a food concession run by a free colored man, and sit down on a bench and eat. There are blue-bellies sitting twenty yards from me. There is also a Yankee gunboat moored behind The Shadows, and Yankee officers living in The Shadows. In fact, I pay my rent to the officers in The Shadows. There is no question; we are not only occupied, Billy Yank has his boot on our necks. But he also has his boot on the slaves' necks. Announcements have been nailed up along Bayou Teche from Opelousas to the salt water that slaves are still under the authority of their masters. If you ask me, they got genuinely screwed.

No matter how the war ends, nothing will change. There are only two forms of income here—sugar cane and cotton. Who will work the fields? The people who own these mansions up and down Main Street that are fit for Napoleon? The big mistake the blue-bellies have made is their treatment of civilians. They let the enlisted men rape black women and loot the houses and businesses downtown and push the pews together in the local Episcopal church to make horse troughs. How's that for smart thinking? Little towns have long memories.

As I walk away from the food concession, somebody nails me with a pinecone between the shoulder blades. I turn around and see three blue-bellies on a bench grinning at me. They look like they've been on the grog all night.

"Could I help you fellows?" I say.

"Heard you got shot at Corinth," one of them says.

"Not exactly," I answer. "I was shot at Shiloh. At Corinth I was injured in a wood-chopping accident."

"*Excuse* me," he says. "I heard you were shot in the back."

"That is correct," I reply. "I was so far ahead of everyone else, the enemy had to shoot me in the back."

The three of them are laughing now, and I let it go and walk away with a smile fixed on my face. But that's not how I feel. I do not like blue-belly humor. No, sir.

I go home and heat some water on the stove and shave and try to clean myself up. As I look at my face in my little mirror on the drainboard my hand is trembling, my razor unsteady on my throat, the whites of my eyes still pink from all the busthead whiskey I consumed last night. Hannah Laveau made a fool of me. The funny thing is, I don't blame her. In fact, I admire her. She could sell hot chocolate to the devil and snow to the Eskimos in Alaska, just with that humble smile she has.

However, the times and the society we live in do not allow for charity of the spirit. North or South, a pound of flesh is a pound of flesh. You either buy it or you sell it. Textile mills, gun factories, cotton gins, or a colored family on an auction block, the Bible gets short shrift when it comes to money. Take a stroll through the graves at Shiloh and ask those underground what they think of things.

I have another problem, too. Thinking about Hannah fires up certain elements in my construction that do not resolve themselves easily, unless I visit the tents on the edge of town that light up at sunset. I was always a mess with women, probably because I didn't have a father and my mother was blind and taught me there was no greater sin that violating a woman's purity, and that meant keeping my hands to myself. So somehow I always ended up with women who were of an unusual nature. My first wife was a Chickasaw half-breed who gave her own height as seventeen hands, the way you measure a horse, and whose face could make a train turn on a dirt road. My second wife was a cleaning woman at the state asylum. I thought that was a big step up, until I forgot our first anniversary and she almost beat me to death with a bedpan.

I walk down to the saloon at the end of the street, not far from the tents that light up at sundown. Bayou Teche is rising with the tide, the fog rolling off the water, cold and smelling of fish roe and so thick I can hardly see my hand. It should be a grand moment, because in many ways southern Louisiana is the Garden of Eden and to be enjoyed to the fullest. But I know my drinking has already mortgaged the day, and I will spend my hours figuring out my alternatives and end up at the place where I started, sick and weary and just plumb disgusted with myself.

It's not that bad, you say? I'm afraid it is. I can let Old Man Lufkin get away with rubbing my face in it, or I can condemn Hannah Laveau to a horrible death, or I can let her go, even if she is guilty of killing Minos Suarez, ensuring I will live out a life of penury.

These kinds of thoughts hurt my head. The saloon is wreathed with fog and has ventilated batwing doors, as though to prove there is nothing to be afraid of inside. It's warm there, and clean, and the bartender is smiling at me. I hold up four fingers to show him how deep I want him to fill my mug.

"A gentleman has been looking for you, Mr. Cauchon," he says.

"Oh?" I answer. "Someone who owes me money?"

He points at a figure behind me. It's Wade Lufkin. Two other men are standing close by; all three have the certitude and posture of educated men who wear expensive suits and can look at people such as myself as though gazing at a bug on the end of their noses. One man carries under his arm a thin, flat, dark-stained wooden box with brass hinges.

"I told you I would call you out," Lufkin says. "Are you prepared, sir?"

"Prepared for what?" I say.

"Said like the coward you are," he says.

It is truly a bad day to have a hangover.

9

WADE LUFKIN

"These gentlemen are my friends and attendants," I say. "The pistols are sixty-five-caliber flintlocks of the finest manufacture. We can fire simultaneously or draw straws to see which of us will fire first. Or, in your case, sir, whether one of the participants wishes to run away."

Cauchon has the expression of a goldfish staring out of a bowl. "Flintlocks?" he says.

"They work quite well, as several vile fellows will vouch."

He pauses as though inspecting each of my words, then bows and sweeps his hat inches from the floor. "I am honored, sir," he says. "But why would a man of your station waste his time chastising a man of my humble origins?"

"A healthy community should tidy itself up from time to time. I am only too glad to help. Is there a particular place you would like your remains delivered?"

He raises one finger in the air, as would a professor lecturing in an auditorium. "Sir, I am amazed by your eloquence and the way you do not contract your words, as people have been doing since the seventeenth century. I do the same in order to sound smarter than I am. But I am a poor example compared to you, good sire. My congratulations."

I do not know if the problem is inbreeding, congenital syphilis, or a benighted seed spread by the prison colonies in Georgia, but there is a group in the Southland for which there is no cure. I am not being unkind. They have been with us since Ham left the Ark and fouled a continent.

He is still waiting for me to speak. "This morning you reduced the rations of water and food for Hannah Laveau. I have known some loathsome men, but you, sir, are the lowest of the low."

"I did not reduce her rations."

"The jailer told me he was acting on your orders," I say.

"Your people put that man in charge of the jail, not I."

I am holding my gloves in my right hand. They are made of felt, but with a quick snap of the wrist I sting him just below his left eye. A solitary tear runs down his cheek. It's not from pain. It's from something else. He never blinked. In my life no one has ever looked at me in the way he is looking at me now.

He turns his head and looks out the window. "Is that a hearse outside?" he asks.

"It is," I reply.

He nods. "Sixty-five caliber, you say?"

"You mean the pistols?"

He doesn't answer.

"Yes, they are sixty-five caliber," I say.

No one else is in the saloon, except the bartender and my two attendants. The felt on the billiard table has a strange glow in the light of the oil lamps and makes me think of an open casket. The cuspidors and foot rail at the bottom of the bar have the soft look of butter. The .58 Minie in my leg is throbbing, as it does sometimes when pressed against the bone. I can smell the coldness in the fog outside and the smoke from a cookfire where the prostitutes have set up shop on the edge of town. The horses hitched to the hearse are nickering under the trees, the plumes on their browbands bobbing in the grass. "Mr. Cauchon," I say. "Just promise me you will leave the area."

"No, sir, you will not receive that promise," he says. "But if you do not object, let me get down a hardboiled egg and a pickled pig's foot before we go outside."

There are only two kinds of people who talk like that. Those with damaged brains and those who have nothing to lose. I think in my wisdom I have picked on Job in order to have my duel.

10

PIERRE CAUCHON

We are under the trees now. I know the fog is cold, but I do not feel it. The only feeling I have is where the tips of his gloves touched me. I feel as though he has extracted a divot of skin from my face. There is no pain. Only deadness. He has remade part of me into nothing. It is what his class has always done. They make people into nothing.

I cannot think of anything other than my nothingness, so others have become more aware of the proceedings than I am. The tent camp of prostitutes has come to life. They have dragged chairs and milking stools and blankets to the edge of the oak grove and are eating fatback with their fingers and drinking a brew of parched corn and chicory that has been substituted for coffee since the blockade. Among the various spectators are members of Colonel Carleton Hayes's Red Legs, some still drunk from the night before. I can see no blue-bellies, though. I suspect they are at church.

This is a very strange war we are having. Yankees and Rebs come and go. White trash like the Red Legs attack and terrorize and rob both sides and see if they can outdo William Sherman in scorched-earth diplomacy. Most of them breathe through their mouths and think the words "Dred Scott" are a warning to stay away from Scottish people. Colored troops are captured and sold into slavery so they can stoke up all the other slaves. The Yankees have sunk boats up and down Bayou Teche, and now cannot get past the boats they chopped holes in. I am convinced this war was caused largely by people who had too much time on their hands.

By the way, the Yankee general overseeing the invasion of southern Louisiana is Nathaniel Banks. He was a bobbin boy in the textile mills of Massachusetts when he was twelve. Guess how he is getting even with rich people?

I look about me and have only one thought: I hate to die for the entertainment of a bunch like this.

Lufkin's attendant has opened the box containing the two pistols and now walks toward me with the solemnity of a funeral director. He offers me the box as though it holds the Holy Grail. "The protocol requires you be given first choice, sir."

"Can I have both of them?" I say.

"Should I repeat myself, sir?"

"No, you've done your job." I don't mean it badly. Frankly, I am very afraid. I lift one of the pistols from the velvet molding; it feels as though it is magnetized and will not allow me to raise it in the forty-five-degree position the duel requires. My heart is beating, my throat as dry as an ashtray. But I'm determined to brass it out. "You can go back to your owner now."

The attendant looks me dead-on and leaves no doubt about his feelings for me.

"And be sure to give your wife my best," I add. "The lovely thing surely knows how to give hers."

He turns and walks stiffly back to Wade Lufkin. I think the attendant wants to get it done and go back to his home, but something is amiss. Lufkin is angry about something, looking past the attendants at me, placing his hands on their shoulders, as though comforting them and explaining something to them. He doesn't pick up the remaining flintlock from the box, and instead limps toward me, his jaw set, probably because of the ball in his leg.

"Stop where you are, sir," I say. "I will have no more of your guff."

"Are you a Christian, sir?" he asks.

The prostitutes and their patrons are getting irritable and starting to heckle us. A buggy driven by a darky with a white woman in formal dress pulls off the road and stops under the trees. "Am I a Christian?" I say. "Let me think. On occasion I have dropped by a local church or two."

"Which denomination?"

"I did not get the details. They were definitely against sin."

"Just after Fredericksburg, I killed a Yankee officer, a fellow probably the same age as I was."

"Be done with your message, sir. Or better said, be done with your bloody shite."

"Fair enough. I believe if I kill you under these circumstances, I will forfeit my soul. And if you kill me, I will still be responsible for a murder because I forced the situation on you, and the consequence will be the damnation of us both."

"You slapped my face with your glove, you bastard."

"I apologize."

The woman in the buggy is getting out, the darky helping her down. She wears a long dress made of purple silk and lace round her neck and a burnt-reddish wool coat, and she carries a bag stuffed with clothing. I cannot see her well, but I know she doesn't belong here. She is someone who is everything we are not.

"Did you hear me, Mr. Cauchon?" Lufkin says. "Let's work things out in a sensible way."

"Oh, you speak in a grand fashion," I answer. "If only I possessed your education and manners." I clear my throat and lean forward and spit in his face with all the power I can muster. "There," I say. "How does it feel, Mr. Lufkin? How do you bloody well feel?"

We take our positions. There is no going back now. Our audience has quieted down, as though death has a greater behavioral influence on them than life. I suspect that may be the case with all of us. The funny thing is, you do not learn that lesson until you walk over that last hill in your life and see an infinite glare in the sky and realize that the greenness of the hill on which you stand has already gathered you to its breast.

As I stand under the oaks, I know the die is cast. Oddly I cannot get my eyes off the woman who descended from the buggy. I know her. Her name is Florence Milton. She is from Massachusetts and runs a private school in New Iberia and was one of the protesters at the hanging of the gambler by the blue-bellies at the U.S. Mint in New Orleans. There are also rumors that she has helped slaves escape into the Atchafalaya Basin. I do not doubt it. When provoked, she could make the devil join the Baptist church, or at least that has been my impression.

I do not know why she attracts my attention at this moment in my life. I am sure in her mind I am a centerpiece in the slave culture, a sweaty white man hired by the plantation class to lay the flagellum on the African's back, a slithering creature escaped from Eden, a molester of black women. I do not believe I am those things, but so be it. If I had to choose a witness in this entire crowd, it would be her, a New England pilgrim if there ever was one.

I look up through the limbs of the live oaks, but the fog is so dense I cannot see the sky. I ask the Creator to have mercy on my soul, and wonder if I will see my blind, dead mother again. I say her name under my breath, and hope that no one sees me, not because I am ashamed but because I think Florence Milton and possibly her driver are the only people in this oak grove worthy of hearing my mother's name.

We have agreed to shoot from a distance of fifty feet and to fire when the attendant drops a handkerchief. The strangest aspect of this duel is the fact that my opponent is an honorable man who would probably turn his weapon on himself rather than cheat. Would an army shoot itself to prove it is honorable? This may be the reason we are losing the war.

The woman from Massachusetts is causing a disturbance. In the corner of my eye I see her using her whip on the bartender and a Red Leg and some drunkards who can hardly stand up. But I have to keep my attention on the attendant with the handkerchief dangling from his fingers; he has already started his count, beginning with "ten," dragging his voice, my heart sinking with the silence between each number. The wind has come up, shaking the drops of water out of the trees overhead. The backs of my legs are quivering, my colon puckering. I cock the hammer and with one eye aim at Wade Lufkin's chin so the ball will have two kill zones, the center of his face or the top of his chest.

"Eight . . . seven . . . six," the attendant counts.

"This is a pagan ritual!" the Milton woman shouts. "Have all of you lost your minds?"

"Five . . . four . . . three," the attendant counts.

"This is a blasphemy in front of God Himself!" the woman yells. "Shame on all of you!"

"Two . . . one," the attendant says, almost in a whisper.

As soon as his fingers open and the handkerchief drifts into the wind, I pull the pistol's trigger. The flint strikes the steel next to the pan, then there is a spark and a flash and a split-second pause before the charge explodes and the sixty-five-caliber ball leaves the barrel. Wade Lufkin fires almost simultaneously, and the air fills with smoke and the smell of cordite. I cannot tell if either of us has struck his target. I lower my pistol and keep waiting to die, but nothing happens. Nor do I hear Wade Lufkin cry out. Maybe I have missed him altogether or maybe he is dead. In honesty, I hope it is the former.

I walk toward him, off balance, drained of energy or strength of any kind, my right hand tingling. Lufkin is on all fours, looking up at me as a surprised dog might. No, that is not true. He sees nothing. His face is scarlet with blood, his eyes pooled with it. Pieces of his scalp are gone. His pistol lies on the ground. The barrel is split, the hammer and flash pan blown apart. He tries to get to his feet, then falls with one leg twisted under the other. He seems to have gone mad, grinning and rotating his head blindly at the crowd.

"Stop your moaning, ladies," he says. "Break out the champagne and give me a big kiss. Fuck Jefferson Davis. I love every one of you."

11

FLORENCE MILTON

Yes, you heard me right. I called it pagan. If the Irish are not shooting one another, they are fist-fighting. When they are not fist-fighting, they are drinking. That is why I called this business under the trees an offense against God. Duelling is a ritual designed to hide a murder. The superstitions of Rome and the Celtic race in general have no place among us. That is why St. Paul warns us about blood sacrifice. Read 1 Corinthians 8:1 to 11:1.

My driver Jerome takes me straight to the courthouse, which is only a short distance from the Negro jail, another blister on our souls. I have given money to Jerome so he can buy his breakfast from a street vendor, and I am now entering the sheriff's office. Be advised. The sheriff, Jimmy Lee Romain, is not a bad man but, unfortunately, a nincompoop. More unfortunately, he was elected to his office not in spite of the fact that he is a nincompoop but because of it. In Louisiana we elect unintelligent and corrupt people to public office in order to keep them busy in distant cities. The worse they are, the farther we send them. Have you visited our national capitol?

Sheriff Romain sits behind his desk like a sack of potatoes and makes me think of someone who has just run up a stairs, although he has not. Maybe Mr. Darwin is right about the fish crawling onto the land and becoming simians and eventually the human species. If so, I suspect that someone stepped on the head of Sheriff Romain's ichthyological ancestor. I am also convinced that men such as the sheriff are created by God to prove that the superiority of the white race is not a tenable belief.

His eyes slide up and down my clothes.

"Stop that," I say.

"Stop what?"

"Looking at me in that fashion."

"You're holding a whip."

"I just watched two men fire duelling pistols at each other. One is that white trash Pierre Cauchon. The other is Wade Lufkin. I cannot believe his uncle has allowed him to do this."

The sheriff is slumped horizontally on the chair, as though his spine has been surgically removed. He pushes his ring of keys around on his desk blotter. There are tiny blue and red veins and blond whiskers on his soft cheeks. "Four slaves took off last night from the Suarez plantation," he says.

"Yes?"

"Don't make me arrest you, Miss Florence."

"How dare you."

He yawns, then finally puts a hand to his mouth. "Wade Lufkin wasn't hurt, was he?"

"Why don't you go out on East Main and see?"

"I could certainly do that," he says. "If it will change anything."

But he doesn't move. Instead he looks at the cemetery through the window. Most of the crypts are built of brick and mortar.

The ground is soft, and the weight of the caskets has cracked the concrete at the bottom of the crypts and is taking the entire structure down. Most of the dead are victims of yellow fever, a scourge whose origins are a mystery. We have even fired cannon into the swamps in hopes of diminishing the terrible toll it has taken in our community.

"I have clothes for the colored woman in the Negro jail," I say. "I am talking about Hannah Laveau."

"What's wrong with what's she got?"

"Sir, have you no shame?"

He gets up, his eyes rheumy, pale blue. "Whatever you need, Miss Florence. What's the condition of young Lufkin?"

"His face is horribly disfigured. He babbles with the coherence of a parrot and his eyes are cups of blood and misery."

"It's that bad?" he says.

"Sir, did you suffer a cerebral injury as a child? Were you beaten by a parent? Would you at least straighten up in your chair and not lie there like a giant earthworm?"

He stares at me in bewilderment. And rightly so. I have no idea of what I am saying or why I should ever place myself above others, particularly this bumbling creature who probably cannot count his toes with an abacus. God, please forgive me for my terrible thoughts about my fellow man.

The sheriff walks me to the jail with a parasol over my head, then says goodbye and leaves me with the jailer. His name is Louis Boudreau. His body odor is overwhelming, like an invisible presence that can steal your breath. With his eyepatch and slinking walk and grovelling manners, he could be a creature transported from the

Middle Ages. "I am honored, Miss Florence," he says, rising when I enter his small office.

"I would like to speak to Hannah Laveau. I have also brought her some clothing and a blanket."

"She already has those things," he replies.

"I have been told that. I would like to give her these, regardless."

"Certainly," he says, bowing his head. "Place them on the table. Be assured I will give them to her."

His good eye is aglitter as he waits for me to leave. The dirt on his skin could be matched only by the interior of a chimney.

"I would like to speak to her, please."

He looks at a watch on his desk. "I do not know if that is possible now. She is going to be questioned shortly."

"Questioned?"

"Some officers of the law from New Orleans are here."

"Are you harming that girl?"

"No, we do not do that kind of thing," he replies, grinning. The gums of his teeth are eaten by tobacco juice.

"Two Negro men have told me that the Laveau woman has been denied food and water."

"Which Negro men are we speaking of, Miss Florence?"

"Please don't address me as 'Miss Florence,' Mr. Boudreau. This tradition is intended to indicate familial fondness coupled with social formality. That is *not* our situation."

He makes a sucking sound and lifts a ring of keys from a peg on the wall, his solitary eye focusing on me like the point of a spear. "Coming, Miss Milton? It is *Miss* Milton, isn't it? I'm pretty sure I got that right, didn't I?"

* * *

Hannah is sitting on her wood bed. Her feet are bare and dusty. The hem of her dress rests on the tops of her little feet. She looks thin and sad, her knees close together, her hands folded in her lap. She raises her eyes to mine but does not speak. I have no doubt what has been occurring in this wretched place called the Negro jail.

"I need to examine the clothes and blankets and such before I go," Boudreau says.

"These were given to me by Mr. Charles Lufkin for his servant Hannah Laveau," I say. "Do you wish me to tell him you had misgivings about his charitable actions?"

"You know how to make a man's job hard, Miss Milton. I would not dream of offending Mr. Lufkin. Let me know when you are ready to go."

He goes out of the room, leaving his odor behind, and bangs the door in place and locks the chain, then drops the keys loudly on his desk. I sit down by Hannah and put my arm around her. "Tell me what he has done."

"I cain't."

"You don't trust me?"

"If I talk about it, it becomes real. When I go inside my secret place, it's not real. That means God has been taking care of me. That means I'm going to be all right, Miss Florence."

I stroke her shoulders and the back of her neck. I want to cry. No, I want to kill Louis Boudreau and I want to kill all the other men who empower him.

I pull her close to me and whisper in her ear. "Hannah, inside the clothing I have brought, you will find a bottle of homemade wine. Do not drink it. When I leave, I am sure Mr. Boudreau will come in your room and find the bottle. He is a drunkard as well as a degenerate and will take the bottle for himself and consume it in his office. When he does, he will pass out. You must hide the key I am putting in your hand. It is for the padlock on your door. You can reach it through the bars."

"How did you get the key, Miss Florence?"

"I paid money for it. Money is at the center of this war and the bondage of your people. Do not let anyone tell you otherwise. I suspect Mr. Boudreau will drink the wine this afternoon. We expect rain today. I will have people waiting for you."

"Miss Florence, is something real bad going to happen to me? Is that why you are doing this?"

"You are an intelligent, brave woman, Hannah. That is why these men fear you. That is why they wish to degrade and molest you."

"I might have killed Mr. Suarez."

"Good. He deserved it."

"I ain't ever heard you talk like that, Miss Florence."

I pat her on the back. I can feel her heart beating all the way through her body and her thin dress. "We ladies have to stick together."

12

WADE LUFKIN

I have decided that my ride in the back of a vegetable wagon to the physician's office is like awaking on a cross at Golgotha. I also believe someone has given me laudanum. If so, that might explain the red skein that has afflicted my vision. The limbs of the live oaks overhead have the color and design of a disemboweled animal.

I fear I no longer know who I am. I always believed I was an ornithologist and an artist who subscribed to the charitable ideals of Walt Whitman and Ralph Waldo Emerson. However, in a rage I killed a young Union officer, then left the war to others and returned home and let my uncle Charles take care of me, forgetting that his wealth was made on the backs of enslaved Africans.

Then, in a burst of martial sentiment, which is the most poisonous drug a human being can ingest, I looked down at the remains of my three cousins in their coffins and challenged Pierre Cauchon to a duel, giving no thought to the possible loss of my soul and the fact I had just become the thing I hated.

Ask Our Savior for forgiveness and be done with it, you say? Do you think I have not tried? That goes to the very heart of my problem. When I solicit forgiveness, I get angry simultaneously. I asked the Lord's help before the duel. But the duel went forward regardless. I could not stop it without besmirching the Lufkin name. Where was Our Lord then? He said his yoke was a mild one. My opponent, a crude and licentious man, was left unscathed. My face will probably remain a study in horror, one that will make the kind at heart weep and children flee. A mild yoke? Really.

You say I manufacture sorrow and loss and deliberately seek morbidity. There is something I haven't told you. When the .65 caliber pistol blew up in my face, another event occurred, one that was more startling than my wounding. The young officer I killed in Northern Virginia took physical form right next to me, squatting casually by my head as I lay on the ground, my ears deaf from the powder's explosion. His blue wool jacket was stiff with dried blood, his long johns showing where I pierced him with the bayonet.

Are you here to guide me to a better world? I asked.

Oh, no, laddie, he replied in a Celtic accent. *You have hell to pay.* Then he laughed.

Because I killed you? I acted in self-defense.

Your problem is of another kind. You think you're a bloody saint.

I didn't want to go to war. I became a non-combatant. In some ways I took greater risks than the soldiers who had weapons to protect themselves.

That's rot. You punctured my organs with glee.

You lie, I said.

Ah, listen to yourself. The genteel Evangelical, the defender of the slaves, particularly when there is a lovely African thing waiting to be picked off the tree. Yes, I am talking about the darky delight named Hannah Laveau who has your lower aspirations tingling.

I was never improper with her. You have no right to say that.

Maybe not, he said. *But you're still a fraud. You take no side and place nothing of value in the arena. You will probably end up a school-teacher, telling tales about yourself to children, sometimes hitting them when you're angry.*

I don't think you're the man I killed. I think you're an evil spirit.

Could be. You'll be finding out soon. Here's an addendum for you: You will not be going to the place where your cousins are, the ones who died at Chickamauga. Goodbye, laddie.

The wagon wheel hits a pothole like a ball-peen hammer snapping my collarbone. I can feel blood issuing from both my eyes. The tree limbs overhead are still red, but are now shuddering with the cawing and shite of carrion birds.

I slept on and off for five days in my bedroom on the second floor of my uncle's house. I ate little because the stitches in my face began to tighten, so that chewing was a torment, as though my head were covered with a wet leather hood that was shrinking by the hour. My closest companion was the laudanum on my night table, and I no longer cared whether I became an opium addict or not. In fact, the "pink lady," as we used to call it, was a lovely friend to have at my beck and call.

Now I am in my sixth day in my bedroom, and my vision has somehow been returned. One of the surgeons has said that blindness can be caused by emotional trauma, and its restoration tenuous and not to be taken for granted.

A servant removes the chamber pot from under my bed. He is elderly, bent over, his hair gray. He wears a faded black coat and a white dress shirt with frayed cuffs.

"What is your name?" I say.

"Christopher, suh," he says, standing by the bed, holding the chamber pot with both hands.

"Do I know you?"

"Yes, suh. For many years."

"I am sorry you have to do this for me."

"It ain't no trouble, suh."

I am propped up on my pillows. Through the windows I can see the swamp and the hard blueness of the sky and a long yellow bay that is white-capped, as if thousands of seagulls are flying low over the water.

"Is it warm outside, Christopher?" I say.

But he's gone and I don't know where. I hear footsteps on the stairs, then Uncle Charles sits down by my bed. "Are you feeling a little better, my fine young boy?"

"Yes, sir."

Uncle Charles speaks more endearingly as each day passes. All of his children are dead. The remains of his three sons who died at Chickamauga contained bits of iron as thick as your thumb. He removed them from the bodies with his bare hands.

"You may be an idealist, but you're a grand one," he says. "My wife and I love you as we would a son."

"As I love you and Aunt Ezemily, Uncle Charles."

"The surgeons have high hopes. But we must be patient."

"Patient about what?" I try to smile, and my face tightens with pain.

"The surgical remedies that are available."

He has removed all mirrors from the room. Nor would he allow the servants to bring silver vessels or wide-bladed silver knives near the bed.

"You have been very kind to me, Uncle Charles. You mustn't worry."

He leans forward. His breath is like a feather on my skin. He has reached that elderly stage when the breath is always sweet. "A great shadow has fallen on our way of life, son," he says.

He has never called me "son."

"The last of my children have been killed by the Yankees. You have been mutilated by an evil man. Eventually the servants will run away, and our home will be taken from us through the guise of taxation."

"Maybe it's God's will," I reply.

"No, the devil himself has his hand in this, Young Wade. That is why we have to undo his snares and not flinch at the methods that have been forced on us."

He has the soft features of the colonial patricians from whom he descends; his hair is silvery blond and looks almost angelic hanging in his eyes. For just a moment the strident figure who ripped a fortune from an Edenic land is gone from the room. In fact, his voice is as soft as his face. "Do you understand what I mean?"

"No, sir," I say.

"We have to fight back in kind and pray it not be held against us," he says.

I do not want to quarrel with him. Nor do I have the strength. "Uncle Charles?"

"Yes?" he says.

"Could one of the servants bring me a mirror, please?"

He takes a breath. "The body heals itself. But we have to give it time."

"I need to see who I am, sir."

The light goes out of his eyes. "You are a brave soldier and a fine young man, Wade. Don't ever forget that, no matter if misfortune should take you to the grave. You're a Lufkin."

I fall into a warm sleep and do not wake until afternoon, when shadows are on the ground. The window is half open, a breeze ruffling the curtains. I can hear a pig squealing and know that it is being slaughtered and is fighting for its life. I also hear shotguns booming in the swamp, killing the ducks and robins and raccoons that will go into the huge cauldron of gumbo that will be the field workers' supper. But this is the world in which I live. Pain and the killing of harmless creatures not only sustain us, they have made my family rich. But what is the alternative? A monastic life? Do the monks not kill small creatures? What about the Yankees and the burning of our homes and the rape of the colored women? Is this the place where we work and play in the fields of the Lord?

I sit on the side of my bed and pour a tablespoon of the pink lady and put it to my lips. Then through the window I see an image I am sure is a mirage. A cavalry officer is leading a column of perhaps two hundred men onto Lady of the Lake Plantation. The officer wears swashbuckler boots and a tall hat with a wide, finger-smeared brim. Uncle Charles has given me a telescope to watch the birds through the window. I focus the lens on the officer's face. His beard is dark red, his cheeks festering or glistening with a liquid of some kind. He leans from his saddle and spits.

At the back of the column is a mule-drawn cannon. The teamsters are black men. One has no shirt; another wears Yankee trousers. There is no question about the rest of the column. They're Red Legs, unshaved, their uniforms weather-faded, their expressions either dissolute or vacuous, some sleeping in the saddle. They wear every kind of revolver and broad knife and musket and cut-down shotgun imaginable, the sign always of irregulars and robbers; they also carry Spencers. And some have human heads tied to the cantles of their saddles, the hair so long it could belong to women.

The column forms a huge noose around the house. Its leader gets down, a saber on his side, and walks to the front door, out of my line of sight. Then I hear his fist pounding on the front door and the walls of my bedroom vibrating. In my mind's eye I see Uncle Charles opening the door, berating a misfit for the disgrace that he is, and telling him to get off the plantation. But that is not what is happening. I hear their feet coming up the stairs, then my bedroom door opens and I am looking at a man whose face seems luminescent with disease, his mouth misshapen with scar tissue.

"This is Colonel Carleton Hayes, Wade," Uncle Charles says. "He is going to help us."

"I understand you have had a go of it," the colonel says.

"Not really, sir. A scrape that I brought on myself."

"You have a brave attitude, then. I've gotten into a sordid situation or two, but I didn't handle it as well as you."

"I am familiar with your background, sir."

He nods, then says, "Do you find my background objectionable?"

"He's not a judgmental sort, Colonel," Uncle Charles says.

"Oh, I know he's a good lad," the colonel says.

"What is your business with my Uncle Charles?" I ask, more brazenly than I have ever spoken in my uncle's house.

"You're out with it, are you?" the colonel says. "My business is with you. Pierre Cauchon is spreading rumors that you are a liar and a functionary of the blue-bellies and a practitioner of miscegenation. More specifically, he says you have been intimate with a black wench named Hannah Laveau."

I look at Uncle Charles. He is staring out the window.

"Your men have human heads hanging from their saddles," I say to the colonel. "Maybe the heads of women."

"No, that is not correct," Hayes says. "Those are redbones who raped a white woman. Their heads will be on pikes outside St. Martinville before the sun is set, a reminder to the Negro population as well as the redbones."

"Uncle?" I say.

But he continues to stare out the window.

"Uncle Charles?" I say.

"The enemy of my enemy is my friend," he says, turning around. "Our boys gave it their best, but they're outnumbered and without food and ammunition. In a short time we will be at the mercy of the Unionists, many of whom are depraved. Colonel Hayes will not let us down."

"That's right, son," the colonel says. "In Missouri and Kansas I rode with both James Lane and William Clarke Quantrill. You know the lesson I learned? Ride for yourself and your family. No one else gives a bloody fuck."

"Sir, you're in my uncle's home," I say.

"It's all right," my uncle says. "These are troublesome times, Wade."

"Think this over, Uncle," I say.

"We haven't told you everything," he replies. "Hannah escaped from the Negro jail. Before she left, she emasculated the jailer, Louis Boudreau. I'm sorry. I know you had kind feelings for her."

"Hannah wouldn't do that," I say.

"She did it, Wade," he says. "There's a good probability she did the same to Minos Suarez. You have to be a realist, son. It's comforting to believe the pen and the paintbrush are mightier than the sword. But those are the words of dead Quakers."

13

HANNAH LAVEAU

I was scared after we got free of the jail. We hid out and paddled two days in the Atchafalaya looking for the island where we would be safe. The gum trees and tupelos were in full leaf in the bays as far as I could see. When the sun broke on the horizon, a red light travelled across the water like a flame, turning the world into a place of dancing shadows and fish roe smells. Then God tole me not to be afraid, the Atchafalaya Basin was nothing but a big bowl He made by His own hand after the Flood. It was a special place, He said, because it changed all through the day and night, the bayous and bays rising and falling with the tide, the waves chucking against the tree trunks, the gators floating like logs in the current between the islands, the deer and the li'l animals watching us like they weren't sure if we were to be trusted.

It was on the second night that everything got bad, and it was because of Miss Florence. There are some people who have too much faith, and some people who are too brave. Then there's the kind who are brave and faithful and so stubborn you want to hit them in the head.

It was dark when we got to our island in our pirogue, with just enough moonlight to see the outline of the shack and the shiny damp on the trees and the footprints of creatures big and small where the tide had slid back into the Gulf. Miss Florence got out of the pirogue first and drug it up on the silt, almost knocking me down, then tole me to finish getting it out of the water and to unload our food and clothes and blankets. I tole her to let me get a fire started. That it ain't good to walk in the dark, no. But she would not listen.

"Miss Florence—" I started.

"Stop being a fussbudget," she said. "We need to get you something to eat. Louis Boudreau tried to starve you into doing his will. Don't tell me he didn't. One day I'm going to whip the daylights out of that man."

"Miss Florence, I lived in the West Indies and Devil's Island. There are things you do and things you don't do. Don't be running in the jungle in the dark. Also, I ain't a fussbudget."

She went straight into the shack and started throwing junk out the windows and the door. Then I heard her scream. I ran to the shack. She was standing inside, slapping at a cottonmouth moccasin wrapping itself around her neck and arms, one that was almost three feet long. It must have fallen off a shelf where a cypress tree had grown through a window.

Oh, God, don't let me fail now, I thought. Even though I know I ain't that brave, let me be brave now. Miss Florence is a good lady, and even though she's contrary and sometimes makes me want to hit her, she doesn't deserve this.

So God made me mad at the snake and I slung it around and hit its head on a chair and flung it on the floor and stepped on its face and jumped up and down on it until it stopped squirming. Then it squirmed one time and I slammed the chair on its head one more time and it opened its ugly mouth and died.

I know I have to help Miss Florence or she's going to die. Field workers and the ones who log and clear swamps know about snakes. Bending over is work that nobody wants. If you get snake-bit in the neck or the face, the chances are you will not make it back to the overseer. He will not be happy to see you, either, because he will probably be blamed and he will also have to clean out the nest.

A coral snake's poison goes into your brain and makes you crazy and unable to care for yourself. A copperhead will go after you when it doesn't have to. A rattlesnake will coil and warn you first, but when he lets go, it's with force and dedication.

Cottonmouths ain't like other snakes. They try to swim away or duck under the water when they see you; in the swamp they work their way up on low-hanging tree limbs and sleep on them. But if a cottonmouth is coiled and it shows you all that white inside its mouth and you don't see it and you reach down to pick up your fishing line or crab trap, it will pop you in the face and spread its jaws across your cheek and hang from it. Even when you get it off, there is no place to tie a tourniquet.

I throw the snake out the window with my bare hands, then put Miss Florence on a blanket and another blanket on top of her and my coat under her head. Her face swells up so big she can't close her mouth and chokes on her spit. I turn her on her side and drain her throat, but all the things I need to save her life—the suction cups, the medicine, a knife to cut an X on the punctures—those things are not there.

So now I put my mouth to her wounds and begin sucking as much blood and poison as I can. It tastes different than I thought it would. It tastes clean, like vegetables just pulled out of the soil. I spit it out and do it over and over again. All the while Miss Florence's eyes are two inches from mine; they remind me of my mother's eyes before she was taken to be executed, as though she was asking someone to explain the terrible thing that was happening to her. Miss Florence's hands are resting on my back, like she wants to crush me against her but cain't because she would lose her life.

She's breathing up and down now, her breath hot on my cheek. Then she whispers in my ear, "Let me pass, child. I'm not afraid. The Lord is my shepherd."

I brush my hair out of my eyes with my arm. "Don't be talking like you're a sheep, Miss Florence. When it's your time, the Lord will tell us. So far I ain't heard him say anything on that subject. So be quiet and stop bossing people."

I'm lying, though. Miss Florence is dying. I stay with her all night, fanning the mosquitoes, washing out her wounds, changing her undergarments, trying to feed her pieces of cornbread and salt pork to build her strength. At first light a boat with two sails and four men rowing goes right past the island. I could wave them down, but I know they're slave chasers. How can I tell? They all look angry. Why? Because they know what they're doing ain't right.

It's midday now and the sun is straight up in the sky, bright and hot and white, and all the shadows are burned away on our li'l island. In the distance I can hear a drumming on the water, then it gets louder and louder, and I know it's a boat with a boiler. It's like a machine that doesn't belong here, one that wants to tear up what the Earth is supposed to be.

I put a cool cloth on Miss Florence's brow and go to the window and look through the trees. The people who were supposed to meet us and take us north never showed up. Miss Florence says they are probably in jail. I don't believe that. Rumors were being spread about me. That I killed Minos Suarez. Abolitionists will lose their lives for an escaped slave, but not for a colored woman who killed a depraved man who ruined her life.

The boat is just on the other side of an island covered with willows now, the water splitting on the bow. For me boats have always meant freedom, or at least the chance of freedom. This could be a Union boat, one that has medicine and soap and poultices on board, one that could get us to the Mississippi. Vicksburg has fallen. That means runaway slaves in the Deep South can make it all the way to the Ohio River and real freedom and never have to fear the branding iron again.

But the boat has rounded the willow island now and I can see the dirty black smoke coming from the stacks, and the paddlewheel in back, and an empty cage on the deck, and a swivel cannon on the bow, and the flag that's flapping above the wheelhouse, and suddenly I am very afraid, because I have no place to run. Not even a place where I will have time to drown.

Any hope I had a few seconds ago has vanished. If I do not give myself up, Miss Florence will die for sure. If I do surrender, I will be put to death after the men on that deck get through with me. I would rather die by my own hand.

I back away from the window and squat down by Miss Florence. She turns her head and opens her eyes. "What is it, child?" she says.

"It's a Confederate boat, Miss Florence. I'm going to turn us in."

Her hand creeps up on my wrist. "No. Do not do that."

"I got to. You're going to die, Miss Florence."

"I have already made my peace. I will not let you give up your life for me."

Her hand squeezes my wrist so hard my blood cain't go through my veins. I try to pull away from her.

"Do you understand me, child?" she says.

I jerk my hand from her and get to my feet and go to the window. A man is on the boat's bow looking though a telescope. To end everything all I have to do is go out the door and through the trees onto the sandbar where the tide has pooled, and I will no longer have to make choices. Like my mother, I will be undone by the world and time will go by and I will never have lived.

Then I hear the voice. It's the same one I heard when I escaped the West Indies and the same one I heard when the Minie balls and the cannister were killing everybody around me at Shiloh Church.

The voice says, *Abide with me and fear no evil.*

I do not know where the voice has come from. It did not originate inside my head. Or out on the water. Or in the trees. "Who are you?" I say.

But there is no answer. The boat is turning toward our island, the paddlewheel churning up water that is as yellow as paint.

"Who are you talking to?" Miss Florence says.

I start to answer. Then I see. Like a veil has lifted from my eyes. The voice isn't from God. Not at all. It's from my li'l boy Samuel. In his bassinet. The one he slept in when he was a li'l baby. His glow fills the whole shack. Even Miss Florence can see him. I know that because his light is shining on her face.

"Tell me what to do," I say.

But he doesn't. He just keeps smiling, and the more he smiles the brighter he becomes.

Then everything stops. Miss Florence's mouth is half open, her hand in the air, like a claw. The boat is aimed at the island, the keel tilted in the chop, the spray on the bow and the smoke from the stacks frozen in midair.

Then I know what Samuel is telling me. He does not say it. Neither does God. The things he says inside my head have meaning that words have not caught up with. The message is even on the backs of my eyelids and is also in my heart and soul.

"I will," I say to the shimmer of light that still hangs in the shack.

"Will what?" Miss Florence asks.

The boat swings away from the island and heads toward the Gulf of Mexico. A deckhand pours a bucket of garbage over the gunwale.

"Answer me, child," Miss Florence says. "Why do you have that strange look on your face?"

"You're going to get well, Miss Florence."

"How do you know this?"

"Because it's already happened. It's that way with everything, Miss Florence. The things we need are already there. We just have to find them. Can you do me a favor?"

"What?"

"Don't call me 'child.'"

She puts her fingers on my cheek. The look I saw in her eyes earlier is gone. "I think you have a fever," she says. "You must take better care of yourself, Hannah."

14

PIERRE CAUCHON

I do not think things are working out for me. Wade Lufkin blew off his own face, but nonetheless the blame will be placed on me. Lufkin society doesn't just screw down and marry up; they screw everybody they can. The first thing they do is find out how much money you have, then they proceed to take every dollar of it. You know how my regiment got blown to hell at Shiloh? The officer who was supposed to be on our flank was Major Ira Jamison. He didn't show up. Just like that. In the middle of a war. He was somewhere else. We went up the slope, into cannister and mortar fire, with the evening sun in our eyes, and got enfiladed. Their firing line cut us down like wheat in a field. In fifteen minutes 40 percent of our boys were dead or wounded. I could hear them in the dark all night. Pray you never hear that sound. It's like the wind moaning, or people sobbing under the ground.

I have heard rumors about Major Ira Jamison. People say he knows the future. We will lose everything we own. King Cotton will be King Poverty. Without slaves, there will be no cotton crops, at least not ones that produce over three thousand bales a season, such as Angola Plantation. The rumor is that Ira Jamison already has an answer for our labor problems. Convicts will be the new slaves. These are the leaders we serve and admire.

But I cannot change these things and should not brood on them. As a constable who serves the governor of the state, I am obligated to enforce the law. Unfortunately, I struggle with three impediments. One, I bear enmity toward the Lufkins and would like to see termites reduce their home to sawdust and the lot of them blown out to sea. Two, in order to get even with Charles Lufkin, I have to prove he sent Hannah Laveau to murder Minos Suarez because Lufkin owed Suarez money. Three, the information I have gathered about the murder of Minos Suarez and now the jailer Louis Boudreau has come from slaves. Nothing slaves say about anything is trustworthy. This is not their fault. When they tell the truth to their masters, they are usually whipped.

I forgot my conversation at the jail with the sheriff, Jimmy Lee Romain, who found Boudreau's body. He said there was a broken wine bottle on the floor, but no splatter, which meant he had drunk it all when he hit the deck. The padlock on the door to Hannah's cell was open, the key still in the hole. It was raining hard, and wet footprints were around the body. It was hard to tell if one or two or three people had trekked in and out. But one thing was for sure. The person who sexually mutilated Louis Boudreau made sure it hurt, because poor Boudreau's eyes were open, sad and stupefied, a tear sealed in one eye, as though he could not believe the thing that was being done to his body.

When the sheriff stopped talking, he stared out the window at the rain. His red-and-white whiskers and blue eyes and baby flesh made me wonder if enfants can be a half century old.

"You have any candidates in mind, Jimmy Lee?" I asked.

He looked out the bars at the smoke and fog on the bayou. The sky was blue-black, and oil lamps were burning in the windows of The Shadows, where the Yankees now have their headquarters, even if the owners are walking around in their midst. "I have my speculations," he replied.

I waited for him to go on.

"Hannah Laveau could have done it," he said. "Or anybody who's been around his stink. Hell, take your choice."

That's our sheriff.

This morning I went to the home of Florence Milton and knocked on her doors and even looked in the privy. Everything was locked up, including the privy. Whenever a slave takes off for the Atchafalaya, I usually find a way to talk with Miss Florence without putting her under suspicion. That might sound contradictory considering the vocation I'm in, but Miss Florence volunteered in a Reb field hospital when we got our butts run through the grinder along with Sterling Price at Corinth. It was a son of a bitch. Our battalion station tents had no laudanum. You have never heard a scream until you have listened to a man whose arm is being sawed off. I watched her. She stood her ground and didn't flinch, blood all over her dress and face. I don't care if Miss Florence frees thousands of Pygmies or Watusi and marches them into the governor's mansion or into my backyard, I will always be on her side.

Also, she has a roomful of books in the back of her home, and before the secession she would have soirees on her back lawn on the bayou and serve lemonade and read Nathaniel Hawthorne to us. She looked much younger then. I think her worries about mankind have taken their toll. Most of the audience was illiterate, and many couldn't speak English, but they always seemed the better for the experience. In reality, I have never understood her kind. She doesn't have a self.

Now my mare Varina and I are on our way to the Suarez plantation on Spanish Lake. As I mentioned, I have been there before. It's a handsome place, built in the 1790s, with twin chimneys and a second-story verandah, but it's not a happy one. Visiting there is like visiting a home where you know the children are treated badly, maybe even beaten or subjected to incest, and for whatever reason you can't do anything about it. The day can be bright, the azaleas blooming, the four-o'clocks scattered in the grass under the live oaks, the surface of the lake glinting in the background. But when you enter the gates and go down that long carriageway, you immediately realize the family members or the overseers are looking at you with a frown, unsure of who you are, perhaps glancing over their shoulder to see where Old Man Suarez is located or not located before making any concession to an unexpected visitor.

I tether Varina to an iron post and look about. None of the family come out. Perhaps they are in mourning. The overseers seem to be gone as well, although I know that is not the case. The Suarez plantation is run by fear. The chief weapon they use is the invisibility of the owners and caretakers and the awareness among the slaves that at any moment an angry white hand might knock them to the ground.

There is another aspect that is different among the Suarez slaves. The women wear dresses that are washed almost as colorless and thin as cheesecloth, and the men wear clothes that are hardly more than rags, particularly the elderly, since their time on this Earth is almost over.

I walk behind the house, where I have a view of the lake and the cane fields and the darkies hoeing out weeds in the rows. There are no overseers in sight. The darkies look right through me. A fat mulatto woman opens the back door of the main house and pours a bucket of slop into a wood barrel, one that will be carried down to the hog pen. She looks at me, but only through the side of her vision.

"Hello, there!" I say.

She pauses, wary, and doesn't speak.

"Is Miz Suarez home?"

"Ax her," she says.

"How can I ask her if I don't know where she is?"

She goes back inside, without answering, slamming the door.

I walk down to the barn. It's by the water, the ancient red paint barely evident, many of the boards streaked with rot. A free black woman whose name I can't remember is setting down a milking stool and a bucket of water and an empty pail next to a cow. The cow's tail hits the woman in the face. She slaps it in the butt. What is her name? Darby? Dauterive? The memories I have of her are not entirely pleasant. Babineaux? No, that's not it. Darla? Darla Babineaux? That's it.

"How you doin', Miss Darla?"

"Just as fine as can be, Mr. Pierre."

"You remember my name. I am very complimented."

"Well, of course, a handsome man like you," she says.

She has eyes the same color as Hannah's, right out of the Caribbean Sea. Except she can mess with your head. After a couple of exchanges with her, you don't know if she's laughing at your thoughts or inviting you to do something you shouldn't have on your mind.

Her hair is as black as silk, her skin light, her mouth red. She wears brass rings in her earlobes and fluffy purple-and-white dresses and Mardi Gras beads. When she stands up she's shorter than you think, but she turns up her face to yours and makes you step back, whether you are white or black. That doesn't happen a lot around here.

What I could never figure about her was her staying on with the Suarez family after she had a chance to leave, not leave just here, but leave the South. Four or five years ago a German man with two sword scars on his cheek visited Old Man Suarez for a couple of weeks, then paid him eleven hundred dollars for her manumission and left without any explanation. Instead of going with him, she stayed behind and shucked corn and cleaned thunder mugs and milked cows and cooked for a nasty old man who should have been dropped upside down in his privy's honey hole years ago.

"Would you be knowing where Miz Suarez is, please?" I ask.

"Is that what people call lace-curtain Irish, Mr. Pierre?"

See what I mean?

"I would appreciate if I could just find out where Miz Suarez is, Miss Darla."

"Miz Suarez is in town. So now you know," she says, and winks. Darla is seated on the milk stool now. She dips a rag into the water bucket and wipes off the teats on the cow's udder. She looks at me over her shoulder. "Can I do somet'ing for you?"

I clasp my hands in front of me and look up at the clouds, my face meditative. "I wonder if you can tell me about Hannah Laveau's situation with Mr. Suarez."

She begins to pull on the cow's teats, the milk pinging inside the tin pail. "Situation?" she says abstractly. "I don't know exactly what that is."

"I think you do, Miss Darla."

"Not me, no," she says. "I would like to help you, though. Are you sure I cain't help you, Mr. Pierre? Just a little bit?"

I hate to admit this. My face actually gets red when women talk like this. And they do—I mean, the ones in the saloon. I try to stay away from that kind. That is definitely what I have no need of.

"Did you know Louis Boudreau?"

"The one who ran the Negro jail? No, not really. I know he didn't have no friends."

"Would Hannah have any reason to hurt Mr. Suarez?"

"No, suh," she replies, her eyes veiled.

"That's not what the other darkies say."

"Don't be calling me that, Mr. Pierre. I'm a free woman now. I ain't a darky."

"I didn't come here to offend you, Miss Darla. Mr. Suarez was murdered in a horrible fashion. I have to find out who did it."

She stops pulling on the cow's teats and wipes her fingers on her cloth. "No, suh, you got somet'ing else on your mind. It ain't giving you no sleep, is it?"

"There is nothing wrong with my sleep."

"Then why are you acting so nervous?"

"I am not acting nervous. Do you have reason to think that Hannah Laveau killed Mr. Suarez?"

The wind is blowing and the sunlight through the oak trees is shifting on her skin and hair and clothes like a net of gold coins. "Sit down next to me."

"What?"

"Get a wicker chair from the barn and sit down."

In the distance I can see an overseer watching us from the edge of the cane field by the lake. I try to stare him down, but he doesn't move. I get a wicker chair from inside the barn and sit down beside her. The overseer is gone now. Darla's thigh is next to mine. I have lost my train of thought. "You want to tell me somet'ing?" she says.

"No," I reply.

"You got Hannah Laveau on your mind. She's a conjurer woman, Mr. Pierre," she says. "It don't matter how much she prays in front of people, she's had the gift passed to her. The gift has to go from a man to a woman or a woman to a man."

"What gift?"

"How to put spells on people."

"Hannah Laveau is not a conjurer, Miss Darla. Neither is she a violent person."

Her eyes are jittering as they rove across my face. "She's already inside you. You just don't know it."

"No, she is not."

"Come see me when you're ready, you." She starts pulling on the cow's udder again, humming a song.

"Did you hear me?" I say.

She rubs her foot on mine, then recommences squirting milk into the pail, her thigh against mine.

15

COLONEL CARLETON HAYES

I am well known for my egalitarian views. My flag is the Cross of St. Andrew, which is the flag of Scotland, and does not represent the South or the North. Documents and governmental mandates are little more than words written on the wind. The world you live in is the one you carve, and I have carved it with my sword from Missouri and Kansas down into Texas, and now in Louisiana, and have not lost a battle or the loyalty of one soldier, and I have drawn them from every kind of background and race.

I make no claim on philosophic knowledge, but I have come to several conclusions about the nature and travail of mankind. We are born alone and die alone; in between we can think about Heaven or Hell and which is to our liking; I plan on visiting both. When the smoke of this war clears, the name of Colonel Carleton Hayes will be branded on his enemies and lauded by the common man. Because that is what this war is all about. In the meantime, many have told me there is no better tactician in the war than I, not Forrest, not Sherman, not Jackson, although they are very good.

I will be a little more specific. The Jews in the synagogues mocked Jesus and said, "Physician, cure thyself." Jesus gave them the dust from his sandals. I will give Jews and Gentiles alike a lot more than dust. When I cleanse a town, it stays cleansed.

You ask about the affliction on my face? It is the work of the devil and the wenches in his hire. But I wear my disease as I would a trophy I have pulled from the flames. I lift my face to the light and let it shine as a testimony to my purgation of all that is evil in the world. I glory in the scars on my body, the blood-red color of my beard, the crossed eyes others have mocked me for, until I came to town.

It's night now and we are encamped along the edge of the swamp at the foot of the Lufkin property. Lufkin's workers are allowed to build a bonfire to cook their food and play shadow games and drive the mosquitoes back into the swamp. I have just been told that three of my young fellows drifted down to the cabins and gave a quart of whiskey to the overseer in exchange for an African woman. Behavior of this kind is deeply disappointing and causes me great concern.

I have these fellows stripped and tied to tree trunks and have ant beds poured on their bare feet, then I head up the slope on my horse, with the overseer, a pitiful creature nicknamed Biscuits-and-Gravy, walking behind me, a bullwhip binding his wrists and looped around his neck. Mr. Lufkin is playing croquet by lamplight in the yard with his grandchildren. It doesn't take him long to shoo them in the house. "What's going on here?" he says.

"One of your employees seems to be running a business on the side, Mr. Lufkin," I reply. "I think it's called 'procuring.'"

"Take the whip off his neck, sir. Do it now."

"Surely."

I get down from my horse and unwrap my whip and roll it up and place it my saddle bag. The overseer rubs his throat, waiting for me to apologize. Or somehow to restore his dignity. I remove a pine knot from the bag. It has a foot-long tail on it, as rough and coarse and dry as a blonde hag's unwashed hair.

"What are you doing?" Lufkin says.

I smile at him, then kick the overseer behind the knee so he collapses forward, then I beat him the way I was beaten on a fo'c'sle at age sixteen, drawing blood with each stroke, tearing fresh strips, clipping off ends, soaking and weighting the whip's fibers until he's whimpering and the remnants of his shirt are lost inside his wounds.

"That ought to do it," I say, and drop the pine knot on his back. "Did you have any questions for me, Mr. Lufkin?"

"Questions?" he says.

"About taking it to the blue-bellies, sending them a message or two about who's in charge. You haven't seen my lads in action, sir."

Lufkin seems dazed. He takes off his coat and kneels by his overseer and places it across his shoulders. "I'll get you into the house, Mr. Comeaux. I'm so sorry this has happened."

"He'll be fine, sir," I say. "Why don't we have breakfast tomorrow?"

They both stare at me, their eyes blinking, afraid to speak.

"No?" I say. "Have it your way. I say, let bygones be bygones. I'll knock on the door tomorrow."

I turn my horse and head back down the slope. The night is beautiful. Stars are dropping out of the sky. The darkies are dancing around the bonfire, their shadows jerking on the grass, like spirits trying to rise from their graves. I get under my mosquito net inside my tent and pull my coat over my head and sleep the sleep of the dead.

* * *

As you probably realize, I am not entirely taken by the Lufkin family. I think they're cabbage Irish who mustered the money to hang lace curtains on the windows and now find themselves drowning in their own piss. Young Wade seems half Nancy. It is hard to believe he took a ball on the Rappahannock. Maybe he was running in the wrong direction. Regardless, this is how I see the war. It's a business. The Yankees are not trying to defeat the South militarily. That's for show. They plan to starve it to death.

I learned a strategy from Bill Anderson and William Clarke Quantrill. You do not need ordnance to fight a war. Ordnance is a pain is the ass. You travel light and think of fire as your friend. It costs nothing, is immediately available, and leaves an unforgettable scar. Look at what that cocksucker Sherman does. His boys shoot livestock and throw them in the wells. Disease can work marvels. Look at what the blue-bellies have already accomplished. They call it the Anaconda Plan. There have already been two bread riots in Richmond. Not among the darkies, either. White ladies were ripping each other's clothes in the street over a loaf of bread. I am talking about the capital of the Confederacy.

The Yanks want to seal off Louisiana from Texas and stop the flow of food and gunpowder and Enfield rifles from the rest of the South. They have done a good job of it, too. But I know how to put them out of business. My boys can put Nathaniel Banks in a pot of hot tar. They know how to decorate a tree, too, and I'm not talking about conventional ornaments, either. Almost all my boys carry a bowie or an Arkansas toothpick. Many of them were apprenticed in North Texas, and taught a Comanche or two that there are lots of ways to die.

We could burn out Nathaniel Banks in New Iberia and draw troops out of New Orleans and free the city and bring a flotilla into

Baton Rouge and Vicksburg. I say keep the iron hot. The flesh cannot contend with it. We can have them on their knees.

If you think all of this is an abstraction, you might look at your local newspaper today. Quantrill just burned Lawrence, Kansas, and killed up to two hundred males, and not one was under sixteen. That Quantrill is a stickler if I ever saw one.

It's the next morning now and awfully hot. After coffee, I sit down on a stump with a pair of bare-chested darkies holding a parasol on each side of me. They are devoted to me because I liberated them from a place called Misery Plantation that actually had Pygmies on it because they were slaves of slaves that were captured in Africa by Dutchmen. I call for my master sergeant to bring up the three boys I had to tie to the trees overnight. Their feet are so ant-bitten and swollen they are blue and as bloodless as stone, the toes fused and inseparable.

"You boys have anything to say for yourself?" I say.

Their heads are bowed and their hair hanging in their faces. They probably haven't had a wash since their mother tried to throw them out with their first bathwater. Their wrists are still tied behind them. One has wet his pants. I cannot remember where we picked them up. I think it was somewhere around the Red River. That area tends to foster nomads who are born with six toes and gills on their necks and monkey tails. I've seen them.

"Are y'all baptized?"

One of them looks up, just enough for his hair to part over his nose. "Yes, sir," he says. "By immersion."

You could fool me, I think. "Then why did you decide to purchase an African woman for immoral purposes?"

"I seen others doing it," he says. "During that raid on Ville Platte. They said you didn't give it no never-mind as long as nobody got killed."

Nobody can be this ignorant. "Say that again?"

"My folks are churchgoers, Colonel. Our preacher says the Africans are on the same level as the beasts of the fields. Except we have to be a little kinder to them. Actually, Moses run them off before he went into Canaan Land. That's how come they ended up slaves in America."

I nod and put a piece of molasses candy in my mouth and click it over my teeth and suck on it. "Sounds like you have special insights. Scholarly research and such. What's called a bibliophile."

"Sir?"

"Don't worry about it. Y'all look like brothers," I say.

"We are, sir, and we will fight to the death in your cause."

I take the candy out of my mouth and flick it in the dirt. The stump is hurting my bottom. I also have to admit I cannot believe the stupidity of the people who follow me. It's astounding. There is no equal to poor white trash when they get their hands on a Bible. I'm surprised we don't have people practicing infanticide on street corners.

"What's your opinion on this, Master Sergeant?" I say.

He has a black beard and black eyebrows that are as bristly as rope, and wears a sun-faded Union kepi that somebody spit tobacco juice on. He stares at the bay; the reflection of the sun on the surface is like hundreds of knives. "We're in bivouac, Colonel," he says. "There's blue-bellies crawling all over that swamp. These boys knew better."

"What do you recommend, Master Sergeant?"

His eyes are receded, his jaw tight. Like a drill sergeant. "That's a hard one, sir."

The sun is in the boys' eyes. Their wrists are obviously hurting and their upper arms shaking. There is salt on their lips and their armpits are soggy with sweat.

I address the only boy who has spoken and who I am sure is the oldest. "Your parents are devout, which means they will understand the level of mercy with which I am treating you. We can either execute your two brothers and let you take the news and their belongings back home, or we can shoot you in their stead and let them carry your remains home so you can have a decent burial."

I open the cover on my pocket watch and squint at it. "What is your answer, boys?"

They are terrified. One of them groans, but I cannot tell which because the wind is blowing off the bay now, hot and dry and smelling of dead shellfish, flapping the canvas behind me. The groan is like the sound an animal makes when it's caught in a metal trap and knows it will have to chew off its own foot. One of them, I know not which, starts sniffling.

The oldest boy straightens his shoulders and flips his hair back with his head. "Take me," he says.

"What's your name?"

"Private Shaye Langtree."

"I did not hear the word 'sir' or 'colonel.' Or is that just my poor hearing at work?"

"My name is Private Langtree, *sir*! You are a son of a bitch, *sir*!"

I shift myself on the stump again. The two Africans holding parasols over my head are black as tar and running with sweat. Their eyes seem to have no color, like zombies that clawed their way out of a grave.

"Cut them loose and put them on latrine duty, Sergeant," I say.

"Yes, sir," he replies.

I wait for the boys to react. But they don't. I suspect they're afraid I will change my mind. I look directly into the eyes of the oldest boy and feel a twitch in my face, like a rubber band snapping. I tell my sergeant to report back to me in fifteen minutes, then I go into the shade of my tent and take a seat on a soft cane chair and relax my bottom and drink a glass of warm lemonade and wipe my face and the back of my neck with a soiled towel that is not mine. It's got a god-awful stink on it.

My master sergeant comes back up the slope and steps inside the tent and salutes. I throw the towel at his chest. "Find out who left that here."

"You did, sir," he says.

"That's mine?"

"It has your initials sewed on it, sir."

"Oh, yes. I forgot. A lady friend gave that to me. Watch that boy."

"Which boy do you mean, sir?"

"Take a guess."

"Shaye Langtree? I've got him digging a new latrine, sir. How about I just bury him in it?"

"That's not funny."

"No, sir, it's not."

"Get out of here."

"Yes, sir. Do you want me to take the towel?"

What towel? What is he talking about? Why do I have to always depend on an ignoramus like this? "What's your name again?"

"Master Sergeant McNab, sir."

"I thought so. Good work, McNab."

16

HANNAH LAVEAU

We ran out of the li'l food we had, and I made do with a flying fish that smacked the side of the shack and crabs I bought from some fishermen. They spoke only French and didn't seem to know much about the war or even care about it. But there's a reward on runaway slaves, and I cain't be sure that they won't report me to the slave catchers who prowl the Atchafalaya and have no mercy.

Miss Florence is not quite right in the head. She wakes up and doesn't know where she is, and walks out in the sunlight and waves at boats passing by. I had to pull her inside a couple of times and sit on her once and threaten to leave her. She keeps saying her people will not forsake us. I have a feeling Miss Florence doesn't know a lot about human beings. Ask Jesus. Out of all his men, only John went to the cross.

A storm is coming. There are no black clouds in the sky yet, but you watch. The wind will die and the sun will glow the color of tarnished brass and the air will smell like salt and wet sand and seagull nests toppling in the waves, then you'll see a glassy funnel wobbling far to the south and flickers on the horizon that turn out to be lightning that makes no sound.

I'm awful tired, not the kind of tired you get picking cotton, but the kind when your soul has got pneumonia, when you hear voices in your head telling you to go to sleep and not wake up. I love Miss Florence, but she's headstrong and fights with me, and in the morning I wake up so tired my eyes are red and I can hardly gather enough firewood to fix a decent breakfast. I got mad at her once when I shouldn't have, and I gave her a good shaking after she started to wade out in the channel where a gator was hanging in the current, just waiting to rip her apart. I shook her so hard I almost snapped her neck. And I'm mad at her now, and I'm mad at God for the weather that's coming up, and I wonder if it isn't time to look the storm in the face and let it have its course.

I'm sitting on my pallet in the corner, staring at her.

"What's on your mind, child?" she says.

I start to correct her for calling me child again, but she's too fast for me. She says, "I'm sorry, Hannah. I would never belittle you."

"We may be looking at a hurricane, Miss Florence."

She gazes out the window at the yellow density of the sky. Her hand flutters to her throat. She sounds like something is caught in her windpipe. "That looks like sand blowing out of the water. How can that be?"

"Hurricanes got their own rules."

She clears her throat again. Her nostrils are white around the edges. Miss Florence ain't a coward. But this is a special moment. I have seen it many times. This is that moment when people hear a whisper that comes out of nowhere and suddenly know they're fixing to die.

"What do you suggest?" she says.

"The pirogue."

"It doesn't have enough draft."

"It's our only choice, Miss Florence."

Her eyes linger on mine. She shakes her head. "No, I won't do it. You can make it by yourself. If you see my friends, tell them where I am."

It's a temptation, but not because I am afraid of the storm. If I get caught by bad men on our li'l island, there will be no escaping my fate. You know what I mean, too, don't you? Or maybe you don't. A colored woman in the hands of white men doesn't have a chance.

"Why are you frowning at me, Hannah?" Miss Florence asks.

"You're going to get in the pirogue with me, or I'm going to hit you upside the head with my shoe, Miss Florence."

We paddled for four or five hours, heading due north, so we could reach dry land and find shelter before lightning or a waterspout caught up with us, the wind growing stronger and stronger, the tide rising. But I was worrying about the wrong things. I was in the back of the pirogue paddling on both sides because Miss Florence had blisters on both her hands, mean ones with the skin already popped, when the wind gusted and she looked at something behind me and her face changed and she reached for her paddle. "We must hurry!" she said. "Oh, Hannah, I fear this may be it. I have failed you. I am so sorry."

I did not know what she meant. Then I turned around and I knew. I had heard about these but had never seen one. The wave was over ten feet high, rushing toward us, scouring up the sand

and shale and rotted vegetation in front of it, crowning but never toppling or flattening, instead streaming with baitfish and a dirty yellow froth, feeding itself, uprooting dead cypress trees like they were celery stalks.

Then it was under us, lifting us into the sky, twirling us like a stick, pushing us through trees that were flooding to their tops, their limbs crowded with small animals that were drowning. The clouds broke open and poured down on us, so hard the rain felt like drops of lead. My head was spinning. In the corner of my eye I could see another boat. It had a paddlewheel and two smokestacks and a cage on the stern and a Confederate flag on top of the pilothouse, and I knew that something terrible was about to happen, the same way I felt when Master Suarez removed his clothes and used his body to take away everything I owned.

Suddenly I am in the air, and so are Miss Florence and the pirogue. The tidal wave is swelling under us, like the back of a whale, alligator gars six feet long belly-up in the froth, their backs broken, their gills as red as razor slits, a stink like offal rising from the water.

Then I see the Confederate boat directly below us, its deck sloshing, the steel door on the cage swinging in the spray, white men clutching the bars to keep from going into the water. The pirogue crashes on the deck and breaks in half. For a moment I think my spine is broken. Miss Florence slides by me, clinging with her nails to an empty wood box that wouldn't stay afloat two seconds.

I always thought I would accept death when it came. That's when I believed li'l Samuel would be waiting for me. But there is nobody on this boat except the kind of men who wear dirty clothes and raggedy beards and have hungry eyes. One of them grabs me like he's grabbing onto a log and is going to float me underneath him so he can keep himself from sinking.

Then the wave is gone, rushing northward through a bay of flooded tupelos that look like grave markers in a cemetery. The water is flat now, the rain gentle, the sun shining. Dead fish are everywhere, and others are skittering around sideways, like they're only half alive. Miss Florence is trying to get up but slips down twice and hurts her knees. There are two men on the deck and one in the pilothouse, and all of them are laughing at her. One of them was onboard the boat that delivered Mr. and Mrs. Lufkin's dead sons to the dock at Lady of the Lake Plantation. His eyes are locked on mine, his teeth white when he grins inside his beard. I know his thoughts before he has them. I know what the sunset will bring that evening. And I know what it may bring for Miss Florence, too, because men like these are hunters and do not share, and if they do, they leave no evidence lest their companions use it against them.

We are placed in the cage, the door padlocked behind us. Pieces of a reddish-brown seaweed called sargassum hang on the bars. It grows in the waters around Devil's Island and in the West Indies, places I never wanted to see again. It's wet and ugly and thick and has white creatures in it. And now it's here, dripping on the tops of my feet because I have lost my shoes. *It's here.*

17

COLONEL CARLETON HAYES

The Creator surely does have mysterious ways. We went through a tidal surge and then a hurricane and a chain of storms that could have provided bathwater for not only Louisiana but the entire state of Arkansas. I put a captain and a couple of my lieutenants and my master sergeant in charge of the enlisted men and went up to the Lady of the Lake big house in case those old people and their Nancy nephew, Young Wade, needed some support, which turned out to be the case.

My father always taught me that a genuinely strong man is a kind man, but a kind man is often weak and hides his failure inside false acts of charity. My father was a profound man, and was part of Andrew Jackson's escort of the Cherokee to their new home in Oklahoma in 1838.

Old Man Lufkin had come down with a fever and a pain in his right arm that left a tremble in his face, and his wife tripped on the staircase while she was carrying his food up, instead of using a servant, and in the meantime Young Wade got hold of a mirror and saw what he looked like and went out in the hurricane and started shouting and shaking his fist at the thunder.

I am getting the feeling this is not your normal crew of plantation nobility. Or maybe it is. How about Jefferson Davis? The whole goddamn Confederacy is under his thumb, the same man who as U.S. Secretary of War imported camels from Arabia to the United States and delivered them to cavalry units in the American West. I understand they're still running loose in the desert and causing many a prospector to take the pledge.

I latched all the shutters, put bricks on the storm doors to the cellar, lit candles and oil lamps all over the house, and had the cooks fix food for everybody, including the other servants. Then Mrs. Lufkin asked me to go after her nephew and bring him inside. She was wearing a black mourning dress with a ruffled white collar. The darkies say she recently buried three sons in the cellar because the Yankees believe the plantation owners have been hiding their silver in graveyards.

"Miz Lufkin," I said. "Let the boy shout and holler and get rained on a while, then we'll dry him off and fix him a toddy and put him to bed. Right now he seems a bit touched. Or is that just his way?"

"No, it is not."

"Hmm," I said, like people do for lack of words. But she kept staring at me, as though I were a bat that had just flown into the house. It made me very uncomfortable. "Is it true you're related to the Booth family in Georgia?"

"No, I am not *related* to the Booths. I *am* a Booth. From Wilkes County. Why is it you ask?"

"You know, Edwin Booth and all," I said.

"No, I do not know. What are you saying?"

"He's a famous actor."

"Sir, you talk like an idiot."

I definitely think this family has a problem.

Anyway, that brings me up to date. I hang a slicker over my head and go out in the thunder and the wind. There are lamps lit in the tents where my men are bivouacked. Some of the tents have been blown flat. Some of my men have probably quartered themselves in the shacks of the darkies. Well, that's what I taught them. An army marches on its stomach. You get your victuals where you can.

The skies have quieted down; flashes of electricity ripple through the clouds and die on the horizon, and stars twinkle in the blackness. I get a hand on Young Wade and march him back to the house and upstairs to his bedroom. He feels like a pile of sticks. I also send a servant downstairs to bring me a bottle of whiskey. I have to admit I love whiskey. I love it so much I don't abuse it, because then I would have to give it up. I pour myself three inches and let the servants undress Young Wade and dry him off and put on his nightshirt for him. In his nakedness he's a sickly-looking fellow, with a puckered scar where he still carries a Minie ball. But, oh Lord, that face. I doubt if even a blind woman could deal with it.

A book of poems by Robert Browning lies on his bed. When I pick it up and open it, the glue in the binding cracks.

"Could you hand me my sedation, Colonel?" he says.

The laudanum bottle is on a table by the wall. "Do you have particular times during the day you take it, Young Wade?"

"Yes, the particular times when I am in pain. When I feel I have nails in my face. Would you hand it to me, please?"

I sit on the side of his bed and feed him a tablespoon of laudanum and touch his mouth with a napkin. When I try to put away the spoon, he grabs my wrist. "Give me the bottle."

"The Orientals are flooding our country with their opium, son. Let me give you a shot of whiskey. Or better yet, I'll mix you a little whiskey with the laudanum, then gradually you can get rid of them both."

He's sitting up in the bed. His face looks like a broken flowerpot. There's a need in his eyes he cannot hide, and a hatred for both himself and me. "You have it worked out, do you?" he says.

I stand up with the laudanum bottle in one hand and the whiskey in the other and walk to the French doors that open onto the balcony. "The sky reminds me of black velvet. The Milky Way looks like snow blowing in the wind. There's a lesson in the heavens, Young Wade. It's about beauty and power and ephemerality."

I turn from the window to see if my words have had any effect on him. His eyes are fixed on the laudanum and whiskey bottles in my hands.

"Where is your Uncle Charles?" I ask.

"Resting in his bed."

"I would like to speak to him about your medication. I think we should have some caution about its use."

"My aunt does not want him disturbed," he replies. He wets his lips, then wipes them with the back of his wrist. "I'll take the mixture of laudanum and whiskey, Colonel."

"Maybe we should reconsider," I reply.

"No, I want it. It's generous of you to wait on me."

"Maybe you should go to sleep now. I'll check on you tomorrow."

I put the laudanum bottle in one coat pocket and the whiskey bottle in the other and walk out of the room, letting my gaze slide off his face. I close the door softly, just as he throws something at it, maybe the unread book on his bed.

Then, as fate would have it, I hear Mrs. Lufkin calling out and the feet of the servants running down the hallway. I follow the servants into Lufkin's room. Over their heads I can see the old man jerking in the bed, his arms flopping, his genitalia exposed, his feet gray and curled like claws, his tongue as thick as a pig's bladder halfway down his throat.

I see nothing I can do to help, so I go back to Young Wade's room to get out of the way of others and serve the family in that fashion. A lad like Young Wade needs an authority figure in his life, a boost of the spirits, a kind word. That's what my father used to say. In fact, he said it again and again and again, all the days of my young life, until the day I shot him.

18

HANNAH LAVEAU

The boat is rocking in a lagoon, bumping against a sandbar, the evening sun a red coal beyond the flooded trees on the western horizon. The three men are getting drunk in the pilothouse. They speak in both French and English, but only in French when they speak about Miss Florence and me. They have dirty minds and dirty ways, and keep looking over their shoulders at us. Earlier they shot an alligator for fun. The pistol is British, like none I have ever seen. You can cock it or not cock it. They took turns using it.

Earlier they put a canvas tarp on one side of the cage and gave us some newspaper and a bucket to use for our waste. Miss Florence has refused to use it. She is indignant and believes that her anger will force our captors to either put us on land or turn us over to a constable. She does not speak French, and I do not tell her what the three men are saying when they talk about us. In fact, the men themselves are probably not aware of the plans they are making for themselves and us. They are the kinds of cowards who use one another to become somebody else, someone who can do things they would not do on their own.

I ain't smart. I have just seen too many women hurt by bad men. See, they cain't abide what they are; it's not *who* they are, it's *what* they are. They are full of hate when they come out of the womb. And if they're not, it's taught to them. The only thing valuable in their lives is the belief they are better than us. We ain't got souls. God gave ownership of us to them. It's in Leviticus 25:46.

The men are laughing louder now, swigging down more liquor, laughing so hard they cain't stand up, coughing up phlegm. It won't be long now. They'll flip coins. I don't think Miss Florence is going to get through this. Maybe me neither. I'd like to go over the side and swim into deep water and stay on the bottom of the bay and let the light shine down on my face one last time, then open my mouth and drift down into a dark, cold place where nobody can get me.

Way out on the Gulf a fiery ember is still burning below the rainclouds, like the flames on a sinking ship. But that's not all I see. I stand up in the cage and look through the bars and see a seraphim descend upon the ember and pick it up with tongs and fly across the water and touch my lips and eyes with it and forever purge wickedness from my life, and not just my life, either; I am also freed from the evil of the men on the boat, no matter what they do to my body. I know none of these thoughts seem rational, but that doesn't matter. I know these things are real.

I feel Miss Florence's hand on my shoulder, then her breath on the back of my neck. "Can you make out what they're saying?" she asks.

"Yes."

Her lips are dry and gray. "What?" she says, not wanting to hear the answer to her own question.

"They're making fun of us, Miss Florence. They're saying ugly things, too."

"What do you mean by 'ugly things'?"

"Things you don't want to talk about."

She takes her hand from my back. "They plan to take advantage of us?"

"They're telling jokes about it. That's how it starts."

"We won't let that happen," she says, straightening her shoulders.

"Don't try to fight them, Miss Florence. Keep your eyes shut. Go to a place inside yourself and stay there. Then it will be over."

She's breathing hard now, her hands opening and closing. "You're not telling me everything, Hannah."

"They don't care what they do to me, because I don't count."

She pushes her hair off her forehead with the heel of her hand, grinding it into her skull. "We will not allow this to happen. They will not do this to us."

"Miss Florence, these ain't 'people' you're talking about. Maybe they come from under the earth. They come from someplace cruelty and meanness is made. Maybe in a forge. Where the iron is beaten on the anvil with a hammer. They ain't human, Miss Florence."

She starts hitting me on the chest with her fist. "Tell me what they are saying!"

"Their kind don't leave witnesses," I reply.

"I have to relieve myself in front of you, Hannah. Please forgive me."

I feel so sorry for Miss Florence. She has been such a nice lady and done so much good for people. She ain't prepared for what's about to happen. It ain't right. I guess I'm saying that to God.

"You know the story of Perpetua and Felicity in the Roman arena?"

"I don't recall," she says, irritable.

"One was a slave, one an owner. They died together in Carthage. Awful things happened to them before they died. We got to be brave, Miss Florence."

It wasn't the right thing to say. Miss Florence never thought she would have a day like this, or be on a boat like this, or be with men who have the claws of crabs instead of hands.

"After I finish my business, I want to have a talk with the captain," she says.

It ain't going to do any good, I think. But I don't say it.

One of the deckhands throws a brown bottle into the current. It bobs up and down in the water then floats away from the sandbar, the bottleneck stiff and tinkling with light in the sunset.

19

FLORENCE MILTON

My dress has not dried; my skin and hair are matted with debris. The sun is completely gone, but the bay is still lit, as though the Earth has pulled the light under the water. I have to make a confession. My behavior and my rhetoric are largely a pretense. I am afraid. And I am ashamed to admit that. As an educator I always taught my students, who are members of the plantation culture, that they should never bear an animus toward their "servants" or the poor, because a lack of charity is the sister of fear.

Now I find myself sick in the stomach, weak in my legs, and dry in the mouth; my eyelids feel like sandpaper. The mental image of these men putting their hands on me makes my scalp shrink and tests my continence. I am not only afraid and ashamed, I'm angry at myself. I was in a surgical tent at Corinth, and cannister with lead balls in them were exploding all over the cottonfield, the canvas jumping each time a ball went through the tent. I stayed with the surgeons and those poor boys on the stretchers while their friends were running; even when the tent was burning, I stayed. And I was proud of myself.

I press my forehead against the bars of the cage. Hannah does not think I understand these men. But I do. They will take me first, and because I am plain and have never used cosmetics, and because I am educated and have a New England accent, and because there are rumors I am part of an underground railway, they will sexually degrade me and pretend their desires are irrelevant and they are simply straightening out a Yankee abolitionist who had no business south of the Mason-Dixon.

Then they will kill me and weight my body with chains or more probably eviscerate me and fill the cavity with bricks and sink my remains into the depths of the Gulf. When they tire of raping Hannah, they will sell her into a brothel in Galveston or for a great deal of money to French aristocrats in Mexico. These are not simply dark imaginings. I was an idealistic girl in Boston when I decided to go to Louisiana and fight the good fight of Saint Paul. I do not regret my choice. But I regret that I took too much for granted and now face a death for which I am not prepared.

Hannah did not have to tell me the story of Felicity and Perpetua. They are two of the bravest women in the history of the Western world. I always admired them, even prayed to them. That is what I do now. Then I pick up the waste bucket and clang it against the bars.

"You men come down here!" I say. "I have a few thoughts to share with you."

Gathered around the cage, they call to mind a trio of partially evolved apes—muscles flexed, simian hair on their skin, tattoos, a fecal odor in their clothes, their breaths soaked in alcohol.

"I am a personal friend of General Richard Taylor," I say. "If you do not know who that is, he is now trying to retake Baton Rouge for the Confederacy. He is also the son of President Zachary Taylor. I doubt that your antics here will be appreciated."

The captain of the boat wears a filthy cap on the back of his head and laughs in my face and hooks his hands on the bars, releasing a stench like cat urine from his underarms. He's the biggest of the three men, his shirt rolled up on arms that are as big as hams, the back of his neck sunburned, his stomach hanging over his belt. "You make a fine show of it, you," he says. He drops one hand and squeezes his genitalia. "How would you like to suck on this? That is, after you clean up the mess you made with your bucket."

"I know Sheriff Romain. I also know the Suarez and the Lufkin families in New Iberia and St. Martinville. Hannah Laveau is the property of Charles Lufkin. Do you want to be accountable to him?"

The three of them look at each other in mock surprise, then begin laughing again.

"Why not just have a drink with us, and we'll talk things out?" the captain says. "Come on, I'll unlock you and let you clean up."

"You speak French and English," I say. "I suspect you have had some education. Don't do what you're thinking. In a few hours from now you'll realize the mistake you have made. And from that time on these two men will have power over you for the rest of your life."

"Really?" he says. "I like your accent. Let me open the door."

I step back from the bars, but I have no place to go or hide.

"Come on," he says, inside now, reaching to touch my face. "Let's talk about lobsters. I was a fisherman up in Nova Scotia."

I keep stepping back from him.

"You're a spinster, aren't you? You're also a member of the Underground Railroad."

"Do not put your hand on me."

"There's two things you don't quite understand. The man to your right is my son. The one on the left is my brother. And I'm Claude. Glad to meet you."

Then his fist explodes in the middle of my face.

They drag me by my clothes and my hair across the deck, picking me up and throwing me down, hitting me everywhere they can. The sky is black now, like soot, the stars barely glimmering. The deck is as hard as table rock, or perhaps ancient stone, the kind that Felicity and Perpetua suffered on seventeen hundred years ago. I know that Hannah tried to fight the captain and his son and brother, but she was no match for the three of them, and they flung her to the deck inside the cage and kicked her and locked the door.

The captain drags me into the pilothouse and shoves me down beneath the wheel and unbuttons his fly.

"Where do you want it first, girlie?" he says.

My breath is gone, my nose bleeding, my hands and face trembling with trauma. I want to say something to him, but I don't know what it is. I want to tell him that the Almighty will be his judge; I want to tell him that Hell waits for him. I want to believe that the elements themselves will tear him and his family apart, that justice always finds and gives solace to the meek and punishes evil. But I cannot speak. My tongue is cut and I have swallowed a broken tooth. I am strangling on the blood and phlegm in my throat.

I know my heart and my lungs are about to give out, and my death is imminent.

Then something happens that has never occurred in my life. A wind blows across the bay and the swamp, roiling the clouds, spreading the moonlight through the willow and cypress, spangling the water, the reflection wobbling inside the pilothouse. I can see animals on the islands that surround us, big ones, some that make sounds I have never heard before. Inside my head I hear the roar of a crowd and the ring of swords being pulled from their scabbards, and I smell an odor like blood and warm sand and animal dung.

I see two women dying in an open-air stadium by a sea that is the deepest blue I have ever seen. They are dying incrementally, by flagellation, by the claws and teeth of wild animals, by the swords of Romans in gladiatorial dress. Suddenly the women point at me, and one of them, the slave girl Felicity, says, *Your time is not now.*

I get up from the floor in the pilothouse. The wheel is inches away from me. Heat lightning flickers through the clouds, and I see a leather belt hanging from the bottom of the wheel. A holster is attached to the belt, and inside the holster is a cap-and-ball revolver. I pull it from the holster with both hands. The weight alone tells me this is not an ordinary revolver. It's huge. The chambers are loaded; the caps are clean. I lift the sight on the barrel into the face of the captain and pull back the hammer with both thumbs, then squeeze the trigger. The flame is a foot long. I have never seen a man so surprised. His mouth looks like a fish's when the fish is skimming across the surface of the water. His hands are in front of him, the palms vertical, as though he is trying to prevent a train from running over him. Then the back of his head splatters across most of the helm.

The other two men are backing away from me. They're speaking French, then English, then French. The only word I hear over and over again is "no." I cock the hammer a second time and shoot one man through the throat and the other in the stomach. They are both on the floor now, curled into balls. A red bubble puffs from one man's mouth; the other man has his arms clapped over his ears and tries to speak but cannot. I cock the hammer with both thumbs so as not to slip, because I am shaking all over now. I touch the muzzle of the barrel to each man's temple, then look away and with one hand squeeze the trigger.

Each man's head bounces from the velocity of the discharge, and the ball goes out the other side and through the floor and ricochets inside the boiler area.

I work a set of keys out of the trouser pocket of the captain, then unlock the door on the cage. I try to explain to Hannah what has happened, but my hearing is temporarily gone and the words I speak are better lost on the wind. The vision I had of an ancient Carthaginian amphitheater is one that few will believe. Maybe that's better. My story about the two women might sully their legacy. Also, there are those who will take me to task for not sparing two of the men. But what if they had other weapons on their boat? Or what if they got the upper hand on us again? I wonder how others would like that?

I sit by Hannah's side inside the cage and stroke her hair, and perhaps secretly wish that she would stroke mine. The tide is coming in now, and I can feel the boat rising from the sandbar. The sky is black, the stars as smoky as melting hailstones. The animals and amphibians have gone, and so have our fears. I kiss Hannah on the forehead, then undress and ease over the gunwale into the water and wash myself cleaner than I have ever been. Then I wait in the stillness of the world in hopes I can re-teach my heart that all streams flow into the sea but the sea is never full, and, like my pilgrim ancestors, I should not question the ways of God as I shelter in His hand.

20

PIERRE CAUCHON

How in the name of suffering Jesus am I supposed to fix all the problems that have been dropped on my head? Everybody in nine parishes is on my butt. Three slave catchers are shot to death on their boat in the Atchafalaya, and their boat burned, and somehow it's my fault. I knew all three of those sons of bitches. The only question for me is why somebody didn't shoot them a long time ago.

Anyway, people are spotting their underwear and think there's a slave insurrection about to bust loose any minute. A few think Florence Milton had a hand in the escape of Hannah Laveau from the Negro jail and in the killing of the jailer and also in the killing of the slave catchers. I am afraid they are probably right. Frankly, if I have anything to do with it, I'm going to see both women get a lot of gone between here and the Ohio River before a lynch mob gets to them.

What I am saying is I am plumb fed up. None of this is about war. It's about money. I wish I was a greyback again. At least I would have some dignity. At least I could legally shoot blue-bellies. That's my problem right now. My superior in Baton Rouge has told me to do something about blue-bellies confiscating livestock on civilian property. I'm supposed to stop them? I fired the first shot at Fort Sumter?

So here I am again at the Suarez plantation on Spanish Lake, unarmed, with a spinal wound from Shiloh and a limp thanks to an ignorant cracker who chopped off three of my toes. Blue herons and pelicans that have lost their way are flying over the lake. The four-o'clocks are blooming pink and gold and red at the bottom of the tree trunks in the pecan orchard. And last but not least, at the barn I can see a mess of blue-bellies, eleven enlisted men and one officer, all of them mounted. Thank you very much.

Darla Babineaux, the freed slave woman, is arguing with them. I swing down from my saddle and take Varina's reins over her head and keep walking through the orchard. Why do I get down? Blue-bellies are blue-bellies. General Banks has given them permission to do whatever they want. If you're smart, you do not challenge them. General Forrest said he won his battles by "getting there firstest with the mostest." I am mostest happy to hear that. Let me be the firstest to congratulate the general. However, Pierre Cauchon arrives with the leastest, thank you very much again.

Defeat does not go down easily. Particularly when the victors stick your face in it. I wonder sometimes why the slaves do not cut our throats. That's how I feel sometimes when a few blue-bellies push me off a walkway or step in front of me in a store. I think about ax handles.

I walk out of the trees and doff my hat to the officer. He's a captain, a handsome man with a straight saddle posture, his hands resting on the pommel. He looks like a pleasant man. Inside the barnyard are seven cows, three calves, and two hogs. They have obviously been assembled there and are about to be herded off the property. Darla seems to welcome my arrival. Maybe even the officer does. "Good day to you, sir," he says.

"And to you, suh," I say.

"Can we be of help to you?" he asks.

Darla cuts him off. "You can get this whole bunch of Yankees off Suarez land and tell them to stop picking on people ain't done them nothing," Darla says to me. She's wearing trousers and Mexican boots and a purple shirt with white trim on it. Her face is lit, her eyes flashing. Miss Darla should have been an actress.

"I'm Pierre Cauchon, the oversight constable for Negro legal problems in this area," I say to the officer. "Can I be of service to you?"

There's a ripple of laughter among his men. "You're who?" the captain says.

I repeat my full name.

"That's the name of the bishop who burned Joan of Arc alive," he says.

"I have been told that on many occasions," I say.

"Are you his descendant?"

"I am not certain, sir, but if I can find out, I will surely contact you."

He stretches against his stirrups. "Perhaps you can convince Miss Darla that we have the right to impound the animals you see before you. If she or members of the Suarez family wish, they can make application for reimbursement in New Orleans."

"There are small children in the cabins, suh," Darla says. "Some of the mothers cain't nurse no more. Please don't take the cows."

The captain removes his hat and huffs air out of his nostrils. His hair is thick and bronze-colored, a contrast to the leanness of his face. I have no doubt something is going on. Maybe he has an eye for Darla, or she has an eye for him. As you have probably sensed, I think most human beings are somewhat thespian.

The captain puts his hat back on. "Wish I could help you. Would you move aside, please?"

Too bad, Miss Darla. As corrupt as he was, Old Man Suarez wouldn't put up with this. With one punch he broke the neck of a man twice his size in a saloon. I look up at the officer. "I didn't catch your name, Captain."

"Endicott. Captain John Endicott."

"I think we have met before, Captain Endicott. It was on the evening of April seventh, just last year."

"Where would that be, Mr. Cauchon?"

"At Shiloh Church. More specifically, at Owl Creek, on General Beauregard's left flank. You enfiladed us and cut us to pieces when we marched uphill into your cannon. I think your fellows had a grand time of it. Are these lads here part of the unit you commanded?"

"That is correct," he says.

"What a jolly bunch you are," I reply. "Blowing the shite out of farm boys, then knocking around barnyard animals. Does West Point have classes in that?"

"Maybe it's time you traded in your sword for a plowshare, Mr. Cauchon."

"Thank you for the suggestion. Tell me, have you ever met Major Ira Jamison? He's the slop jar who didn't show up and left us to your mercy. A bit like that other slop jar Beauregard, who sent us up a hill to get killed by a worthless fucker such as yourself."

"I think you're a bitter man, Mr. Cauchon," he says.

"Why don't you step down so we can chat a bit? Your lads can have a pail or two of the milk they're about to steal from enfants. I didn't know the yellow-bellies were doing that. Oh, excuse me. It's 'blue-bellies,' isn't it?"

He glances out the side of his eye at Darla, his cheeks red. I was right. He's here for more than rifling food from the darkies. His men are watching him, hoping he will turn them loose and perhaps rope-drag me around the Suarez property or put a ball between my eyes and plant a pistol on my body.

Darla places her hand on his thigh, her fingers spreading across his trouser leg. He looks like his rooster just woke up. "Mr. Cauchon don't mean anyt'ing," she says. "You're a nice man, Captain Endicott. Miz Suarez had got the dementia, and the children is all living in the Nort'. Dat just leaves me. What am I gonna do if dose children don't have no milk?"

Her Acadian accent is growing by the second. Acadians cannot make the *th* sound. You can beat them to death and they can't make it.

"I will be back next week," the captain says. "The livestock are not to be moved from this property. I also want Mrs. Suarez's physician to contact me. I can be reached through General Banks's headquarters at The Shadows on Main Street in New Iberia. Are you listening to me?"

"Yes, suh," Darla says, her head bowed.

"I am making an exception for humanitarian reasons."

"Yes, suh," she says again. "Anybody can tell that for sure."

He tries to force her to look at him. But she doesn't. She has beaten him. I also think his plans for a tryst that evening have just splashed into Spanish Lake. He jerks his horse's reins and points a stiffened finger at me. "You!" he says. "I don't care if you were at Shiloh or not. You are not worth the sweat on the balls of my men."

"Thank you, you arrogant, tea-sipping bastard," I say. "May the worms not vomit you up before the devil knows you're dead."

Until that moment, I didn't realize how deeply the canker of war had buried itself in my soul.

I could have gone on my way. But I didn't. Sometimes at the end of the day I go to a dark place I cannot rid myself of. I think about my blind mother, and want to be with her. I also want to be with the children with whom I played. We were a tattered bunch, but the best children, white and colored, and old people I ever knew. They told us stories on their galleries in late summer while the fireflies flickered like pieces of burning string in the trees. I also think about the boys who were at my side when we went straight into Union cannon, twelve-year-old drummer boys rolling the attack, the Stars and Bars flapping, the flag-bearer undaunted by the fusillade aimed at his chest.

Strangely, I want to tell Darla all these things. I am not predatory. I live celibate and have never visited a brothel. Nor do I wish to capitalize on my race. I would just like to be with Darla, the way children are together. Or with Hannah, who to my shame I was willing to sacrifice to get even with Old Man Lufkin for treating me as he would white trash.

I think people of color are superior to us in many ways. They are a kind and loving people, and that is why we seek them out when we are ill. But I cannot deny my lower passions. I wake throbbing in the morning, my dreams filled with images that are embarrassing.

By anyone's measure, I am a foolish man. I long for my child-hood and my mother, even though we lived in penury, and yet I work in servitude to people I despise. Also, I fought for a cause I don't believe in, but nonetheless I wish to be a greyback again and hear my commanding officer shout in his paternal fashion, "Form on me, boys! Form on me! By God, we've got them licked!"

"Mr. Pierre?" Darla says.

"Yes?"

"You don't look good. Come sit wit' me. It's a nice time of day. I'm fixing to crack some pecans."

And that's what we do, well into the evening, when the entire sky is aflame. "Can I tell you a secret, Mr. Pierre?" she says.

"Sure you can."

"I saw Master Suarez dump a fortune out there in the lake."

"How would he do that?"

"Soon as New Orleans fell, he said, 'We're gonna lose.' He collected all the gold and silver in the house and nailed it in a bar-rel and rolled it down the slope and sunk it out on the lake. I seen him do it."

"Don't tell this to others, Darla."

"I ain't. I'm just telling you."

The lake and the flooded trees in it look like they are on fire. I stand up from my chair. "I have to go now."

She stands up also. "Take me inside the barn, Mr. Pierre."

"That would be an abuse of power, Darla."

"No, it ain't. Men did that to me many years ago. I killed one man and almost killed another. They were both white. Ain't nobody bothered me since. You're a different kind of white man, Mr. Pierre."

"I have to ask you something."

"What?"

"Did Hannah kill Old Man Suarez?"

"I ain't got nothing to say about that."

I look at the sunset. I feel like I am watching the end of the world, but I don't know why. I pick up her hand and kiss the back of it.

"Nobody ever done that to me," she says.

"See you later."

"Why'd you do that?"

"I fear for you. Good night, Darla."

"Come back here," she says. "Please, Mr. Pierre. I don't know what you're doing, you."

But I keep walking and don't look back. The dark energies within the society I serve are unpredictable and can be so cruel you question the existence of God. I hope I haven't opened a door I can't close.

21

WADE LUFKIN

I have told the servants to hang blankets on the mirrors in the upstairs hallway and the bathroom, and I no longer grieve upon the damage done to my features by Pierre Cauchon. The pain in my sleep is another matter. Laudanum and a tablespoon of whiskey have become my recourse, and I look upon them as friends, although some believe there is habituation associated with some of the elements involved.

The summer is coming to an end. The light no longer climbs into the evening sky, and in the early morning there is a hint of gas in the swamp. Uncle Charles is only a few feet down the hallway, but I see little of him, perhaps because I don't like to witness infirmity or hear the rasping cough in his lungs that precedes a respiratory death. My contact with the outer world has become Colonel Hayes. He dotes on me and brings me gifts and speaks of taking back the Mississippi River, even though most of the cities on its banks have fallen.

It's Sunday morning now. My bedroom window is open, the curtains riffling, the air surprisingly cool, the swamp maples in the bay already turning red. Colonel Hayes knocks on my door, then peeks in, a mug of coffee in his hand. "How are you feeling, young fellow?" he says.

"Just fine, sir. And you?"

He sits on the side of my bed and puts the coffee in my hand. Coffee is a treat these days. He picks at something on his fly, then releases it. "I have to be out and about, so I thought I would check in with you first," he says.

"Out and about where, sir?"

"You'll be hearing about it. It's nothing to worry about. I may be bringing some units from Missouri, fellows who have already made their mark."

I nod my head. I give little credence to the colonel's stories about Missouri raiders. Yesterday he was speaking of Cole Younger and Frank James. Who are Cole Younger and Frank James? "Thank you for the coffee, sir. Have you visited this morning with Uncle Charles?"

"Oh, yes, and I have made sure the darkies do their jobs well."

"Sir?"

"You have to be on top of them. Give them an inch and they'll take a mile."

"That is not our way here, sir."

"Oh, I know. I meant no harm." He gets up from the bed and pats my shoulder. "Keep your ear to the ground, Young Wade. You will not only hear a thundering of hooves. You will hear history in the making."

"I am sure that's so, Colonel."

After he's gone, I pour my whiskey-and-laudanum from my cup into the coffee mug and drink it to the bottom. In no time I'm asleep and in a pink garden that is free of thought or consequence, where nymphs float in the trees and an organ-grinder plays to children who run through the flowers and do not fear a man whose face is hideous. Yes, the organ-grinder is me.

I do not wake until afternoon. When I walk to the window and look to the south, the entire encampment of the colonel and his men is empty, except for the trash and liquor bottles and dead campfires they have left behind. I hear no thunder of hooves on the ground or horns blowing along the road to Roncesvalles. I see nothing other than a dirty scar on the earth left by a man who picks at his fly.

Maybe I have learned a lesson. Maybe for the Lufkin family, this is the end of the war. Maybe for us that day has come when the lamb will lie down with the lion and there will be no more death. We are religious people. These things are in Isaiah and the Book of Revelation and in the promises of Our Lord, so how can we deny them? And if these prophesies are true, why should they not occur here, at Lady of the Lake Plantation?

I wonder if indeed an enormous change is about to take place in my life. One that is spiritual, one that will rid me of the young officer I bayonetted to death in Northern Virginia.

It's four days later, after dark, when I hear the horses outside. I look down from my window and see my Aunt Ezemily standing in the yard with an oil lamp, surrounded by twelve to fifteen mounted Yankees. A rainy mist is blowing out of the bay, and the light shines on their faces and slickers. They keep looking over their shoulders, their horses stamping, as though flies are biting their underbellies. The enlisted men are armed with Spencer carbines, lovely seven-rounders with which a single soldier can wreak havoc.

I put on my robe and slippers and go downstairs and out the door into the mist. Two of the servants are standing behind Aunt Ezemily, their eyes on the ground. This is the first time I have been outside since the duel. The officer has removed his hat, obviously in deference to my aunt. His face is shiny in the lamplight, his features clean, his hair the color of copper. I can see no weapon on his person. He wipes his face with a kerchief and puts his hat back on.

"So, if I understand you, madam, you have no idea where Colonel Hayes has gone?" he says. "Nor do you remember when he encamped on your plantation, with two hundred men and wagons and an artillery piece? Nor do you know where they might be? They went just puff, like dandelions?"

"The totality of my time, sir, is devoted to the care of my husband, Mr. Charles Lufkin, who is in his last days," Aunt Ezemily says. "We lost three sons at Chickamauga. They were transported and buried here just recently. You can see their graves in the grove of live oaks. Since their interment, we have taken no more interest in the war, and leave others to their own concerns."

"How long was Colonel Hayes bivouacked here?" the officer says, turning in the saddle, looking down the slope.

"I do not know, sir."

"You took no interest in two hundred Red Legs strolling about, building bonfires, probably getting drunk, slinging trash all over the place, all of this in your front yard?"

"I do not appreciate your mocking tone, Captain Endicott."

"That is not my intention, madam."

"Please do not address me as 'madam' again. My name is Mrs. Ezemily Booth Lufkin."

"Are you related to the actor?"

"Would you please leave my yard?"

"My orders are otherwise, Mrs. Lufkin. I have to confiscate your livestock and also I have to search your house for weapons and any documentary evidence of your complicity with Red Legs."

"Search my house for *what*?"

"You may indeed be innocent, Mrs. Lufkin, but in the last few days Carleton Hayes has burned colored settlements, robbed the bank in Opelousas, lynched three people he believed to be abolitionists, and fired a cannon at General Banks in New Iberia. How would you like this jolly fellow to do the same for you?"

"I have nothing else to say to you, sir," she says. "You have killed our sons. Now let us mourn."

She turns down the wick of the lantern and extinguishes the light, then walks back inside the house, her eyes straight ahead. The servants follow, leaving me in the mist with the soldiers. The soldiers have paid no attention to me, and I have no idea what they are thinking. The officer is intelligent and educated, and probably what we call well-bred. He tugs on his hat brim, his jaw flexing, his horse stamping. Perhaps he's about to bid us adieu. But that is wishful thinking. He's fighting inside himself, and I know the outcome will not be good.

"Sir, may I speak with you?" I ask.

"What did you say?" he snaps. Then he sees my face for the first time. And so do his men. "Excuse me, sir. How can I be of assistance?"

"My aunt and uncle had no choice about the presence of Colonel Hayes. I was not able to help them, either. I was with the Eighth Louisiana Infantry and the Army of Northern Virginia and seriously wounded and declared an invalid at Malvern Hill."

"Go on."

"I am familiar with General Banks's policies. They are not those of General Grant."

"Please do not speak derogatorily of my superiors, sir," he replies.

"We are not insurrectionists, sir."

His back is as straight as a bayonet, his arms propped stiffly on his pommel, his horse's agitation growing. "You have made my case, sir."

"Pardon?"

"You have served in the military under Lee and Jackson. You know the rules of war. You also know that Lee has excoriated brigands and trash like Carleton Hayes. You and your family have aided and abetted, sir. Stand back or be arrested."

"We are a house of sick people," I reply. "We have to feed the servants and the field workers."

"Then free them and let them go their way."

"Where should they go, sir? Tell me that. Should they eat the bark on the trees?"

A sergeant moves his horse in the space between the captain and me. His kepi is pulled down on his eyes, his expression somber.

"Get your goddamn horse out of my face," I say.

He makes no acknowledgment of my statement but eases the reins just a little and touches his horse's belly with the heel of his boot, enough to make his horse knock me backwards in the dirt.

Then they go to work, some in the barn, some through the front door, some through the back. I can hear glass breaking, a desk being thrown through a window, my aunt's piano being torn apart. An enlisted man is on the second-story verandah throwing clothing in the air.

I try to get to the officer, to pull him from his horse, or beg for his charity, or apologize for my aggression. But the horses of his men are swirling about me, knocking me down again, stepping on me, splattering me with mud. I feel a rage that is greater than any in my life. I grab a mounted enlisted man and rip him from the saddle. He goes down with the Spencer in his hands. I get a hold of the reins and kick him in the face and try to pull the Spencer from him, but his hands are gripping fiercely onto the stock. The only good fortune in my situation is my closeness to his friends; they cannot shoot me without shooting one another. I swing onto the saddle of his horse and pour it on, I mean flat hell-for-breakfast, bending low, slashing the reins, kicking up mud, the lungs of my stolen horse chugging like a train.

In seconds I have broken free and am pounding down the slope, passing the abandoned encampment of Colonel Carleton, racing past the quarters, hoping my unfortunate horse does not stumble, hoping I can reach the far side of the lagoon and intersect the road that will take me to St. Martinville, where I can ask the help of the sheriff. Then I hear gunfire behind me, fusillades of it from the Spencers. The rounds that go long make a pinging sound like a banjo string snapping on its peg; others clatter in the tupelos and die over the lake; a toppling round whirrs like a pinwheel past my ear.

But thanks to Our Lord I have beaten the devil at his own work. I feel a sense of exhilaration that is like rising into the cold-white purity of the stars. I cross the countryside, my stolen horse now my friend, galloping steadily over the softness of the earth, and sleep in a boathouse on Bayou Teche. In the morning I wake with an entirely new perspective of the world. I have not used opiates, yet I feel the Earth is a grand place after all, resilient and welcoming, the way a mother can be, the fruit of Eden an arm's length away. And if my face has been marred, so be it. Is it not better to wear a scar on the skin, one that was honorably earned, than carry a lesion on the soul?

I cannot find the sheriff, for which I'm glad, for he's a worthless man, and I reach Lady of the Lake just before noon and slide down from my horse and pull off the cavalry saddle and throw it in the swamp and walk toward the quarters with my stolen horse in tow, the house in the distance. The Yankees did not burn it. The damage they did inside can be repaired. We will start over and find a way to release the slaves and care for the poor and live the lives of true Christians. In one way or another, we will indeed be at work and play in the fields of the Lord.

A solitary darky walks toward me from the quarters. His name is Alcide. He has no other name. He's a tall and dignified man and wears a frayed suit and a soap-yellowed shirt pinned at the collar. But something is amiss. It's not Sunday.

"I'm glad you got back home all right, suh," he says, taking the reins from my hand.

"Thank you, Alcide. Is everything all right?"

"No, suh."

"Say again?"

He looks over his shoulder. He scrubs his forehead with the heel of his hand and cannot look me in the face and starts to cry.

"Is it Mr. Charles or Miss Ezemily?"

"At least fo' bullets went in the quarters, Mr. Wade. A baby and the mother got kilt."

"The Yankees shot up the quarters?"

"I don't know, suh. I ain't seen it."

"Tell me the truth, Alcide."

"It happened when you went flying by the quarters, Mr. Wade."

I start walking again, my hand empty of the reins, the long green grass on the slope flattening under my feet, the horizon tilting.

"I'll fix you some breakfast, suh," Alcide says. "Them Yankees done it, Mr. Wade. Come on back, suh. You a good man. Ever'ting gonna be all right."

22

HANNAH LAVEAU

I have been hungry sometimes. Once in the hold of a galleon off Devil's Island, when the bilge got into the water kegs and the fruit and salt pork spoiled and there was plague on shore. And once when the overseer got mad at my mother and cut off our food. And another time after a storm, when my mother waded out in the sea and picked up coconuts bobbing in the waves and brought them back on the sand and broke them on a coral rock and fed all the li'l children before she fed herself.

But this is a different kind of hunger. After Miss Florence took care of the slave catchers, a pistol ball blew up the engine and set the boat on fire and we had to wade to a sandspit when the tide was out. Some French fishermen, the French we call "*les Acadiens*," took us to land and gave us some bread but no money or clothes because they didn't have any to spare.

We walked miles at night along Bayou Teche, and hid out in the day, and stole clothes off wash lines and food from plantation cook shacks. Miss Florence has never lived like this. Now the stars are out, and we can see the lamps in Brashear City, close to the Gulf, and once again we don't know what to do because we don't know if the Yankees or the Confederates or the Red Legs are in the city. And all the time my stomach is hurting, like a rodent is eating at it, and I know Miss Florence feels the same hollowness inside, because the bones show in her face, and her eyes are small and look like an animal's.

See, the Yankees have occupied New Orleans since last year, but not far out in the countryside. Creole soldiers who enlisted in the Confederate Army changed sides and became Union soldiers who guard the railroad tracks going out of the city. There are tents and shacks outside Brashear City where women sell themselves and don't care to who as long as they got money that's in coin and not paper.

Miss Florence and I are shaking in a blanket because of the damp and the mosquitoes. The only thing we took from the slave-catcher boat is the pistol and some powder and shot and caps in a leather bag. I have told Miss Florence we should sell it or throw it in the bayou, because for sure it can get us hung. Or worse. I'll tell you what I mean by "worse."

The man who led the New Orleans slave rebellion in 1811 was captured and taken to a barn, where the mob cut off his hands and shot him in each thigh and then in the stomach, and after that, while he was still alive, piled straw on him and set it afire.

A lot more died, too, their heads put on pikes up and down the levee on the Mississippi River. But I don't want to think about those things anymore. I just want my li'l boy Samuel back. More and more, I think it ain't much to ask, so why cain't God let that happen?

Miss Florence has her part of the blanket looped over her head, like a monk. "Miss Florence," I say. "I think the mosquitoes are taking over you. That's how they work. They suck your blood till you're so weak you cain't swat them anymore."

"Don't be silly. I'm fine."

"You saved us on the boat, Miss Florence. I ain't going to let you lose your life."

"Of course you're not," she says. "We'll trudge on to New Orleans, then go to the homes of my friends, who will give us the wherewithal to get you emancipated."

Miss Florence is trying to fool herself now, and sounds like a clock with a broken spring running down. I don't want to hurt her feelings, but I cain't lie to her and get us killed. "We have already seen posters on the trees with sketches of our faces on them," I say. "With five-hundred-dollar rewards, too. People around here don't make that in a year."

"Those posters were put up by meretricious individuals to whom one pays no attention."

Before she can go on, she starts coughing. I place my hand on her forehead. It's hot as a clothes iron. "I'm going down to those tents, Miss Florence."

"No, you are not!" she replies.

"I'm going down there with the pistol and sell it. I bet I can get ten dol'ars for it."

She starts to argue, then looks up at me. The light from the stars and the moon has gone out of her eyes. It's the kind of dark look people have before they die. I want to cry.

"I'll be back soon. Are you listening to me? Ain't anything bad going to happen. I ain't going to let it."

* * *

The tents and shacks are set back in the trees along the bank of the Atchafalaya River, which runs on down through Brashear City and through swamps and marshland into the Gulf of Mexico. Brashear City has been a bad city since the war started. Outlaws running from both sides pay money to get on fishing boats that dock in Mexico. There's a flotilla of Yankee ships out there, also, and sometimes at night a blockade runner tries to slip through, and you can see cannons firing out of the gunwales, and if you're close enough on the bank you can see the faces of the gun crews lighting up in the dark, like Halloween masks.

Miss Florence didn't have to warn me. I know the kind of people who are in these tents and shacks. The women are poor and live under their pimp's thumb. Some are crazy because their syphilis has gotten into their brains. The pimps beat up the women, and the bouncers do it to the customers who give the women trouble. Darla Babineaux, my friend at Suarez plantation, worked in one of these places when she was a girl. I always admired her for that. They got her body, but she kept her soul. That ain't easy.

I have the pistol wrapped in a shawl. The soldiers drinking outside the tents and shacks start to notice me as I walk toward them. Most of them are Union men, not Red Legs, and older than you would think. The young ones still remember their learning. The older ones have forgotten who they used to be, and act like it. In the shadows their noses look like pig snouts.

I stop before one group of five sitting on pine stumps in front of a tent that has a lantern burning inside. All of them are drinking. The flap on the tent is closed, but I can see the shadows on the canvas and know what they are doing inside. Lord, I want to run away. But I cain't let Miss Florence starve.

"Come on over here," one solider says. He has two chevrons on his sleeve and a blond beard that looks as stiff as goat hair. His eyes are red and lazy when he takes a drink from his canteen. "Where did you get your suntan?"

"I want to sell a gun."

I unwrap the shawl from the gun and turn it over on each side so he can see the blueness of the metal. "I'll take twelve Yankee dol'ars for it."

"Come over here and show it to me," the same soldier says.

"Let's see your money."

"I got it in my pants. Come on, darlin'. You show me your gun, then I'll show you mine, and we'll talk business."

They all laugh.

"Walk out here in the dark and talk with me," I say. "Unless you're afraid."

"You'd better get your cunny out of here, love," he says. "I hear the management is protective of its interests."

"Did your family teach you to talk that way?" I ask. "Did you come down from the North to use bad language and insult people who haven't done you any wrong?"

He grins and gazes idly at his lap, like he's drifting off. The others look away from each other, tired of whatever it is that makes them tired.

"Eleven dol'ars," I say. "The name Beaumont-Adams is on the barrel. I have a feeling it's special."

"Where did you get it?" he says.

"The Confederates left it in a ditch after the fight at Nelson's Canal in New Iberia."

"I need a better light," he says.

He gets to his feet. A lantern hangs from a tree trunk ten yards from us. By the side of the lantern is the same wanted poster we saw nailed on at least a half dozen trees along Bayou Teche.

"I don't like the way some of the people here been acting," I say. "Walk down with me by the water. The moon's bright there."

It is, too. There's a lagoon where rowboats have been scraped up on the sand. Out on the river the moon clatters like a chandelier on the water's surface. The Atchafalaya here is as wide as the Mississippi.

"You ain't afraid, are you?" I say.

"All right, girl, let's take a walk," he says. He brushes off his pants.

"I ain't a girl, suh."

"No, I reckon you're not."

He walks ahead of me, down the slope to the water's edge, maybe protective, so I don't fall. I just ain't sure. He looks back at his friends, then at me. "What's your name?"

"My name ain't important. You want to buy the pistol?"

He takes a drink out of his canteen, then says, "Sorry, want some?"

"No, thank you."

"I want to apologize for the way I talked up there. I was acting smart. Hit me if you want."

"I ain't interested in hitting people. You got eleven dol'ars?"

"I have seven. That's all. I'll turn out my pockets and show you."

He seems smaller than his uniform, like somebody gave it to him and he shrunk inside it, like he wasn't supposed to live inside it in the first place. "Did you fight around here?"

"I did at Second Fredericksburg. At Marye's Heights."

"It was bad there?"

"I don't like to talk about it. Can I hold the revolver?"

"It's loaded," I say, and hand it to him.

"Are you a slave?" he asks, looking down at the gun, touching the initials cut into the grip.

"Do I look like one?"

"I ask you because I think you're a runaway. If you are, I hope you get free on your own because I don't think this war is going to end."

"Why won't it?"

"Because it was crazy to begin with. My family has a farm in Pennsylvania. It looks just like the farms in Virginia and Maryland. Same limestone walls, same barns and silos, same churches and language. Now the fields are burying grounds, but without tombstones." He hands me back the gun.

"You don't want it?"

"I want it, all right. Just let me get my money out of my britches."

He's unsteady as he works the coins out of his pocket. I feel sorry for him. He's younger than I thought. His kepi slips off his head, and he barely catches it. He laughs at himself, then gets his kepi back in place and his coins and pocket straightened out. "I got to tell you something," he says.

"What?"

"I'm glad I met you. I got drunk with those other fellows and strolled along without paying attention to where we were going. If it wasn't for you, I would be feeling real bad in the morning. You want to tell me your name?"

No, I don't. But I don't want to offend him, either. "My name is Hannah."

"Like in the Bible?"

"Yes, suh."

"You're a nice lady, Miss Hannah." He's smiling, He reaches out and squeezes my hand. He makes me think of a li'l boy, maybe the kind I want my li'l boy to be. Then his eyes shift. "But you had better go along now."

"Suh?"

"Just go, Miss Hannah."

I look around, my heart staring to trip. "I don't see anything. What's wrong?"

Then I hear feet running and noise from the shacks and tents, then a shrill laugh and somebody baying at the moon.

"An extra show, boys!" somebody yells.

"Hannah, get out of here!" my soldier friend says. "Don't just look at me! Run!"

It's too late. A big man comes charging out of the slash pines, his black hair and beard as wild and thick as a lion's mane, his skin grimed with coal dust, probably from a ship's boiler, his boots hard-tipped, probably with steel. His eyes are burning with rage. "Thought you'd steal our business, did you, girl? I'm gonna split you up the middle!" he says, grinding his teeth and crashing over my soldier friend, then driving his fist into my face, wrapping me in his stink.

I have never been hit so hard. I feel as though the bone behind my nose has been pushed into my brain. Nor have I ever felt such pain, except when Master Suarez took me. I'm on my knees now, the gun and the one-dol'ar coins scattered around me, my fingers splayed on my face, blood sliding in rills down my forearms.

But I cannot put together what is happening. Miss Florence is next to me. Her mouth is opening and closing, but her words sound like they are being spoken underwater. The soldier has gotten to his feet and is swaying back and forth, his forehead split. Something is wrong with his arm; one shoulder is lower than the other. He's inches from the big man, patting him, his mouth making words that are as round as walnuts, but making no sound. Why is the soldier patting him and dusting him off? I thought he was my friend.

Then I understand. He's trying to quiet the big man down. But Miss Florence has picked up the revolver. Since she shot the slave catchers she's learned she doesn't have to cock the hammer to pop the shell. She squeezes the trigger, and the big man goes straight down, as though through a trapdoor in a scaffold, his jaw hanging open, one eye blown through the back of his head.

Then she turns the revolver on the soldier.

No! I shout. I am waving my arms now. *No! No! No! He's a friend! Listen to me, Miss Florence! Don't hurt him! Oh God!*

But I feel I'm imagining my words rather than saying them. Miss Florence fires the pistol again, and the ball goes right through the heart of the gentle soldier from Pennsylvania.

I think I scream, but I am not sure. I run through the trees, slipping on the pine needles, the lower branches slapping my face and tearing my clothes. I run and run until my lungs are on fire. Then suddenly my hearing returns, as though someone has clapped his hands on my ears. Miss Florence is calling my name, puffing her way up the incline. She lifts her right arm in the air. Her hand is clutched in a fist, her face bright with victory. "I've got the money, child," she says. "Enough to find our friends. Those men back there can't hurt you anymore. Did you hear me, dear Hannah? Why are you crying, child?"

23

PIERRE CAUCHON

The news is on the telegraph and in the newspaper. A teacher named Florence Milton and a runaway slave named Hannah Laveau are suspects in the shooting deaths of a Union solider and a procurer in Brashear City. The motive is thought to be robbery. The Union soldier's pocket was turned inside out.

This doesn't fit together. Neither one of those women is a violent person. Miss Florence's idea of sin is accidentally stepping on the cat's tail. But I can't understand why they were around a pimp. My guess is someone tried to kidnap them. The woods all over Louisiana are filled with people like Colonel Carleton Hayes, a man I would more and more like to see turned into lamp tallow. In fact, because of him I am about to enter The Shadows and sit down with General Nathaniel Banks and Captain John Endicott.

Did you grow up listening to stories about the greatness of our leaders, whether in business or the White House or churches where people drink poisons and then submerge their arms in boxes of copperheads or return home and kill their families and burn all their belongings?

I'm sitting with leaders of that sort right now, on the verandah, surrounded by live oaks. Captain Endicott has polished all his brass and is wearing his saber. The complainant who has brought the meeting is Mrs. Lufkin. She is still wearing her mourning clothes. Her lot has not been a kind one.

Maybe I can explain something that is difficult for others to understand. With regularity, North and South, we give power to people who have no interest in us. A short distance from The Shadows, down by the bridge on the Teche, a nice lady named Ellen Lee Burke reared three sons by herself after her husband, a survivor of the Goliad Massacre, died of yellow fever. They were poor Irish immigrants and also abolitionists. The three boys enlisted in the Confederate Army. Willie Burke and I went up the slope together at Shiloh and later into a fusillade at Corinth that would daunt the devil himself. The Yanks took Ellen Lee's cows. Who the fuck would believe this?

There is nothing about this war that is rational. The owners of the textile mills in Massachusetts do not care about the children who work in them. The builders of the railroads do not care about the Slavs they dump on a prairie wasteland. The makers of our arsenals do not worry about the hundreds of thousands their products blind, maim, and kill. But the people I am with are about to tell me that none of this is so.

General Banks is trim and wears a mustache and has allowed three or four days of whiskers to grow on his chin, but he gives me the sense his brain is not entirely functional. He wears a Hardee hat and a dusty uniform that looks like he just came from the firing line. However, he is known mostly for his incompetence and the record number of cotton bales he has kept safe and sound for businessmen everywhere.

"Would you like more tea?" he says to Mrs. Lufkin.

"No, thank you sir," she says. "I would simply like your word that you will indemnify me for the damage done my home; then I can be out of your way."

"Yes, Captain Endicott has told me about that," the general replies. "Tell me, though, because I am quite curious, are you related to Edwin Booth, the famous Shakespearian actor?"

"Why is it that so many of you, and I mean those with a military background, have this obsession about Edwin Booth?"

"I am not aware that is the case, madam."

"I wish you would not refer to me as 'madam,' sir."

Captain Endicott puts down his teacup. I have the feeling he has chosen this moment to occupy the high ground. I think the good captain should take up thespian studies himself. "Mrs. Lufkin, I am deeply sorry for what has occurred in your home."

"Excuse me. The destruction of my home did not 'occur,'" she says. "You brought a collection of Visigoths inside our home and tore it apart. Our piano was brought from Hungary. Franz Liszt composed on it."

"What you do not understand is our history with Carleton Hayes, Mrs. Lufkin," Endicott replies. "He and his marauders have killed and wounded Union soldiers and civilians all over central and southern Louisiana. Some of those soldiers were under my command. Their fellow soldiers took their anger out on you. They will be reprimanded for that, and at some juncture you will be indemnified. But your indignation and self-righteousness are embarrassing."

"Your men fired blindly into the servants' quarters," she says. "One of the servants and her infant were killed."

"Your 'servant' and her child were slaves, not servants, madam," Endicott says. "Take your disingenuous vocabulary somewhere else."

"That's enough of that," the general says. "What is your perspective on this, Constable Cauchon?"

"I don't have one, sir," I say.

"That's interesting. You do work out of the governor's office, don't you? You do investigate the legal rights of the Negroes? I believe that is a meritorious pursuit."

"Yes, sir," I say, and gaze at the Spanish moss swaying in the trees, the spangled sunlight like a thousand eyes on the verandah. "But we all know better than that."

"I beg your pardon?" the general says.

"I do no good for anyone, General."

"Then what are you doing here?"

"I believe some innocent people are going to be killed. Their names are Hannah Laveau and Florence Milton. Your soldiers are putting up reward posters wherever they can."

"Do you have evidence of these women's innocence?"

"I know them, sir," I say.

"Unfortunately, they seem connected to five dead bodies. Do you have an explanation for that?"

"Three of the dead were slave catchers," I say, and immediately put my foot in it.

"You admit they might have had a motive?" the general says.

"I meant that this particular trio of misfits were hated by many people, sir."

"You sound like you may have a bias, Mr. Cauchon," he replies. "But no matter. Mrs. Lufkin, please accept my apology for the behavior of a few men. I will try to make it up to you. In the meantime, I have to deal with a particularly ugly presence in our midst, this depraved creature who calls himself Colonel Carleton Hayes, the man you and your husband empowered to burn down two Negro settlements, rob a bank, lynch three white men, and shoot a cannon at me."

I don't know how the general has done it. But somehow he has become the victim.

"Is there anything else I can do for you, madam?" he says.

"Yes," she says, rising from her chair. "Please do not enter our property again."

"Mrs. Lufkin, in another year or two, your world will end and will never be restored. It will also live in infamy. The rest of the nation will go on, and places such as Lady of the Lake will be curiosities. I am sorry for the loss of your sons."

Endicott drops his eyes. I do, too. I don't like Nathaniel Banks. But his words make my heart sink, the same way I felt when I sat beside Darla Babineaux cracking pecans while the western skies were aflame with a dying culture that no one can explain.

24

COLONEL CARLETON HAYES

It's evening now, a special time of day. The light draws down into the woods, like the Earth is trying to undo Creation, like it wants to start all over and admit a mistake was made at Eden or when Cain cracked his brother's skull and tried to fling the stone and blood from his hand but instead put the stone in the foundation of his home, causing it to collapse upon him.

Like Cain, I have my weapons—fire and such—at my fingertips. The fire burning the farmhouse by the woods is spreading now, scattering the shadows with sparks, flame, and the curds of smoke from a whiskey still we did not know was in the barn. Rogue Confederates fired at us from the house and forced the situation on us. Now we sit by a deserted road lined with ten mule-drawn sugar-cane wagons aimed at the Red River. The wagons are full of darkies, their faces mournful. Soon they will be sold to a slave broker from Texas, an unnecessarily violent man, a Comanchero I do not like to deal with. However, in war one has to make concessions to practicality.

Some of the slaves are descended from Pygmies. That's what I said. The original group in Africa owned Pygmy slaves themselves, and when the Dutch raided the village, they chained and packed the bunch like lines of butterfly cocoons in the hold of the ship and sent them on their way, in this case to a place called Misery Plantation. I didn't make up the name. Now they are mine, and soon they will be the property of our Comanchero friend, Little Boy Roy.

Hardened and indifferent, am I? I knew Robert Lee down in Mexico in '46. He was a young artillery officer who blew the shite out of women and children. He also allowed his men a frolic at Chambersburg, Pennsylvania, and rounded up the darkies, escaped and freeborn alike, and shipped them to the auction block in Richmond, along with that study in egotism Jeb Stuart, who captured sixty black Federal teamsters outside Washington and sold them into the cottonfields. In their mind, I am ill-bred and coarse. I guess they are right. Also, I guess it's permissible for a gentleman to kill children and women as long as they are peasants.

What am I really talking about? The owners of the farmhouse and their little ones are all dead. I think they were dead before we fired the first volley through the windows, although I cannot be certain. We took sniping from the windows, then responded with grapeshot, guaranteeing no one would leave the house alive. Yes, it bothers me. I don't like these moments of introspection. They make my head hurt.

There's Little Boy Roy now. He's the meanest little bucket of goat piss I have ever known, and puts me in mind of an insect. He has a pinched face like he's constipated, and wears a Hardee hat, a stove-pipe affair mashed at the top, like General Banks's hat, and pointy Mexican riding boots and oversized canvas britches always falling off his ass. I will admit I don't get into this boy's path. There are stories about him I don't want to think about. And neither do you.

If I get through this war, I am going to make sure Little Boy Roy is put in an insane asylum.

I mount my horse and meet Little Boy upwind from the burning house. I raise myself in the saddle and doff my hat. "How do you do, sir?" I say. "I hope you had a pleasant journey."

His face is in shadow, and I have no idea what he is thinking or what kind of mood he is in. He doesn't acknowledge my greeting.

"Is something wrong, Little Boy?"

"What's that stink?"

"Dead people."

He chews on his lip, his eyes contemptuous. "Were you born cross-eyed or did someone drop you on your head?"

"It's hard to say."

He looks at the wagon train, no longer interested in the subject of our conversation. He wears a colorless cotton shirt that is swelling in the wind. His skin is as sunbaked and rough as dried mud.

"How many niggers did you get me?"

"About thirty-five."

"About?"

"A few took off. I haven't had time to do a recount."

He's staring at the house now. His eyes are empty. "You killed civilians in there?"

"I didn't go inside."

His lips are caked. He tries to wet them, but his mouth is dry. "I don't like the way this is shaping up. My name better not be attached to this. Understand?"

My horse is blowing, his sides swelling, his feet shifting. "Let's talk money."

"It's in the bank in Shreveport."

"In Shreveport?" I try to laugh. "Where did you get your schooling, son?"

I know, I know, I shouldn't have said it. But I cannot abide people who try to take advantage of me in a business situation, particularly one that is linked to the Constitution itself. I start to speak. Then I take one glance at his face.

"Want to say that again?" he asks.

"I always enjoyed doing business with you, Little Boy. I would never get on your bad side. You're a gentleman and a man of honor."

"Was there Rebs in that house or did you just decide to burn it up?"

"They were deserters. Not Rebs. No-accounts living on the fat of the land while we fight their war."

"Tell you what, Carleton. In recognition of your patriotism, I'm gonna pay you in Confederate money."

"Hold on there, now."

It's dusk now, the sparks from the farmhouse brighter than the remnants of the sun. A horse is coming hard from the column of cane wagons, the rider bent low in the saddle, dust rising from the horse's hooves.

"I hear you shot a cannon at General Banks," Little Boy says, as though he wants to distract me from the rider.

"Repeat that, please?" I say.

"How many black women are in the wagons? Breeders are in short supply."

I strain my eyes at the wagons. There are several figures I don't recognize. "Who did you bring with you, Little Boy?"

"Drovers."

"Where did you get them?"

"Out of my morning shit pot. What do you care?"

"I wish you wouldn't speak with such vehemence, Little Boy."

"Don't you start showing off your vocabulary with me, old man. Just looking at the pus on your face gives me the runs."

He swings down and blocks the line of sight between me and the rider bearing down on us. A holstered army .44 hangs from Little Boy's pommel, but on the other side of his horse, where he cannot get to it easily. He puts the reins in his mouth and removes his Hardee hat and combs his hair. It's shiny and thick with grease and dandruff. The last of the sunlight is flickering on his face. He puts away his comb and hooks his thumbs in his belt and sucks his teeth. I have never seen him more relaxed.

"What are you up to, Little Boy?" I say.

He cocks his head, a crooked, idiotic smile on his face. "I was just toying with some business ideas. Have you thought of starting a leper colony?"

But I cannot keep my attention on him. The rider is Private Shaye Langtree, flying toward us on a buckskin. He jumps off and hits the ground running inside a cloud of dust, the buckskin going on without him.

"Good God, son, who kicked a fence post up your ass?" I say.

He doesn't answer. Instead he knocks Little Boy down in the dust and then piles on top of him, pinning him with his knees.

"He's fixing to kill you, Colonel!" he says, breathless, reaching for a knife before Little Boy can speak.

"He's unarmed," I say. "Back off, son. Let the man talk."

Little Boy is trying to fight his way out from under Langtree's weight and almost frees himself. But Langtree flips him on his stomach and wraps Little Boy's hair around his hand and stretches back his head and slides his knife under his throat.

"Don't—" I say.

"He's got a hideaway," he says. "I heard his drovers say it. They ain't worth your spit, Colonel."

"No—"

He peels back Little Boy's head and rips the knife across his throat, slicing his windpipe in half, then rises from Little Boy's body, staring at it as though he's not quite sure what he has done. I can't deal with this. Little Boy is still alive and is trying to turn on his back and shut down the spigot in his throat.

Langtree steps on Little Boy's right forearm and bends over and pulls something from Little Boy's sleeve. "A two-barrel Derringer and a rig. Just like his drovers said."

"How come they told you?"

"They didn't, sir. I was eavesdropping. I've dealt with them Comancheros before. Every one of them is a sidewinder."

"You're aware you just left me with no market for over thirty slaves, aren't you?"

"No, sir. I didn't think about that."

"Did you hear any talk among the drovers about a bank account in Shreveport?"

"No, sir. But with your permission, I will have a talk with them."

"Yes, that will be fine."

I know how to choose my words carefully, and I also recognize danger in people when I see it. The first warning is always ambition. The second is ingratiation. But I do not know why Langtree bothers me. Again and again I want to excoriate him, then I feel ashamed. I look down at Little Boy. His face lies sideways in a pool of blood that is twice the size of his head.

"I'm promoting you to sergeant," I say.

"*Sergeant?* Me?"

"Are you familiar with the work of Machiavelli, Sergeant?"

"No, sir, I don't think so."

"I think I have an edition I can loan you," I say.

"Yes, sir, I'm sure I'd like that. Do you want me to talk to them drovers?"

"Yes, please do. I think I will take a nap in my tent. Let me know what you find out, then we'll be on our way."

"What about the slaves?"

"Tell them to go back to Pygmy Town."

"Sir?"

"Tell them they're emancipated. What the hell am I going to do with Pygmies?"

"They ain't all Pygmies, sir."

"Let me put it this way: Is it easier to liberate a bank in Shreveport or feed and clothe and doctor people who hate you?"

"I never thought of it that way," he says.

There has to be a better way to make a living than this. The fire has died in the farmhouse and the stars are bright and winking overhead. I fall asleep quickly in my tent, a handkerchief sprinkled with camphor on my face. In the distance I hear men screaming, but assure myself that I am dreaming. I wake shivering in the false dawn and wrap a Union blanket around my shoulders and try to remember my dreams, but I have no memory of them or even of the events that led up to the death of Little Boy or to my freeing of the Negroes. These mental lapses make me wonder if I have some undiagnosed medical problems.

When I step out of the tent I can smell fatback and coffee made from shelled corn cooking on our breakfast fires. I eat with my soldiers and have a jolly time of it, actually. The darkies are gone, I have no idea where. The wagons are empty, the mules still hitched. I mount up at the head of the column just as the sun rises above the trees and streaks across the earth. Five bodies are suspended from the archway of the plantation. They all have on the same pointy boots worn by Little Boy Roy. The archway must be over thirty feet high, and the nooses that hold their bodies were pulled all the way to the beam, so the bodies look unearthly, floating above a world that doesn't want them.

My master sergeant catches up with me. "Where are we headed, Colonel?" he asks.

I stare at him but cannot remember his name. "East," I say.

"East, sir? That's toward Baton Rouge. It's loaded with blue-bellies, Colonel."

"I see," I reply. "Let me think on that a while. Yes, we have many options, don't we? Many indeed. You say there are blue-bellies in Baton Rouge? I thought they moved on. Maybe we should tidy up the place. Cut off a few heads. What's your opinion?"

His mouth opens slightly, but no sound comes out. What a strange fellow. Well, these are odd times.

25

PIERRE CAUCHON

The days pass and the night air smells of burning leaves in the backyards along Bayou Teche. The cabin I have rented at The Shadows is a lonely place, and when the sun turns a soft orange in the west and slips into the dust from the cane fields, I feel a longing that verges on despair, but I do not know why.

As a child, I was often given to spells. My mother said that was because I was "special," that I was given sight into the future because she was blind. Except there was a catch. No one would believe me. When she would tell me this story, her eyes would fill with tears, and she would fold her arms around me and press my face to her bosom and her cheek to my head. Her pain was for me, though, not for herself.

It's at evening tide when I miss my mother most, and I think about the boys in field hospitals I heard cry out for their mothers before they died, and I understand the nature of their loss, like sliding down the sides of the Earth, and I look toward the west and the dying of the sun, and I want someone to drive nails through my wrists and bare feet.

Instead, I saddle Varina and ride out to the Suarez plantation and walk down to the lakeside and the cabin of Darla Babineaux. The sunlight still clings to the cypress and tupelos and the lichen that undulates like soured milk when a fisherman rows past the flooded woods in the center of the lake. An oil lamp is burning inside Darla's cabin, a reckless expense for someone of her means. She opens the door before I can knock.

Her face is swollen on one side, to the extent that her eye is squinched and watery.

"Are you all right, Miss Darla?"

"I have a bad toot'."

I look at the ground around the tethering post. We had rain just two hours ago. "Who tied his horse here?"

"What do you want, Mr. Pierre?"

"To see how you're doing. The horse that was tethered here was shod with Henry Burden shoes. Only Union cavalry have them. May I come in?"

"Why ax me? I ain't got no title on it."

She sits on a cane chair in a corner, away from the lamp. I step inside and close the door and sit down across from her. She has on a fluffy white dress down to her ankles and a purple jacket. "It ain't what you t'ink," she says.

"Endicott hit you, didn't he?"

"I ran after him and fell. I was mad. I tole him I wasn't gonna be no cornbread and lima-bean darky for him."

"You thought he was going to take you up North?"

"That was the way he was acting. Then he tole me he had children and a sick wife, and I deserved better than him. I heard that one before."

"I think you're a fine lady, Darla."

"I ain't no lady. I don't want to be one, either. I'm gonna own a plantation. I don't care who wins this war. I'm gonna be rich. And I ain't ever gonna work in the fields again."

The room is clean, the plank floor probably scrubbed with a brush, her eating table spotless, the clay dishes and cups lined neatly above the woodstove. "Can you take a walk with me?" I say.

"To go where and do what?"

"I don't know. I like you, Miss Darla. I have funny notions. I think you do, too."

"That don't make no sense."

"You remind me of my mother. She was a dreamer. She always said the dreamers are the ones who make the world a better place."

"Can I ax you somet'ing, Mr. Pierre?"

"Sure."

"You t'ink I'm no good? Because that's how I feel."

"What did Endicott do to you, Miss Darla?"

"He had me, then said he didn't want me no more. That's what he did."

I pick up my chair and set it next to hers and sit down again. "You listen to me. You're a strong woman. Endicott is unworthy of you. He's a weak man who seeks approval and uses his power to take food from the poor. He doesn't deserve to wash your feet."

A tear is brimming over the edge of her watery eye. "Thank you, Mr. Pierre."

I smile at her. "I have to ask you a question, though."

"About what?"

"Did you kill Mr. Suarez?"

She looks at the floor. Her hair is parted as straight as a ruler, the ends of it tied with a ribbon on each shoulder, the way a little girl might wear it. She lifts her eyes to mine. She rubs a scar on her throat. It looks like a thread worm that has died in the sun. "I hope Master Suarez is in Hell. I hope he remembers every colored woman who carried his child."

She waits for me to respond. But I don't. She still calls the man who raped her by a title.

"You ain't gonna say nothing?"

"I'm afraid for Hannah Laveau, Miss Darla. What am I going to do about Hannah? Can you tell me that?"

She walks over to me, her hands at her side.

"What are you doing?" I ask.

She presses my head to her chest. I can hear her heart beating and smell the heat in her skin. Out on the lake I can hear the grunting of an alligator in rut, its tail thrashing in the shallows. But the season is wrong. Gators mate in the spring. But this one is tearing into its mate, rolling with it in the mud and salt grass, wreaking havoc, regardless of the consequence.

26

HANNAH LAVEAU

We are inside New Orleans now and protected from the Confederates. The auction at the St. Louis Hotel and Exchange is shut down, and some windows in the building are broken and the pillars scorched, but no matter what happens to it, I will always remember the families that were sold off, one member at a time—a quadroon here, an octoroon there, a full-black Negro here, a child there, a mother crying so bad she was pulled behind the rotunda and slapped senseless.

Rich men and women dressed in their finery drank wine and ate off silver trays while they watched the sale. The devil ain't down in a fiery pit. He's right here.

Miss Florence and I have moved into a back room of my *cousine* Marie Laveau's li'l house not far from the Place d'Armes. There are Yankees all over the square, and we don't go outside in daylight. *Cousine* Marie brings us food and clean clothes and some roots and herbs for Miss Florence, because Miss Florence is looking awful sick. She says it's the malaria or maybe yellow fever. It ain't, though.

She killed the Union soldier by mistake. The other four men she killed are not in her dreams. Yesterday, just before dawn, she got out of bed and ran both of her hands through a glass window and would have cut her wrists if *Cousine* Marie hadn't wrestled her back into bed, with Miss Florence all the time saying, "Why didn't you tell me who you were? Why were you in a brothel? Why didn't you speak up? I am so sorry, young man."

I cain't convince her it was a mistake and nobody's fault except the pimp who hit me in the face and almost knocked my eye out. See, this is what Miss Florence cain't understand. You cain't let bad people put the blame on you for their misdeeds. They bury others in guilt. That's how they get power over you, too. Look at New Orleans. Trumpet vine like strings of gold bells and blood-red bougainvillea drip from the Spanish ironwork on the balconies; the French bread and café au lait vendors roll their carts on the cobblestones at first light, and the fog puffs cold and white off the Mississippi. Then you hear the Angelus ringing at the cathedral and think this is the best place in the world, like Eden was before the snake got loose in the tree, but it ain't.

The executions are still held in the Place d'Armes while people watch. I got caught once in the crowd. There's a smell on their breath you don't forget. It's like the gas you smell when the beetles clog the storm sewers in the summer. The prostitutes live down by *Rue Bassin* and put their red lanterns in their windows at night and open up their shirts so the soldiers can see their breasts. They sell absinthe down there, too. You can tell those who drink it. They don't look human anymore. Their faces are the color of a frog's stomach; their eyelids disappear, and they look at you as though their souls have gone somewhere else.

Flatboat people, the kind way up the river who carry knives and what they call a devil's claw, bring white and Indian and mulatto women down by the water and build bonfires and sometimes get into fights with drunken soldiers and kill one another. The bodies float out to the Gulf, and by morning nobody cares about what happened last night, unless the dead person is a soldier.

Hundreds of black and colored people still dance and make a storm-like kind of music with African drums and bells and banjos and reed pipes on Congo Square. Visitors like to watch them from their balconies, but I believe the music and the dance are about the voyage from Africa in the hold of a ship, and if the visitors knew the thoughts in the heads of the people dancing in the square, they would be afraid.

Only a few minutes ago Miss Florence said she wanted to give herself up. What she doesn't understand is that she will be giving both of us up. There was no witness to the shooting of the slave catchers and no witness to the shooting of the pimp and the poor young Union soldier. Miss Florence would probably go to The Walls, in Baton Rouge, where the women are not allowed to speak and got to wear chains outside the cell, and I would probably be hung. *Cousine* Marie tries to comfort the condemned in New Orleans. She sits all night with them, then walks with them in the morning to the scaffold. She says she has never seen a greater form of torture. They cain't eat; they cain't sweat; they cain't even speak going up the steps. They are so thin and scared that a strong wind could blow them away.

I fussed at Miss Florence this morning. It made me feel bad. She has risked her life so many times for others, even tending wounded Confederates at Corinth. *Cousine* Marie has a tiny li'l dog that curls up on Miss Florence's face. Dogs are a good judge of people. That li'l dog knows a good or bad person with one sniff.

What am I going to do? *Cousine* Marie says she can get both Miss Florence and me on a steamboat going up the river to Saint

Louis. But I've got a big problem with that. My li'l boy is out there somewhere, waiting for his mother. I have got to go back to Shiloh and find somebody who saw what happened to him that terrible day the greybacks went up the hill into the cannon. God ain't going to walk away from us now, is He? He ain't ever let me down before. Why would He start now?

I don't want to think about these things. I feel miserable and want to break things, just like Miss Florence did. So this is what I say to God: You got to help me, Suh. I cain't do all this on my own. It ain't fair. You take me all the way to New Orleans and leave me between the Mississippi River and half the Yankee army. It. Just. Ain't. Fair.

I look out the back window at the alley and the banana plants growing along the rain ditch, and I see a man I think I know. He's wearing a white suit with a shimmering green vest decorated with black diamonds, but he's unshaved and his hair is uncut and he looks like he slept under a train car, or maybe got dragged by it, because his face makes me shudder. It looks like someone gouged it with a spoon and sewed it together with wire, or like the masks people wear on the Day of the Dead.

He hammers on the door with his fist, enough to shake the room. Oh, Lord, that cain't be *him*, can it? Not from Lady of the Lake? The kind and handsome man who wanted tb paint birds and never hurt anyone? God, don't let that be Mr. Wade.

He's pounding again now, and kicking the door at the same time. I ease it open and try not to show my thoughts when I look into his face. Oh Lordy, deliver me up. Don't let me hurt this poor man's feelings.

*   *   *

"Is that you, Miss Hannah?" he says.

His breath is rife with the same smell of sewer gas that *Cousine* Marie described smelling among the people who gather for the hangings in the Place d'Armes.

"What are you doing here, Mr. Wade?"

"I've come to fetch you and the abolitionist woman." He looks up and down the alley. "I can't be out here."

"Please come in, suh."

He steps in quickly and shuts the door behind him, pressing against it with his back. "You know a Yankee officer named John Endicott?"

"No, suh."

"He has a murder warrant on the pair of you. He'll hunt you down. I know his kind. He and his men killed a woman and her child in the quarters at Lady of the Lake."

"Suh, I don't understand. The Yankees might be bad, but they don't—"

"You don't know them," he says. His eyes are quivering. "This fellow is treacherous to the core. Do you have money?"

He's going too fast for me. "Mr. Wade, all we got is our lives. You want something to eat?"

"We don't have time for that."

"Mr. Wade, we got enough grief."

He squeezes himself, as though he's cold. "Well, I can understand. I don't mean to be a bother."

A bother? Mr. Wade is more like a big mosquito buzzing in your sleep. "I'll get you a blanket."

"That would be fine. You don't know how good it is to see you, Miss Hannah," he says. "It's like the old times."

"Mr. Wade, I have to ax you this. What happened to your face, suh?"

"I had a duel with that fellow Cauchon. My pistol blew up. But no matter. I have changed my thinking about many things."

"I don't know what you mean, suh."

"The Yankees have to go," he says. "We'll handle our own problems."

"When did y'all try to handle them before?"

"I guess that's a good question," he replies. "I know there's an answer to it. Well, now is the time to start."

"Suh, none of this sounds like you."

"I've been a bit ill, that's all. I need my medicine and then I'll be all right."

"What kind of medicine?"

"It's sold here in a shop. It's not far away. Can you send a servant? I have money."

Then I hear *Cousine* Marie behind me. "*Qui est cet homme?*" She has a kerchief wrapped around her head and wears two skirts over a petticoat. "*Qui est cet homme?*" she says again.

"*Un ami,*" I say. "*Il est malade.*"

"*Est-il fou?*" she asks.

"*Je crois qu'il est accro à l'absinthe.*"

"What are y'all saying about me?" he asks.

"That you need to sit down and rest, Mr. Wade," I reply.

I hope God ain't listening to this. I hope even more that *Cousine* Marie ain't going to run us down the alley.

"I'm sorry to be a nuisance, but do you have a servant who could fetch my medicine?" he says.

I'd like to fetch it on the side of his head.

27

WADE LUFKIN

They put me on the couch with a blanket and a pillow, and when I awaken they are gone, and through the curtains I can see the autumnal light and the rainclouds stacked like bruised peaches in the sky and banana fronds ruffling in the wind, and I wish for the return of my youth and my conscience and the innocent world in which I was born.

Sleep is not my friend. The rifle and pistol balls that killed the enslaved mother and child were meant for me. They died in my stead. That's what my dreams tell me. In daylight I can convince myself that Captain Endicott and his men are to blame, just as they were to blame for the destruction of my aunt and uncle's home. My regiment never fired blindly with small arms into a civilian area, and I never saw another unit do so, either, though artillery was another matter. With time, atrocities will happen, and one side will provoke the other, and each will take revenge in turn, and we will go home with secrets we share with no one. That's the reality of war, not the quixotic babbling of poets.

A fresh suit and underwear are draped over a chair. In the bathroom there is a tub half filled and a block of soap on a wood table next to it. A bucket of warm water is on the floor. I am not sure when I arrived in New Orleans. I know that today is Friday. I know that I am to meet with men I do not trust but with whom I must make an alliance. I also need to put aside my guilt. My aunt and uncle at Lady of the Lake cannot be abandoned and left to the incompetence and crassness and stupidity of men like Generals Banks and Butler. Would Rome have been a better place if Nero or Caligula or Caracalla had been allowed to continue their madness? How about Aaron Burr? What if Thomas Jefferson had not been there to put the bloody sod in a cage?

I walk down the alley toward *Rue Bassin*. The sunset is glorious. The second-floor balconies groan with potted flowers. All of the apartments and houses have ceiling-high ventilated shutters; the courtyards have arches and wishing wells and piked gates and are paved with bricks and planted with crepe myrtle and magnolia trees, and dark green clusters of spearmint grow in the cracks of the bricks, and you can smell the richness of their scent in the late hours of the day. Above me the sky is ribbed with strips of pink cloud that resemble piano keys arching into eternity. Can we not remake this into a perfect world? Did not Roland feel the same surge in his loins as he journeyed on to Roncevaux, his sword jingling, his armor clinking, his horse swelling and blowing under him.

Are Roland and I so different? Did he not have to use thieves and mercenaries and murderers in a noble cause? Am I worse than Lee, who sent fifty-five thousand men up the slope into cannister at Malvern Hill? My sins are not near theirs, I tell myself. Then I realize the level to which my foolish thoughts have sunk.

As I approach *Rue Bassin*, a fecund odor, one that is similar to decomposition, replaces the pillows of balmy air drifting intermittently off Lake Pontchartrain. Not far away lie a garbage pit and a giant divot of a trench full of offal and a string of houses with red lamps in the windows. In a large courtyard is an ale and wine shop that has outdoor tables and offers escorts for the evening. None of the customers are in uniform, but I know the cadences of Boston and New York and Michigan when I hear them. And that does not mean my own class is not there, because they certainly are, every one of them wearing the spots and sensibilities of leopards.

The clientele includes gin owners who are still selling cotton to the textile mills in New England, blockade runners, pimps, pirates, transporters of the re-enslaved to Texas, and flatboat voyageurs, the aggregate of whose body odors could paralyze an elephant. The waitresses are of all races but are hardly more than prostitutes and are sad for the lives that have been forced upon them. I have often been drawn to them but have never taken monetary advantage of them and believe that doing so is a great sin. Their lives are written in the scars on their skin. Most of them speak either Spanish or French, and they look inured and held together like piles of sticks. Perhaps inured and held together in the same way I am, down at the absinthe shop.

I look around me, then see two fellows I saw many times at Lady of the Lake. The younger of the two has a body as supple as a coachwhip and a face with the angularity of an axe blade. In Georgia his kind are called crackers, and everywhere else, trash. They might make good camel drivers, but other than that, I don't know why they were created.

The other man is named McNab, and acts out the role of a master sergeant for Colonel Hayes, although he is now dressed in a suit stiff enough to contain the smell of a corpse. He's mutton-chopped and has no expression, and I suspect he is on all counts a dolt. However, he always seems to have a hidden thought, one to be wary of.

"Top of the evening to you gentlemen," I say.

"And to you, sir," he replies. He offers his hand but does not stand up. Nor does his companion.

"May I sit down?" I ask.

He pushes a chair toward me. "Sure. What are you drinking?"

"I'll order in a minute." He still has not introduced me. I turn to the young fellow. "Hello, I'm Wade Lufkin."

"I'm Shaye Langtree," he says. His fingernails are rimmed with dirt, his handshake weightless. He remains in his chair. "Pleased to meet you."

"Where are you staying?" I ask McNab.

"The hotel on the corner of Rampart. Just over there. Where are *you* staying?"

"Oh, I haven't found a place yet," I reply.

"A bit cagey, are you?" he says.

I grin and look at empty space. This fellow is a snake, from his fangs to his rattlers.

Our table is in shadow, the brick wall against our backs, the concrete floor abrasive and cold. Uncomfortable or not, no one can hear our conversation. I motion to the waitress and give her my order. She nods and goes away, her hooped earrings swinging, her skirts swishing.

"You drink absinthe?" McNab says.

"Sometimes," I reply. "I take it you do not."

"Tastes like licorice to me," he replies. "Is it really made from wormwood?"

"Let's get you a glass, too," I say, raising my arm to the waitress.

McNab leans forward. "The hell with that. The colonel sends his regards. Get me?"

Then I see the hidden thought in his eye, the slight smile at the edge of his mouth. The waitress brings our drinks. Her skin has the smooth texture and color of the clay in a riverbed. She has a blue tattoo above one eye, a few strands of hair hanging across it. I ask her to leave the absinthe bottle and to bring a clean glass for McNab. He raises a finger. "I need none of that."

She goes away, his eyes following her. "What's this plan you've got?" he asks.

"*This* plan is to take advantage of General Mouton keeping the Yankees tied up while we retake Baton Rouge and force Grant to give up Vicksburg and let Forrest drive every Yankee soldier out of Mississippi. *That* in turn can hinder Sherman's obvious desire to take Atlanta. This can change the direction of the war."

"Sounds like shite to me," McNab says. "Where are the weapons for all this?"

I would really like to give this fellow a punch in the face. "I have access to over five hundred Spencer rifles and the money to buy them."

"You'll buy them with Dixies?"

"No, I will buy them with gold."

"Will you, now?"

There is a potted palm within an arm's length of the table. I pick up his whiskey glass and pour it into the dirt, then put water in it and a splash of absinthe. It bounces off the bottom of the glass in a cloudy green mushroom. "Have a belt of this. It gives a fellow a finer grasp on things. You'll be quite surprised, I'm sure."

"I don't particularly care for the way you're talking to me," he says.

"Oh, sorry," I say. "Would it be better that I see the colonel myself? Perhaps tell him you called my plans shite, plans that are basically his?"

"Let me see if I can phrase this," he replies. "The colonel is often indisposed. In the head, that is. Get me?"

"Yes, I do think I *get* you," I say. "I deal only with you."

"It don't mean that at all," says the young man named Langtree. There's a glare in his face, an odor like a dead rodent on his breath. He turns to McNab. "The colonel has his bad days. But he gets things done." He pauses to drive home his point, then looks back at me. "Where can we get the Spencers?"

"Sir, not far from our table are two gentlemen who have been running Enfield rifles up the Atchafalaya River for the last two years," I say. "There are also spies in this courtyard, and British military observers here. Would you be a little more reserved with your vocabulary?"

The young fellow, Langtree, looks around, then back at me. "I didn't say who. I said where."

"There are people here who can read lips," I say.

But his density seems impenetrable. "You reckon we can actually take back Baton Rouge? I fought there at the graveyard. The blue-bellies loaded their cannons with grape and blew corpses out of the crypts. I never saw anything like it."

"In answer to your question, yes, we can take back Baton Rouge," I say.

Langtree stares at McNab, as though sharing a communal moment, his eyes as bright as Christmas morning. "I say we tell the colonel to light the torch," he says.

"Watch your mouth," McNab says.

"I think the colonel is a great man," Langtree says. "Don't be talking to me like that."

"What did you mean by 'light the torch'?" I ask.

"It speaks for itself," he replies. He pulls back his coat and exposes the butt of a cap-and-ball Remington revolver. "There are people you cain't teach. Read the Book of Revelation."

I drink my mixture of water and absinthe, then pour a straight shot and knock it back and rise from my chair. I put several coins on the table. The clouds look like spun gold against a purple sky; the floor seems to be titling under my feet. "Please tell the colonel I will be in touch in the next few days."

"You've got your dander up, have you?" McNab says.

"Not at all. This has been a delightful occasion."

"How do you know where the colonel is?" Langtree asks.

"Our waitress is a Confederate agent," I say.

I tip my hat to them and walk out of the courtyard. Then I realize that my joke at the expense of the waitress could have a terrible consequence, considering the intellectual level of Shaye Langtree or even McNab. I go back to the courtyard, but both men are gone and I can't find the young woman who waited on us. I wonder if my talent for hurting others will ever cease. I deliberately dig my fingernails into my left cheek and leave a wound I am afraid to look at.

It's dark outside now. I'm sitting in the front room with Miss Hannah and Miss Florence and Miss Marie. The streetlamps are lit, and through the curtains I can see horses pulling a public car down the tracks on the neutral ground. The absinthe has worn off, and I can feel the return of my paranoia and a tightness in my body that is like sinew scraping against bone.

I am not sure that I am altogether welcomed by Miss Marie. She is a handsome woman in a plump way, but suspicious of strangers, I suspect, particularly a fellow with a face like mine.

The great irony of my evening is that I am with women of color who speak Spanish, French, and English, while only a short time ago I was with two cardinal examples of the white race who can barely speak their own language.

There is something you must understand about the contradictions of the South. It is not one society. The elevated and wispy echoes of our mother country that you hear in plantation society have been taught us by British tutors. Listen to their round vowels. You could roll them down a hallway at Buckingham Palace. By the same token, the overseers are usually the descendants of Cockneys who were born not far from Bow bells.

The profanity and coarseness and violent metaphors of a truly pagan race are of course the gifts of the Irish, God bless their souls. But perhaps the greatest contribution is from the people who were brought to the New World on slave ships during the era of the Middle Passage. It's the iambic line. Listen to it sometime. Every other syllable is accented. Any British poet would immediately recognize it.

"I cannot thank you enough for your hospitality, Miss Marie," I say. "I have always heard that you are a kind lady. I hope I have not caused you any inconvenience."

My words seem to break across her face. "Where did you go this evening, Mr. Lufkin?"

I feel a catch in my throat coming. "A courtyard place on the edge of the Quarter. I wasn't there long, though."

"You should not go there, sir. It's a dangerous part of our community."

"You think so?" I say, disingenuously. But she has brought up a subject that has been bothering me since I returned from drinking with McNab and the young fellow Langtree. "I have the feeling the waitress was Creole, bilingual perhaps, maybe from the Islands. She has a blue tattoo above her eyebrow."

"That's Gabrielle Lemoine. She's from Martinique."

She waits for me to speak. "Really," I say, clearing my throat. "Does she have friends? People who walk her home? That sort of thing?"

"Why do you ask?"

"As you say, it's a bad neighborhood."

Her eyes will not leave mine.

"Well, I should be going to bed, I guess."

"What happened there, Mr. Wade?" she says.

"Nothing, really. I was making a joke with a fellow. That's all."

"A joke about Gabrielle?"

This woman should have had a job with the Spanish Inquisition.

"Not anything that was unseemly," I reply. "Just a casual remark about Confederate agents."

"You did that down on the *Rue Bassin*?"

"Yes."

She gets up from her chair. "Goodnight, sir," she says. "I hope you sleep well."

Then she walks out. My throat is dry, my heart thudding. Miss Hannah and Miss Florence pick up the tea dishes and go into the kitchen without speaking. I follow them in. They are washing the dishes in a bucket, their backs to me. Neither will acknowledge my presence.

"I meant no harm," I say.

Miss Florence finally turns around. Her face is gray, her eyes hollow. "Leave the absinthe to the devil. It will drive you mad."

"I know, Miss Florence. I've developed a bad liking for it. I'm not sure what to do."

I wait in the silence that follows, hoping that Miss Hannah will speak to me. But she doesn't. I go into the room that has been allotted me, along with a couch and a blanket and pillow, and lie down and soon fall asleep. But I will get no rest.

In the early hours Hannah Laveau comes to me. I do not know what to make of it, not now, nor probably ever. She kneels by the couch and strokes my forehead with her fingers. I can feel her breath on my skin. There is a glow around her, a soft radiance, the color of butter that has been browned.

"Hannah?"

She doesn't answer. She leans down and kisses my forehead, then my lips.

"God loves you," she says, and walks away, as though she has been subsumed by the darkness itself.

I sit up on the couch, searching the room with my eyes. "Come back, Hannah," I say. "Please."

There's no reply. I spend the rest of the night rolled up in a ball, an unrelieved, unbearable throbbing at work in my lower regions. What is the dawn worth if your nocturnal hours are a torment, your simplest thoughts a tin of worms? Will the touch of a woman's lips always be denied me? Will I never have peace? *What the hammer, what the chain, in what furnace was thy brain?* I say to myself.

Poor William Blake, I have the feeling you suffered the pains of the damned.

*   *   *

I wake early and walk into the gaseous vapors of the dawn and sit
down in the Café du Monde on Decatur Street and order café au
lait and beignets. My words to McNab and the young fellow Langtree were true. The estate my parents left was eventually cleared
of entanglements, and the money was placed in a Minnesota bank
where it would be safe. I have the wherewithal to buy many weapons.
The big issue will be my confrontation with Colonel Carleton Hayes.
I will finance his private army, but it will no longer be under his
control. It will be dedicated to goals that are humane, democratic,
and Jeffersonian, and most of all, to the abolition of slavery.

What's to lose? Sherman is a hero in the North, and Jubal Early
in the South. With leadership like that, the Republic should be an
ash heap within five years.

The fog is so thick I can hardly see the cathedral on the other
side of the Place d'Armes, much less down on the river, where the
blue-bellies and flatboaters cavort at night. Then I realize something is wrong. I hear people yelling and a horn blowing. The
curds of fog and steam are as tangible as cotton puffing across
the river's surface. I walk down the slope, where I can now make
out some Union soldiers throwing ropes weighted with grappling
hooks off the bank. They sink into at least two feet of fog before
they splash on the river's surface, then the soldiers retrieve them
and work their way down the bank.

I feel a terrible sense of alarm. Why? Because we teach ourselves to be unafraid and not to listen to those warnings and doubts
and fears that have been with us since man was created. Last night
I convinced myself that Hannah Laveau's visit to my room and
her kiss upon my forehead and mouth were only a dream, one

that I used as an opiate so I didn't have to think about the danger to which I may have exposed the Creole waitress. For whatever reason, perhaps because my parents owned slaves, my greatest fear has always been the same: I would harm the innocent. Have I done that now? What was the name of the waitress? Gabrielle? Dear Lord, let this be just another dream.

Now I think Hannah's visit was real. I also believe she had a prophetic vision of a tragedy, one that I was directly responsible for, and in advance she was telling me I was loved by God.

I can see the river more clearly now, and the grappling hooks arching in the air and splashing in the water. Then a soldier shouts out, "I got her! Somebody get a net! Oh, shite. You don't want to see this one, boys."

28

FLORENCE MILTON

I have followed Young Wade for reasons I am not sure I understand. Maybe he's a kindred spirit. My life has changed greatly since I shot and killed the young Union soldier near the brothel tents. I see his dying face from sunset to dawn. No, that is not correct. I see the surprise, then the realization that his life has been taken irrevocably. His mouth is open, his eyes fixed on mine, as though he can hold his body erect and prevent his knees from buckling if he can only hang onto the person who has shot him through the heart.

His eyes slide away, and then he curls on the ground like an infant in the womb and breathes his last, at rest somewhere beyond a veil I cannot see or penetrate.

I do not think I will ever sleep again. Hence, I do not try. I lie with my eyes open and let the images of the night have their way. Gargoyles are gargoyles. They are not symbolic. If you invite them into your life, they do not go home easily.

People are starting to come down from the Café du Monde, lifting their feet so as not to slip, cautiously approaching the edges of the Mississippi River. The soldiers are pulling a body from the water in a shrimp net. It's obviously a woman. Her skirts and petticoat are soggy with water and mud and garbage people have thrown in the current. The soldiers drag the body up onto dry, grassy land, then peel back the net from her skin and clothes and hair, which allows her arms to flop dead-cold beside her.

Young Wade is at the front of the crowd, staring down at her.

"Better step back there, fella," a solider says.

"Bring a lantern over here," Mr. Wade replies.

"Do you think you know her, sir?" the soldier says. He has two chevrons on his sleeve. "A coroner will be here momentarily."

"I said bring a fucking lantern here," Wade says.

"Contain your language, sir," the soldier says. "Here, we've got your lantern. Did you know her?"

Mr. Wade takes a kerchief from his trouser pocket and squats by the woman's body and wipes the hair from her forehead.

"What are you looking at, sir?" the soldier says.

"A tattoo. She's a waitress on *Rue Bassin*. Her name is Gabrielle."

"A waitress, is she?" the soldier replies. "They're hard to find on *Rue Bassin*."

"Shut your mouth, Yank," Mr. Wade says.

The soldier is young and makes me think of the one I killed. I want to tell him not to disrespect the dead. I want to save him from the regret that eventually follows callousness and the sneer of the quick. But the boy, and that's what he is, says, "I'm sorry, sir. Something terrible was done to this lady. We see a lot of them like this. It's not fun to pull them out of the drink."

Wade walks away and either ignores or does not recognize me. There seems to be no emotion in his face. I catch up with him on the slope and touch his arm. He turns, his kerchief still knotted in his hand, a leaf or a smear of mud on it. "Miss Florence?" he says.

"Yes," I reply. "Where are you going, Young Wade?"

"To pay my bill in the café and take a walk."

"Would you mind if I accompany you?"

"Perhaps another time, if you don't mind. I need to sort out a few things."

"Do not compound your grief, sir. I certainly do not agree with the politics of your family, but on a personal basis I have always admired them. Your mother's courage is a model for all of us. Haven't all of you paid enough penalty for the society in which we live?"

"That is very kind of you, Miss Florence. Maybe we can have lunch today. Perhaps a picnic. We can take along Miss Hannah and Miss Marie."

"I am in my middle years, sir, so I can say things a younger woman cannot. I think you are in love with Hannah Laveau and for whatever reason afraid to admit it. What I am saying, sir, is that you cannot bring back the woman who was so cruelly murdered. Do not ruin your life. Release your heart. Tell Hannah your feelings for her."

"That is very good advice, Miss Florence. But I have the face of a monster, if not the soul of one, and I do not delude myself into thinking otherwise. Look at the sun on the front of the cathedral. That's the glory of God at work. Now look at me."

"Do not mock yourself, sir. And do not indulge in self-pity."

"I agree. You're a grand person, Miss Florence. Let's have that picnic. In a short time I will be back with a basketful of groceries."

"Sir, Hannah and I are wanted criminals. Frankly, you do not seem to understand the realities that surround us."

"Well, we can eat inside."

I give up. "Good day to you, sir."

"And to you as well," he says, tipping his hat, bowing at the waist.

As a New Englander I have to admit there is no equal to the manners of Southern gentility. They're grand on the field of honor and go down with a sonnet on their tongues. But why are they always on the wrong side?

29

WADE LUFKIN

I will describe some details about the way Gabrielle Lemoine
died only because they are indicators of the kind of man who
took her young life. I think the killer rained his fists down on
her face. He also broke her neck. The sinew was the only anatomical
connection that held her head on her shoulders. The shock in her
eyes showed the suddenness of the injury and the level of lethality
she probably never believed would be visited on her person, like a
camera lens clicking unexpectedly shut on her life.

The fraudulent master sergeant McNab said he was staying at
a hotel on the corner of Rampart. "Hotel" is hardly applicable. It's
a borderline brothel, full of cockroaches and bed lice and flatboaters
who pool their money and install themselves six at a time in one
room. The jakes behind it are positioned on an open latrine, which
once a week is bailed out with buckets and dusted with lime and
ash by prisoners from the city jail.

Between the hotel and the courtyard where Gabrielle Lemoine
worked is a curio and herb and voodoo shop often frequented by Union

enlisted men, most of whom are unaware that the antiquities that fascinate them in particular were probably dug from the city dump.

The bell rings on the door as I enter. The lady who comes to the counter from the back is a woman of color, and very old, her eyes glassy with cataracts. I do not know how she sees. She says something to me in French.

"I'm sorry, I speak only English," I say.

"How may I help you?"

"You have some bookends in the window. They look like the heads of elephants, quite heavy fellows, perhaps made from lead."

"Yes, do you want them?"

"How much are they?"

"Six dollars."

"Yes, I'll take them. Please wrap them up."

"You want both of them?"

"Yes. They are book*ends*. One needs the other, correct?"

"But you really need only one. Isn't that correct?"

"I think one of us is confused. I'll take the pair, please."

She goes to the window, obviously walking by memory, and returns to the counter and begins wrapping them in brown paper. I put the appropriate coins on the counter. "Pardon me, but you seem to be examining my countenance," I say. "It's a bit disconcerting."

"Your purpose here is a pretense. You smell of death, sir."

"*What?*"

"It's in your glands, not just in your clothes."

"I helped with the identification of a murdered woman. Right down there on the river's edge. Maybe you knew her. Gabrielle Lemoine was her name."

The old woman's eyes look as inanimate as fish scales. "Gabrielle is dead?"

"Yes," I reply, swallowing.

She looks down at the coins, then pushes them toward me. "Take them."

"You don't want to sell me the bookends?"

"The elephants are yours. I will take no money for them. You were not here, sir. Please do not speak of my shop."

"Have I offended you?"

She walks through a curtain of beads into the back of the shop without answering. I stare at the beads swinging back and forth, then accept the fact that someone has seen deep into my soul, and I cradle the elephants in one arm and walk to the hotel on the corner of Rampart Street. The fog has lifted, and seagulls are lighting on the garbage behind the building, squeaking like mice, their beaks laden. But I cannot get the old woman out of my mind.

The concierge is a gelatinous creature, his chair about to explode under his weight, his lungs wheezing, his bulging scrotum the size of a bowling ball. "I know no fucker by that name," he says.

"None by the name of Langtree?"

"I just tole you."

"No one registered by the name of McNab?"

"Do you pound shit in your ears for a living?"

I am getting nowhere and am about to give up. "How about 'Smith'?"

"Yes, we have several by that name."

I place a silver dollar on the counter and hold it down with my thumb. "How about a 'Smith' with a lovely girl of color from the courtyard across the way?"

He works the coin from under my thumb. "At the head of the stairs, second door on the right."

"What does this Mr. 'Smith' look like?"

"I am a poor man. My wife is dying, and the two of us live just across from the jakes. Do you want your fellow bad enough or not?"

I place two more silver dollars on the counter.

"He's a walking stump and leaves pecker tracks and food crumbs on the sheets," he says. "He will also gouge your eye and cut out your balls and have them with his eggs. He left with the girl in the early hours but came back by himself. Tell him where you got this and I'll cut your balls out myself."

"Thank you for your candor. I just want to deliver a gift to my 'fellow,' as you say, and I'll be on my way. My best wishes to your wife as well as yourself."

He frowns, his eyes clouding, and tries to figure out what I just said. I walk up the stairs with my twin elephant heads, the banister wobbling in my hand.

I put a pencil across my teeth and tap lightly on the door.

"Who is it?" McNab's voice says.

"Message from Colonel Carleton," I say.

McNab opens the door a crack. There are scratches deep in his face. I shove the door and knock him backwards, then close it behind me. "Pardon the ruse, but I had the feeling you might be unavailable this morning."

There are two bunks in the room and trash on the floor and a broken loaf of French bread on a wood table. The air smells like laundry that has soured in a water closet.

His hand is pressed to the middle of his face. "You broke my nose," he says.

"Sorry about that. It doesn't look bad, though. Here's my handkerchief. Or you can pack some cotton balls up your nostrils."

"What are you doing here?" he says.

"I heard you had a romp around the neighborhood this morning. Looks like someone got her nails in your face. If you're not careful, you'll start looking like me."

He pinches his snout to stop the blood draining over his upper lip. "I'm going to let this pass because of the colonel. But don't misunderstand the gesture," he says.

"I don't see your paladin from the wilds of Texas," I reply. "What's the young fellow's name? Long Hedge? Or Hedge Hog? Something unusual."

"Langtree, you idiot."

"Thank you. Where is the lad?"

"He's back with the colonel. Now haul your snooty ass out of here before I notify the authorities."

"I was going to give you a present or perhaps send it to the colonel. Do you have a personal library?"

He has a rag cupped on his nose now. It's bright red in the center. He sniffs loudly. His words are nasal. "I'm done with you. Get out."

I unwrap the elephant heads from the butcher paper. "I had a strange conversation with the lady who gave me these bookends. She seemed to know their future and would have nothing to do with them. She also thought I might have need of only one of the bookends."

He points his finger at me, as stiff as a rod. "Leave."

"Why did you murder Gabrielle Lemoine? My guess is you raped her, then she fought back and you beat her almost to death and then broke her neck and threw her in the river."

"I got into a fight with a drunk blue-belly."

"Blue-bellies fight with their fingernails?"

"Let me explain things for you, Mr. Lufkin. If it wasn't for your money, the colonel would have gutted you and filled the cavity with rocks and sunk you in Bayou Teche. Now get the fuck down the stairs or I will drag you down there myself and stick your head in one of the jakes. In fact, I think I will do that anyway and fill your piehole with a bucket of shite dipped fresh from the latrine."

"You should clean up your language, Mr. McNab."

He takes a gambler's single-shot hideaway from his belt. "Guess who killed the cunt from the courtyard? You. I just hung the bird around your neck."

He cocks the hideaway with his thumb, the beginnings of a smile at the corner of his mouth. But that is the last thing he ever does. I was right about the origins of the bookends. They were definitely formed out of lead. The artisan shaped the trunks of the elephants into comfortable handles so a bibliophile could move them around easily on bookshelves and desks and library shelves and other cozy places. When I insert my right hand inside the circularity of the elephant's trunk, the heft and balance are perfect, the weight comparable to a cannonball the size of a grapefruit. I feel quite snug about my situation now, and wonder if my bookend has ever touched the work of Robert Browning—*Pippa Passes*, in particular—and Pippa's words reminding us that "God's in His heaven— All's right with the world!"

However, I let things get away from me. The first blow was mighty enough. But I guess way leads on to way sometimes, and before it's over I've changed the design on the wallpaper in a dramatic fashion, more than I wish to describe, certainly. I borrow water and a towel from the room and wipe off my hands and coat and some splatter on my face, then toddle downstairs. My gelatinous friend is no longer at his post, although I would not harm him even if he were. Let bygones be bygones. I do not know who first said that. Perhaps it was Browning. It's a wonderful principle to live by.

30

PIERRE CAUCHON

As I have stated, I don't admire the collection of political clods I work for. But they are storehouses of information and get it through the telegraph, female consorts in Baton Rouge and New Orleans, and spies everywhere. The people who still have their money plan to keep it. People like the Lufkins, who believed in the Confederacy and bought the ten-dollar currency called "Dixies," became paupers. The smart people are not philosophically oriented. They know we are going to lose, and they let nothing get past their ken, and that includes the goings-on of unlikely players such as Colonel Carleton Hayes. The word is he has seven hundred irregulars under his command now. Give that some thought. How would you like an army of seven hundred anteaters sucking the ground from under your feet?

I have also heard talk about Florence Milton and Hannah Laveau and Wade Lufkin. It seems on both sides no one wants this unlikely trio killing people, whether that includes slave catchers, procurers, Union soldiers, or the latest one, this fellow McNab, whom, it seems, Wade Lufkin pasted all over a room in a Rampart Street whorehouse.

I don't care what happens to Lufkin, but I worry about Miss Florence and Miss Hannah, particularly Miss Hannah. I wronged her and put her in jail, and because of my false pride I used her to get at Charles Lufkin, who now is paralyzed and bereft by the loss of his three sons at Chickamauga. I have learned a lesson from this. You don't need to seek revenge against your enemies. The bastards eventually fall in their own shite.

I did not mean to use that term in regard to Charles Lufkin. I don't like him, but he's elderly, and the loss of all his sons must be unbearable. The man I have in mind is the fellow who left us enfiladed at Shiloh Church so William Sherman could rip a hole in our flank like a shark tearing meat from the side of a porpoise. The real bastard and motherfucker I'm talking about is Ira Jamison. He was in New Iberia only yesterday, having lunch on the overseer's verandah at The Shadows Plantation. I wanted to shoot him. To simply walk up to his table, pull a pistol, stick it in his mouth, and shoot him.

But that would be letting him off light. Unless you were there, you cannot imagine the carnage at Shiloh. The only ones I have heard describe a similar experience in the war are the Yankees who went up Marye's Heights at Fredericksburg five times in one afternoon and slipped on their own gore, and the greybacks who charged Cemetery Ridge, barefoot and wearing rags, in ninety-five-degree heat, and for one hour and forty minutes were cut down like wheat, until eight thousand of them lay dead or mortally wounded while the blue-bellies at the top of the hill tamped the butts of their rifles and chanted, "Fredericksburg! Fredericksburg! Fredericksburg!"

But it was Shiloh that showed the world the animus we bore one another, brother and child and father, baptized in the same churches, bayonetting one another in a filthy trench that had once been a peach orchard.

I also have Darla Babineaux on my mind. Hannah, too, but it's Darla who has gotten inside me. It doesn't seem natural. She's there when I wake; she's there when I sleep. She's there when I saddle up Varina and ride out to the Suarez plantation for some fraudulent reason I have manufactured. I am not talking about my physical attraction to her, either. In fact, I do not want to think in an unseemly fashion about her, even though she is very attractive and knows a great deal about men. I just like her. I like being with her. I like the way she smells. She's a friend.

Three evenings past, with the sun no more than a spark inside a pile of rainclouds, I placed my face between her neck and bare shoulder, and let it stay there a long time. I breathed on her, and tasted the salt in her skin, and hooked my fingers in her hair.

"What are you t'inking?" she asked.

"I'm not sure."

"Don't lie to yourself, no," she said.

"I think I want to go off with you, far away. Maybe to an island in the South Seas."

"What we gonna do there?"

"I don't know. Grow pineapples and coconuts."

"But you don't want to do nothing here?" she said.

"I don't want to be like that blue-belly Endicott."

"He's nothing like you. You're a good man. Somet'ing else is holding you back, ain't it?"

"No."

"Yes, it is," she said, stepping back from me. "Tell me what it is?"

"Maybe you can't let go of the Suarez plantation. Maybe it's your home."

"We didn't make the world we was born in, no. But that don't mean it tells us what to do. I tole you I ain't gonna work in the field again. I meant it."

Then she went inside her cabin and closed the door. I stood still in the shadows, the cicadas singing, my head drooped. I do not know how long I stood there. Then I went back to my quarters in New Iberia and dreamed about shooting Ira Jamison. Actually, it sounded like a good idea. I have often thought that a short open season on people could rid us of many problems.

Now it's dusk again, and I tether Varina in the pecan orchard and feed her a dried apple, then walk down to Darla's cabin. She loves to bobber-fish in the evening. Tonight is no exception. We put the cane poles and carved sticks we use for floaters and the metal nuts we use for weights and a can full of redworms and nightcrawlers in the rowboat, then row among the flooded trees, the *sac-à-lait* and bream and goggle-eye perch rising to the surface, dimpling the water like rain-rings.

But this evening we do something different. Or rather Darla does. She puts a grappling hook and a coiled rope in the bow of the boat.

"You want to t'row it in?" she says. "Or you want me to?"

"I'll do it," I reply. "But I don't believe Old Man Suarez rolled a barrel of silver and gold into the lake."

"I tole you I seen him do it."

"Oh, I believe he rolled a barrel into the water. But it probably contained his dirty underwear. He was too greedy to separate himself from his wealth."

She laughs, then puts her hand over her mouth. I take her hand away. "Your laughter and your smile are beautiful, Darla. Why do you try to hide them?"

"We were taught not to laugh around white people."

"Now you can tell those white people to kiss your foot."

"I done worse than that."

"Don't talk about it," I say. I know she's talking about the white man she killed and another white man she almost killed, to say nothing of the possibility she helped Old Man Suarez to an early departure. "You hear me, girl?"

"Pull up the hook and t'row it again, and don't call me 'girl.'"

"This is messing up our fishing."

"Just t'row it a few more times."

The wind is cool, the cypresses starting to turn gold, the last heartbreaking descent of the sun sinking into the lake, its red glow wobbling under the current with an eye-watering brilliance. "I love you, Darla."

"You ain't never said that to me."

"I'm saying it now."

"What am I gonna do wit' you?"

"Anything you want to," I reply.

"You gonna get yourself killed, you. Maybe me, too."

"By whom?"

She raises her eyes to mine. "They're out there. Everywhere. They're mean and they're cruel. They hate themselves and take it out on our bodies."

"I know what they are. I enforce the law for them, Darla. There's an island over there."

"Wit' the willows on it? I know where it is and what it is. I know what's on it, too. I tole you before to take me into the barn, Mr. Pierre. You didn't want to, no."

"Don't call me 'mister.'"

"T'row out the hook."

I fling it angrily in a long arc and watch it splash and sink in the current. I begin pulling it in, hand over hand, then it snags, the rope bouncing and tightening, beads of water dripping from the hemp.

"The bottom of this lake is full of cypress logs, Darla. Some of them are two hundred years old. They've turned to stone."

"Get us closer, Mr. Pierre. I tole you I ain't gonna be nobody's cornbread darky. The only t'ing that's gonna make me different is money."

I pull the boat to the spot where the rope is perpendicular to the lake's surface. I don't know why, but my heart is booming. I think it's because I fear stealing from the Suarez family—not because of what they could do to me, but because I would become like them.

"Pull it up," Darla says.

"No."

"Why?" she says, her face filled with disappointment.

"I want you. I don't want the bloody treasure of people I hate, and I hate every fucking one of them."

Her chest is rising and falling, a shine in her blue-green eyes. She wipes her mouth with her hand, then looks into space and then at the water. She works her way past me and sits on the edge of the bow, bumping me with her rump.

"What are you doing?" I say.

"I ain't doing not'ing. When I say I ain't doing not'ing, that means I ain't doing not'ing."

She wraps the rope around her wrist and cinches it across her palm and with both hands pulls the hook free from whatever it had penetrated down below. The boat is caught by the current now, drifting toward the island covered with willows, with no way to accurately return to the spot we have just left.

"Master Suarez used the cabin on that island for duck hunting," she says. "He blew feathers all over the water. He made me watch him do it. He said one day he'd get me a gun. He never did that, no. Know why? He didn't have time because he was dead."

And now I know what Old Man Suarez's fate was, and who killed him, and I don't care that I know this and I'm proud to be with a murderess.

I row us onto the island and feel the hull scrape on the sand. Then I get out and walk through the shallows and help Darla onto the small beach. The willows are bent in the wind, the long, slender leaves flickering like knives. I hoist her over my shoulder and dance like an Indian all over the beach, while she laughs and kicks and pounds my back, her skin turning to gold in the sun's last light.

31

WADE LUFKIN

Miss Hannah and Miss Florence and I disembarked from a paddle wheeler just south of Baton Rouge and went westward in a carriage, back into farmland and the northern tip of the Atchafalaya Basin. I'm afraid we have become an unholy trinity who will find no sanctuary in our beloved state, nor access to passage to the North. Had not a college friend of mine on board warned me that we would be arrested in Baton Rouge, the three of us would already be in chains.

But I guess each of us has his own motive. Miss Hannah wants to find her child in Tennessee; Miss Florence wants to remain with her Underground Railroad friends; and I want to sanitize the state of Louisiana and pretend that honor and spirituality can surmount the horror I see in the eyes of others when they first look at my face. There's a good chance the three of us will be strung high up on a slash pine, food for crows and a warning to all.

* * *

We get out of the carriage in front of a paintless two-story farmhouse surrounded by sugar-cane fields. It's afternoon and the sky is dark with what looks like thunderclouds; however, these thunderclouds have black ash in them and are blowing from the south, actually from a line of flame that stretches across the entirety of the horizon. The air smells like syrup that has dripped on a hot stove.

The colonel is sitting on the gallery in a swayback straw chair, a jug by his foot, a staff in his right hand, a wide-brim hat wilted on his head, his swashbuckler boots supple and rippling with fresh polish.

The young sergeant Shaye Langtree stands next to him, two cap-and-ball revolvers stuck in his belt, the handles reversed for a cross-draw, his eyes as beady as a carrion bird's. He wears a Confederate kepi cocked on his forehead. Flecks of either paint or blood are sprinkled on it. Other men are lying on the lawn, flicking pen knives into the ground, rolling dice on a blanket, or playing a game some call rounders.

This is not a good environment for Miss Hannah and Miss Florence. But I know they will brass it out. No, that's badly stated. They are members of that special group who refuse to flinch, the kind who don't consider bravery a virtue, the kind who stand on a balcony in an electrical storm enjoying the fine breeze. The irony is that they don't know how brave they are.

In the woods I can see perhaps one hundred tents and many more in the distance. I can also see cannons and ambulance wagons and caissons and the tree trunks strung with picket lines, the horses nickering and grazing on grass that is still a bright green. I cannot understand how so many people are willing to follow an idiot like Carleton Hayes.

I tip my hat to him just the same. "Good afternoon to you, sir."

"And you as well," he says. He halfway rises from the chair, then eases into it again, and I wonder if this is a sign of cancer in the colon.

He looks drunk. I can see no one inside the house, no candle or lamp burning, a fact that is making me uncomfortable, knowing his history.

"Who are the people who own this lovely farm, Colonel?"

"Fuck if I know," he says.

"Sir, I am with ladies," I say. "This is Miss Florence and Miss Hannah."

"I noticed," he says. "Get some chairs out here, Sergeant Langtree. Bring some glasses."

"Thank you for your invitation, sir, but we do not wish to encumber your day," Miss Florence says.

I knew we would have a problem. Stalwart as always, Miss Florence is not going to sit down with the likes of Colonel Hayes, even though she is obviously exhausted.

"Suit yourself," he says, then gazes at me. "My informants tell me you literally pounded Master Sergeant McNab's brains all over his hotel room."

"His 'hotel room' was a den of crab lice, sir," I reply. "That said, I take full credit for his eradication. McNab ridiculed you and said your plan to retake the Mississippi was shite."

He twists in his chair and looks up at Shaye Langtree. "Is this true?"

"Yes, sir," Langtree says.

"Why didn't you tell me?"

"I didn't want to hurt your feelings, sir."

I cannot read the colonel's crossed eyes. Nor can I read his face. Half of it is marbled with infection and pus. He tries to blot it clean with a folded handkerchief to his cheek. "You can get me five hundred Spencers?"

"I can also get you Henrys. The ammunition tube holds fifteen rounds. The Yankees load them on Sunday and shoot them all week long."

He doesn't have a chance to respond.

"Colonel Hayes, Miss Hannah and I need to rest," Miss Florence says. "Our journey here has been an arduous one. May we have a room in this house or a tent of our own?"

He looks up at her. "Are you the New England abolitionist who has been stealing the darkies off our plantations?"

Miss Florence's back stiffens, her white blouse now gray with perspiration and sticking to her skin. "No, I am the New England abolitionist who has helped free African families who have been whipped and banded and worked to death in the fields, thanks to people such as yourself."

The colonel stifles a burp. "You know anything about nursing?"

"I studied medicine in Boston and helped care for the dying in two yellow fever epidemics. I also cared for Southern wounded at Corinth."

"You think you can do anything for my rash?"

"Sir, your infection is far more serious than a rash. How and when did you first contract it?"

"Don't worry about that," he says. "I just need the right treatment."

"I will see what I can do," she says.

All this time Hannah has said nothing, a fact apparently not lost on Hayes. "You staring at me, girl?"

"I ain't a girl, suh."

"Why you got that look on your face?"

"Somehow you know where my li'l boy is at. I lost him at Shiloh Church. But you know how I can get him back."

"What is she talking about?" he asks me.

"Miss Hannah hears voices, sir. But I think they are real and not to be treated otherwise."

"Whose voices?" he asks.

"The voices are from God and the angels around Him," Hannah says. "I hear them right now, as you speak. If you don't change your ways, you going to a terrible place, Colonel."

He looks into space with his cross-eyed stare and seems to shrivel in his chair.

"Are you all right, Colonel?" I say.

"Of course I am. Sergeant Langtree, put up a tent for these two women," he says. "Put a guard on it. Give them whatever they want. The man who touches either one of them will have his hands cut off."

Langtree looks at him blankly.

"Did you hear me?" the colonel says. "Get your ass down to the camp and find some bedding for them, too. You look like a scarecrow."

Langtree walks away with Florence and Hannah. I sense this is a dark moment for him. In the shadow of the house, he looks over his shoulder at the colonel, his profile as sharp as snipped tin, his visible eye as cold as glass.

Late that evening I sit by a bonfire in the backyard of the farmhouse and have supper with the colonel. It is not a situation of my choosing, but as Our Lord has taught us, there are times when we must render unto Caesar. Nonetheless, in the warmth of the fire and the sparks rising into the sky, I am eating a plate of pork and eggplant and rice and gravy a few feet away from a man who has committed war crimes I do not want to think about. He is obviously deranged, and probably depraved. It is difficult to have charitable thoughts about him. I suspect his brain is filled with wormholes, and he slides from one to another with great facility because chaos is the only reality he knows. That's about as kind as I can get.

But I am about to find out how far I can push the colonel. I have yet to meet a madman who was not acutely aware of his own needs, his own visceral pleasures, his own indemnification. When it comes to pride, a madman has the sensitivity of an infected gland.

"Are you going to drink my liquor or not?" he says.

"I have been trying to get off the grog, Colonel. But thank you just the same."

"Grog and absinthe are not the same."

"That is true."

"Well then?"

"Yes, sir, please. I'll have a drop."

He pours from his jug into a tin cup and hands it to me. It goes down like kerosene. I'm afraid what will happen if a spark from the bonfire lands on my breath.

"Fried your entrails, huh?"

"Yes, sir," I reply. But I have to admit that I want more and that I have a very serious problem. I set down my plate on the grass. "Gentlemen don't talk business at the table, but these are dangerous times, and if you don't object, I'd like to talk business. Is that all right, sir?"

"I don't give a country shite for that stuff. I got news for you. Your class of people don't talk about anything *except* business."

"Sir, you need to stop using that language."

He cleans his teeth with a rag. "You're a strange one, Young Wade. I think the Yank who put that pistol ball in you pissed on it first. You want another drink?"

"Yes, thank you," I reply, handing him my cup. "Colonel, I will probably never marry and never have the pleasure of children or a legacy. That means I must find another choosing. Do you know what I am saying, sir?"

"That you have nothing to lose?" he says. "I won't argue that." He sips from his cup and watches me as he would an insect. The putrescence on his face makes me think of white mold on a broken tomato.

"I will buy all the ordnance that is available and that I can afford. But there is a caveat. We will share command. There will be no abuse of civilians, private property, abolitionists, enslaved people, or captured blue-bellies."

I wait for his reaction. He is an unpredictable and violent man. I suspect he has weapons concealed on his person. I cannot imagine dying at his hands while he looks on in curiosity.

He stretches his legs and stares at the stars.

"The Creole woman?" he says. "Why does she think I had anything to do with her child getting lost at Shiloh?"

"I don't know, sir."

"Then you find out!"

"Have you heard anything I have said?"

"About sharing command? I'm all for it. You can start with cleaning the latrines and burying the garbage and feeding nine hundred men."

"I thought it was seven hundred."

"That's because you spend most of your time with crazy people like those women." He gets up from his chair and reels in a circle and waves his staff and almost falls into the bonfire. "You talk to the woman, you hear me? I will not go to Hell for the sins of others. Goddamn it, don't you grin at me! I'll brain you."

"I'm not grinning, sir," I said. "I have lost the muscles in my face. I cannot control my expressions."

"I'll brain you anyway. Why have you brought this curse on me?"

"What curse?"

"For the sins of Ira Jamison. For what he did on the slopes above Owl Creek at Shiloh. I hate all these patrician sons of bitches. Don't you lay their fate on me."

The moon is orange and as big as a planet above the trees. The colonel raises his fists and rails at the sky like an ancient Babylonian seeking a god he can blame for the tower he has helped tear down.

32

HANNAH LAVEAU

It's dark now, and I turn down the lantern in our tent and lie down by Miss Florence. Our bedding is made of canvas and straw and long-stem grass and army blankets and a pillow for each of us. The two boys who fixed our bedding were shy and respectful and said they were the brothers of Shaye Langtree, the sergeant who was lectured by Colonel Hayes in front of Miss Florence and Mr. Wade and me. One of the boys asked me if I had been to Mississippi. I told him I had not. He said he had heard it was a big city and that most of the people there were born with six toes.

Miss Florence laughed. I'm glad she could do that because I am real scared for her. Sometimes she cain't hold down her food and she vomits it up and starts shivering, then she has coughing spells and cries when she thinks I'm not around. I caught her burying a handkerchief that had a spray of blood on it. I think I'm going to lose her directly, and I just cain't bear the thought of it.

Somebody hits the side of the tent with a pinecone or a dirt clod, then a rock. I light the lantern again and stick my head and arm out the flap. "Don't you have better things to do than disturbing people's sleep, Sergeant Langtree?"

"Can I come in?"

"Simple mind is as simple does. What is the matter with you?"

"I brought some camphor for Miss Florence. You can rub it on her chest. It's good for coughs. I stole it from Colonel Hayes."

I turn off the lantern. The stars are bright through the tops of the trees, the pine needles spinning down on us. So far no one in the other tents has heard us. I pull the sergeant inside, then put my fingers on his lips before he can speak and place one hand on his shoulder and slowly press him down on the grass. I speak as quietly as I can, hoping he will do the same. The Langtree family has not spent much time schooling their children.

"Don't you give these other men ideas about coming in my tent, no," I say.

"I ain't gonna do nothing like that," he replies. "Will you stop squeezing my face?"

"Then hush your mouth!"

"What is it?" Miss Florence says, her eyes watery in the dark.

"It's all right," I say. "It's just the sergeant bringing you some medicine."

"That's very nice of him," she says.

But I think Sergeant Langtree has something on his mind besides medicine. Except it's not what I think, either.

"Miss Hannah, you was talking earlier about the colonel going to Hell and losing your little boy and such, and it got me scared. I joined up to be on the right side of things."

"You've hurt people?"

"I done worse than hurt. I thought it was okay if it was an order. Then I started avoiding my reflection. Like looking in a window glass or a barrel of rainwater. I didn't want to see my eyes."

"Why not?" I ask, although I already know the answer.

"I looked into a stream just two days ago and I didn't know who I was looking at."

"Who did you think you were?"

"Somebody who made me scared. Me and my brothers signed up and didn't think nothing about it. We lived north of the Red River, up in Comanche country. They burned people and drug people through cactus. White people done it to them, too."

"So you think you're like the Comanche now?"

"Yes, ma'am. I hung men. I see them in my sleep, twisting on the rope."

"You need to get away from Colonel Hayes," I say.

"What are y'all doin' with him?"

I don't know what to say. "Fortune takes you where it wants to take you." But I feel like I am telling a lie now.

"You killed somebody, Miss Hannah?"

"There was a soldier from Pennsylvania. I wanted to sell him a gun. There was a fight, and things got mixed up. That poor boy lost his life because I was meddling."

"Don't cry, Miss Hannah," he says.

"Don't take my hand, either. Nobody got to take care of me."

I cain't believe how prideful I am acting. I feel Miss Florence's hand on my back, the sweat pressing against my blouse.

"I was supposed to be saved when I was baptized," the sergeant says. "I don't feel saved at all. I think I'm goin' to Hell."

I slap him on the cheek, something I have never done to a white person. "Don't you say that! Don't you ever!"

He's stunned. "No, ma'am, I won't. I'll do whatever you say. Just tell me what to do."

But I got nothing to say. My words are used up. I want my li'l boy. That's all I know. Now I know what people mean when they say they ain't got no place in this world.

Then I say something that seems like meaningless words echoing in a barrel. "I'm just a wayfaring stranger and going to see my mother. She said she'd meet me when I come. I'm going over Jordan. I'm going over home."

"What are you saying, child?" Miss Florence says out of the darkness.

"I don't know," I answer. "I got no business he'ping anybody. My li'l boy is dead and I got no home in this world anymore. I ain't any better than the women in those tents where the solider from Pennsylvania died. I'm just a different kind of whore."

I hear the flap close as Sergeant Langtree flings it behind him. Then the heavens break loose and hailstones rain down on our tent, hitting so hard they feel like rocks.

The colonel sends for me in the morning. I put a shawl on my head and shoulders and walk up to the farmhouse, where he is eating on the gallery. He has half a fried egg in his mouth. "You want some?" he asks.

"No thank you, suh," I reply.

"I heard about a man coming in your tent last night."

"It ain't my tent. It's your tent, suh."

"What the hell is that supposed to mean?"

"Nothing. Is there anything else you want to know?"

"Now just hold on there. I just want you to know I don't allow the ill treatment of women. Just give me the name of the man who bothered you and Miz Milton and I will stuff him down a cannon barrel. Of course that is a joke."

"Why did you not ask Miss Florence to breakfast?"

"She looks poorly. I think she might have a disease." He wipes idly at his infected cheek with his napkin. "Sit down with me."

"No."

"What is your difficulty, woman? What did I do to offend you? If you haven't noticed, I have liberated many of your people."

"So they can clean your chamber pots."

"That is not the case. I clean my own." Then he blanches at his own words.

"I hope you washed your hands, suh."

He chokes on his fried egg. The morning is cool and bright, the grass wet. In the distance is a lake, with a plantation and a blackened cane field next to it. A cannon shell bursts high above the lake, its pieces trailing down to the water. The colonel pays no attention. "I want to talk about my soul, woman."

I lower my head and try to hide inside the shadow of my shawl.

"Did you hear me?" he says.

"You didn't see or hear the cannonball explode, suh?"

"It's the goddamn blue-bellies. Ignore them."

"I don't know anything about your soul, suh."

"You said God talked to you."

"The voices talk to me. I don't know where they come from."

"Listen, I'm doing some business with that son of a bitch Ira Jamison. It's just business. I am not responsible for what he did at Shiloh."

"I am."

"What?"

"I should have run away with my li'l boy, no matter how much they punished me. I'm not worthy to hear God's voice."

He looks truly disturbed.

"You shouldn't be talking about yourself like that," he says.

"Truth is truth."

He drops his napkin on his tin plate. "You ruined my breakfast. What's it take to get you on my side? What do you want? And don't tell me 'nothing.' Everybody wants something, no matter how rich or poor they are. Will you stop looking at the ground?"

"Get me to Shiloh Church. Help me find my li'l boy."

"That would take a miracle, Miss Hannah. And I have run out of my share."

Then I do something I cain't understand. I begin walking up the steps.

"What the hell are you doing?" he says, his crossed eyes going up and down my dress, I'm sure searching for weapons on my person. "Stay back, Miss Hannah. I don't know what you're up to, but I don't want you messing with me in front of my troops. It's not seemly. Goddamn it, what are you doing?"

I place the heels of my hands on his eyes and cup my fingers on his forehead. I can feel the disease and the heat and the liquids that ooze from his flesh. "Mother of God, woman, are you trying to humiliate me? Do I have to hit you? I'll do it!"

He shoves his chair backwards. I wipe my hands on my shawl and fold it and place it on his table. He's crouched, as though he fears I will touch him again. Then his face becomes convulsive, and he straightens up and feels his eyes with his fingertips. "What did you do? Jesus Christ, what did you do?"

He runs for the inside of the house, then returns with a hand mirror. "I don't believe this. You unlocked my eyes. My God, woman, where are you from?"

But he cain't finish the sentence. The Yankees explode another shell overhead, the echo rolling across the land, the sunlight and every leaf trembling in the pecan tree next to the farmhouse.

33

PIERRE CAUCHON

I should have known Captain Endicott would come back into my life, or rather "our lives," since Darla Babineaux and I have jumped our own broomstick. For me that's as binding as taking your vows in front of a preacher. Actually, I am disappointed in the captain. There was one lieutenant at Corinth who crawled out on his belly to drag his wounded back home and was so brave the greybacks wouldn't fire on him. I think Captain Endicott is cut from a different cloth.

Anyway, I believe he got wind of us. There are no secrets on a plantation. I don't know if he is moved by jealousy, greed, or just meanness. Bad pennies don't tell you their motivation. They just keep showing up until they wear a hole in your britches.

He woke me up at my rented cabin by The Shadows. The sun was just barely up, like a tiny yellow flame in the live oaks and Spanish moss. It takes me a few seconds to convince myself I'm not experiencing a bad dream. "Excuse me, Captain Endicott, is there any reason on earth that I should be breathing your nasty breath in the early morning hours?"

"You're about two whiskers from a firing squad, Mr. Cauchon," he replies. "I thought you would be interested."

"A firing squad composed of blue-bellies such as yourself?" I say. "No, I am not interested. Most of y'all couldn't hit your foot with a shovel."

"Oh, humorous man! Try this out, laddie. You are a sworn officer of the law. However, your employer, the state of Louisiana, is no longer a state. It is the property of the United States Army. That means you are the property of the United States Army. That means you can be tried for treason." He looks around the room. "I love your décor."

"Would you mind informing me of the treasonous act I have committed?"

"Conspiring with Darla Babineaux to steal the Suarez plantation, which is now in the custody the United States Army. It's not a difficult concept. Maybe with pencil and paper you can work it out."

"You slept with her, you bastard."

"She told you that, did she? But it doesn't matter. You've stepped in it, Reb."

"I think I would like to get up and knock you down."

"Would you?" He drops a piece of paper on my night table. "This is a warrant for her arrest. I haven't signed it yet. But if you give me an eye's blink of trouble, I'll have the pair of you in front of a wall."

Can they do this to me, you ask? They tore up the Lufkin plantation and killed a mother and infant in the quarters. They confiscated

Ellen Lee Burke's dairy cows. They looted New Iberia. Women had to take refuge in the Catholic church in St. Martinville. They would like to put Hannah Laveau and Florence Milton in irons or perhaps in gibbets. It seems that, big or small, the blue-bellies can do whatever they wish.

But the center of his charge, conspiring with Darla to cheat the Suarez family out of their property, disturbs me deeply. The widow Suarez has been losing her faculties for years, and evidently now has no more to lose. She is not alone. There are many women in the plantation culture who stay heavily medicated because of their husbands' behavior. But for me it is awful to think that Darla would take advantage of such a pitiful lady.

Then again, I do not blame her for the death of Mr. Suarez. Any man who strikes a woman is a moral and physical coward and deserves a thrashing and then some. A man who rapes a woman deserves whatever fate is imposed upon him, including a bounce off a tree limb. Old Man Suarez raped Darla, or at best coerced her into lying with him. Since I jumped the broomstick with Darla, I have bad dreams about what was done to her, and when I wake I am possessed with images of his hands on her body, and images of Captain Endicott and the power and control he now has over our lives.

I saddle Varina and ride her out to Spanish Lake, once again entering a fiefdom filled with contradictions—an Arthurian world gone astray, a rejection of Judeo-Christian religion, a moat and drawbridge and castle that will probably become the shelter of Visigoths or simply a pile of burned rubble. Inside the pecan orchard, I can see the hoofprints of many horses. I recognize the print, too. I can also see the stripes of urine where men have recently pissed on the tree trunks.

In the clearing down by the edge of the lake, I see Darla hanging wash. Except she's dressed in her purple jacket and white blouse with ruffles and black dress, her hair brushed and shiny, her face rouged, her complexion darker somehow, even though the sun is shining directly on her.

She turns and looks at me, a clothespin in her mouth.

"Was he here?" I ask.

"Who?"

"Endicott."

"Yes, to see Miz Suarez."

She didn't call her by her first name, with the title in front of it, the way most people here do, showing familiarity and respect simultaneously.

"What did he want?"

"I don't know." Her eyes go away from me. "What are you t'inking, you?"

"Not much. Endicott says he can send us to prison. I heard Ira Jamison is going to turn his plantation into a giant prison farm and call it Angola. Maybe we'll go there."

"I don't know not'ing about Ira Jamison."

I dismount from Varina. "Why was Endicott here? Did you dress up so you could hang the wash?"

"I had to meet wit' de captain and Miz Suarez. About de title on de plantation."

"What about the title?"

"Miz Suarez give me half of it. They say she ain't right in the head and what she wrote down don't count. I tole them I got a lawyer. Right here, in New Iberia."

She gives me the name of the lawyer.

"You think this man is going up against the Suarez family?"

"Don't be talking down to me, no. I know what they can do. Don't you turn against me, too, Pierre. It ain't fair."

"I didn't mean to."

"Your words hurt me. The sound inside them hurts me."

I believe her. And I hate what I am going to say next.

"Did you go into the cabin with Endicott? If you did it, you did it. Just don't lie."

She scratches the top of her chest, her eyes empty. Then she sticks a clothespin in her mouth again and resumes hanging wash, slapping each item on the rope, jabbing each clothespin.

"You went inside. You let him have you, didn't you?"

She takes the pin from her mouth and flings it in my face. Then goes into her cabin and bolts the door.

I lean my ear against the wood. "Darla?" I say.

There's no answer.

"Darla, I can't leave you like this."

"Go away," she says, her voice muffled through the door. "Don't ever come back, either. I ain't gonna be the same after this."

I climb back on the saddle and ride through the spangled shade in the orchard. Captain Endicott and his men and Miz Suarez are on the verandah. So is the lawyer Darla hired. They are drinking lemonade or juleps, except for Miz Suarez, who is wrapped in a blanket and looks like a mummy. Endicott lifts his hat in salute, the sun warm on his tanned features and oiled, bronze-colored hair. I want to put a big one in the middle of his face, one no less than .58 caliber.

*   *   *

I should not drink. When I do, I remember every wrong thing I ever did. Then the next day I feel twice as bad. How smart is that? Just the same, I got loaded. In the same saloon outside of which I dueled with Wade Lufkin and watched his face explode when he pulled the trigger. But that's not the only bad memory I have about Lufkin. He wanted out of the duel. He wasn't a coward. It just went against his grain. He was a gentle person, an artist, a man who tried to avoid violence but brought an inoperable Minie ball home from the Rappahannock. I showed him no mercy and forced him to continue a lethal and foolish ritual. I think I will pay for this. I do indeed.

It's the following morning and I'm still drunk and stumbling around in the mist. The owner of the saloon has barred the door and has threatened to summon the sheriff if I don't get off his porch. I answer his threat by hammering with both fists on the door. Huge amounts of fog are rolling off Bayou Teche. I can't see three feet in front of my face. Even the prostitutes in the tent brothels are shouting at me to shut up. The saloon owner opens the door, slaps a bottle of whiskey in my hand, and says, "If you hit on my building one more time, I will sling this bucket of shite right in your face." Then he makes the sign of the cross. I suspect this is to remind us that he's a religious man and from dear old Ireland, bless his soul.

I said I never visited a brothel. That is true. But that is where I am headed. Until I stop and pull the cork from the bottle and drink at least five inches of it straight down. It might as well have been the backup from a sewage line. The taste is ghastly, the smell enough to burn out your nostrils. I fall backward into the weeds, sure that I'm a goner. I also think I'm having a seizure. My feet are kicking, my spine arching and bucking. Then I see a young woman kneeling beside me, obviously a fallen angel from the tent brigade a few yards away. She has on no coat or wrap, although the fog is as cold and wet as ice water. I can see her shoulders now. They're exposed, and have the soft hue of a candle; a nimbus floats around her hair, as on a Byzantine saint.

I feel her fingers on my chest, then she eases me on my side and holds her palm in the middle of my back, probably to prevent me from strangling on my own saliva or vomit.

Then I realize she is pulling out my pockets.

"I am sure you are a grand girl, and I wouldn't offend you for the world," I say, "but I think between you and the whiskey I have gotten myself a case of the red scours."

Pardon the expression, but I know of no better term for bloody diarrhea.

This lass is undaunted, however, and works my wallet from my pocket and disappears into the fog.

I feel hideous, sodden with my own excretions, laden with guilt over Wade Lufkin and Hannah Laveau and now Darla and my desire to sink my troubles in the girls of the night.

A half hour later I am in the Negro jail. My friend, Sheriff Jimmy Lee Romain, said it was empty and he was doing me a favor. Beyond the bars on the window the rest of the world goes on. The sun climbs into a blue sky, and at mid-morning two boys climb up on the bars and watch me relieve myself. I hope no one else does me any favors.

I paid a fine of two dollars, and had to borrow it from the sheriff. My wages are fifty dollars a month, in Confederate money, so two dollars in coin is hard on my resources. I go back to my rental cabin at The Shadows and bathe with a bucket of water drawn from the cistern and put on clean clothes and eat a lunch of cold cornbread and sorghum. I am determined not to be defined by all the mistakes I have made in my life. I am also determined not to lose Darla. I don't care if she is a murderess. Old Man Suarez had it coming. And so did the other men who molested her.

The fact she took advantage of Miz Suarez's demented condition is more complicated. The Suarez family used up a good part of Darla's life. Also, Miz Suarez must have known her husband was a predator. Portraying plantation owners as victims is a hard go. Put it another way. What if Darla had succumbed to the role the Suarez family had created for her? She would be a wretched and broken woman, if not a suicide. Every time I think of Old Man Suarez, I want to dig him up and hit him in the head with the shovel.

I take a walk down Main Street to the telegraph office. Although my mother was blind and saw light only in her sleep, she gave me a great gift, the kind we associate only with wisemen searching for a star over Bethlehem. She used to say, "Son, if you are a follower of Our Lord, you can start a bad day all over, anytime you wish."

And that's what I do as I walk into the telegraph office. For ten cents Yankee money our telegrapher reads the news from all over the state and sometimes from Atlanta and Richmond. Lee's failure at Gettysburg hangs heavy on many people, but nonetheless there are stalemates in Tennessee and the Carolinas and Georgia that offer promise, at least in the minds of those who have lost loved ones and cannot bear remembering their excitement when secession spread from South Carolina to Texas.

The news right now is about the skirmishes in Louisiana, brought on by a man who would seem, in rational times, to have no power or authority in political events or fighting wars. Or sweeping sidewalks and picking up dead dogs. That person, of course, is

Colonel Carleton Hayes, whose tangled eyes and syphilitic skin are nothing compared to his tangled and syphilitic brain.

The telegraphic news states that Colonel Hayes's "irregulars" are making inroads on Yankee-held territory on both banks of the Mississippi River. Whoever wrote these stories is a numbskull. Hayes's "irregulars" are gutter rats. The Union strategy is not the possession of the South but its destruction. Hayes's troops are feeding off the land. He fights under a black flag; his weapons are fire and fear. What greater gift could the Yankees have? Our uneducated population is doing the Yankees' work. Who needs enemies?

But what bothers me most in the news is mention of Wade Lufkin and Hannah Laveau and Florence Milton. All of them were seen with Colonel Hayes. I wonder if Young Wade has lost his mind. Or more specifically, did pieces of the exploded duelling pistol lodge in his brain, an event that I helped cause?

I said I had started my day all over again. Now I have taken back my worries and my guilt. The telegraph begins clicking, the telegrapher dutifully writing down one word after another. Then he looks at what he has written, his eyes magnified grotesquely behind his glasses.

"What is it, sir?" I ask.

"Grant has just come into Chattanooga. William Sherman's army is expected to reenforce him within days. What's your thought on that, Mr. Cauchon?"

"I wouldn't know, sir," I say. "Thank you for reading me the news."

I walk back down Main Street to my rented cabin at The Shadows. What does the presence of Grant and Sherman at Chattanooga mean? It means the Rebs will be kicked back into Georgia, and it means the battle of Chickamauga and the deaths of the three

Lufkin brothers were for naught. It means that eventually the city of Atlanta will fall and, if Sherman has anything to do with it, be sacked, destroyed, and burned to charcoal.

Let people tell you war is grand, and do not reprove them. Let them tell you the jingle of the sword and spurs and the whooshing sounds of a mounted knight's armor are the music of a medieval balladeer, and do not reprove them. But never let them tell you there is rhyme or reason to war, lest you join the lunatics who have perpetuated its suffering from the cave to the present.

That evening I buy a cigar and take a stroll along the bayou and a short float on the ferry, then head back under the canopy of live oaks that arches over the entirety of Main Street. The sky has turned to lavender and is freckled with birds, a harvest moon above the sugar-cane fields, when I see a number of carriages parked in front of the overseer's house not far from The Shadows. This is not an ordinary overseer's abode. It is grand in its own right.

Who do I see? That malignant Sodomite Endicott, that's who. He's walking across the verandah with a lady on his arm. Other officers are with him, and some of the Suarez family from up North. It is not difficult to recognize members of the Suarez family; they look like frogs. The windows and French doors of the overseer's house are ceiling-high, so I can see the candles burning in the living and dining rooms, and the amber glow of the liquor bottles that the servants are placing on the serving table.

Then I see Darla in the midst of the guests. She is putting a huge silver tray on a serving table. A small roasted pig with an apple in its mouth and a garland of garlic and early potatoes rests in the middle of the tray. Darla is wearing her best dress and her purple jacket and a lavender kerchief on her head, the same beatific color as the sky. I cross the street, not caring if I am seen or not. The humiliation in her face is apparent. Her pain as well. I want to gut Endicott from his belly to his throat.

But as an officer of the law, I learned a lesson. Do not go to prison in order to get even with an enemy.

When Darla snagged what she thought was a barrel full of silver and gold in Spanish Lake, she willingly gave it up to please me. This is a woman who has nothing. I owe her. I not only owe her, I love her. And I love all the poor people we have cheated out of their souls and their lives.

Isn't it time to make the worm turn?

I saddle up Varina and ride out to Spanish Lake, skirting the Suarez plantation, and get down on the lake's bank and walk Varina through the shallows to the dock where Darla's rowboat is tied. This time, however, I'm carrying my cap-and-ball and a treble grappling hook and a crawfish net I took from the barn behind The Shadows. The Suarez home is dark, the stars sprinkled overhead, the lake's surface as black as obsidian. I have no worries about paddy rollers or goons challenging me. Alligator hunters are often on the lake late at night, and so are the fishermen who run catfish lines. In fact, I fire a round into the sky to show the innocuousness of my activities. I begin rowing steadily toward the island where Darla and I consummated our private vows, then dropped anchor in the approximate area where she, in her innocence, had convinced herself that a fortune lay right under her boat.

The treble hook I am using is a superb piece of engineering. The edges of the hooks are filed, the points like needles. The weight gives it heft and also penetration power. The moon is up, the surface of the water riffled by the wind. In my mind's eye I create a clock and use it to cover a three-hundred-sixty-degree circle around the boat, and begin throwing the treble hook out twelve times.

I snag nothing. Not even a stump. But I have to rethink what I just said. I believed Darla snagged *a* stump. In a southern Louisiana lake or swamp, there is no such phenomenon as a single stump. Gum trees grow in clumps or not at all. I pull the anchor and re-create my clock forty yards away, closer to a willow island I remember. On the fourth throw I feel the hooks snag an object that feels as solid and heavy as concrete. It's not deep, either, no more than seven or eight feet.

But I have a problem. If I am hooked on a barrel, I might tear it apart. Darla said she saw Old Man Suarez roll it into the water. That was in April of 1862. This summer we had large amounts of rain, and the lake is perhaps two feet higher. I take off my boots and shirt and trousers and go over the side. The water feels like ice-melt from the Artic. I follow the rope down, hand over hand, into the darkness, until I feel the hooks and whatever they have bitten into. I can feel the roundness of the object and at least two bands of metal around it.

I go back up to the surface and work the crawfish net over the side and follow the rope back down to the treble hook and roll the round object onto the net and then slide the hooks into the netting and head for the surface. I have forgotten the cold, even though my skin is ruddy and as rough as wood rasp. I row into shallower water, then go over the side, up to my waist, and start dragging what is no doubt a barrel up the slope.

Once I am on the mudflat, I tear the slats from the cooper's metal bands and pull out some of the content. My heart is beating and my hands trembling, to the degree I fear my knees will collapse.

"Please let this be Thy design, Lord," I say to the sky. "And neither mine nor the devil's."

The only sound I hear is the wind blowing through the willows, the leaves tumbling in the air, floating down onto the surface of the lake, like stripes of gold.

34

FLORENCE MILTON

Colonel Hayes has "called" for me. That is how his sergeant, Shaye Langtree, has phrased it.

"Those were the words he used?" I ask. "He has 'called' for me? I am under his command?"

"That's pert' near what I heard the man say, Miss Florence," the sergeant replies.

I cannot adequately express how I feel about the colonel. The problem is not simply his odious manner and his venereal afflictions. The problem is the fact he is breathing the air around us, holding it in his chest, degrading it in the phlegm that lives in his throat and the diseases that reside in his gums, the fluids that he huffs out of his nasal passages and smears on the back of his cuff.

However, as I enter the flap, I am surprised by his demeanor. He's wearing white breeches and a red wool coat and a silver vest. His hair is combed, too. And he has risen from his table, his eyes no longer crossed, his fingers barely touching the table, his chin turned slightly so I can't easily see the putrescence that glows on half his face.

"Sit down," he says.

"I'll stand, thank you," I reply.

"Miss Hannah unlocked my eyes."

"I noticed."

"You believe she did it? With her powers?"

"I don't know what I believe."

"If she did, that means all the things she says are true."

"I have no moral authority, Colonel. I killed an innocent young soldier. I may be forgiven, but I will never be the same. Why are you asking me these questions?"

"If she can fix my eyes, why can't she fix my face?"

"Sir, you want to believe she has spiritual power so she can now undo your facial affliction, but you don't want to believe that the gift is really from God, because that would force you to change your ways. Your attitude, sir, is incredibly selfish. Who were your parents?"

He turns his head to show me the other side of his face, oblivious to everything I have said. I can't help but flinch. "It seems like it got worse," he says. "If you cannot cure it, can you make her do it, like she did my eyes? I will give you whatever you want."

"I am not feeling well, Colonel. I do not know if I am showing the early symptoms of smallpox or yellow fever, or if I am being punished for taking a young soldier's life. But there may be another source of my malaise. I have accepted the hospitality of a depraved man, and in so doing I have shown approval of his behavior. However, these things are probably not your fault. You were probably deranged in the womb."

His face seems to dissolve, like a cream pie sliding out of the pan.

"Well, I suspect I should be on my way," I say. "Good day, sir. I didn't mean to be too hard on you."

I turn to go.

"Tell Miss Hannah I'll get her son back," he says. "Tell her I'll kill every son of a bitch from here to Angola Plantation if I have to."

"Repeat that, please?"

He sniffs the air. "You smell of camphor. Close the flap after you. And get rid of those dark clothes. You look like a chimney sweep."

"*What?* What did you say?"

"Stay back, woman. I don't want to hit you. Put that quirt down. Have you lost your—"

I didn't strike him with it. Not really. I threw it in his face and gave him a start, but I did not hurt him. I don't think. He followed me all the way to my tent, his handkerchief pressed to his cheek, explaining that he is a protector of womanhood and ladies everywhere and that his mother gave him a good upbringing, and that I should be aware of his "breeding" and show some respect and come to dinner that evening, and bring Hannah with me.

Sergeant Langtree told me the real reason he was having such a fit. General Lee released a letter or proclamation denouncing murderers and degenerates who are murdering and burning whole towns under the Confederate flag. Evidently the message was aimed at people such as William Clarke Quantrill and Carleton Hayes. I heard him ranting drunk as a loon for the rest of the day. Sergeant Langtree kept him in his tent to keep him from embarrassing himself worse than he already had. Then I did something that was probably foolish and probably because of my attraction to the temperance movement. Hannah and I fixed him some food and took it to his tent at sunset, and poured his whiskey out the flap and literally stuffed food in his mouth with a wooden spoon. He acted like a starving child with a three-hundred-pound wetnurse. I know that's a disgusting metaphor, but I think there is some truth in the theories of Mr. Darwin, although squids may be in our ancestry rather than simians.

Oddly, the days have become warmer, or rather balmier, more like spring, the sky a hard blue, the mosquitoes gone, a slice of moon hanging over the trees in the swamp. I feel better also, but I don't know why. Perhaps because I haven't despaired or given up to the old Grim Reaper. I'm a spinster who believed it was better not to bring more children into the world until we have fixed the ones who are already here. But what have I done? I cannot even think about it. Maybe that is why I feel this moment of peace. My sins are bigger than I am, and as a consequence I leave them with my Creator and think no more about them. That's a strange kind of salvation, I guess.

I wonder if my drunken fellow pilgrim Colonel Hayes, with all his vileness, doesn't feel the same way. It's a horrible thought indeed. I would like to dawdle, but I have a commitment to Hannah and ultimately to my own soul. I cannot put aside entirely the demands that have been placed upon me. I have to make up for the young soldier I killed, and I have to help Hannah find out what happened to her little boy.

In the meantime I have encamped with the very men Robert Lee has condemned, not that the general himself didn't commit atrocities at Chambersburg. If I have learned anything from my experience since the Dred Scott decision, it is this: We are one people, bound by the same Judeo-Christian beliefs, but incapable of living by our own principles; furthermore, we are incapable of living in harmony with ourselves.

The Puritans were not a likable group. They cut off the king of England's head and murdered large numbers of American Indians. They were also good at hanging their neighbors, most of them women. To borrow from my Irish friends, what a fucking mess we have made of our country.

I cannot believe I said that.

I lose count of the days. I believe Young Wade has fanciful ideas about his role in our civil war. Early on a Sunday morning, of all days, the Sabbath, two wagon-loads of rifles show up in the midst of our encampment. The colonel is ecstatic, and the word passes quickly through the tents. From the soldiers' behavior you would think they were witnessing the discovery of the wheel. Young Wade is passing by our tent, wearing black trousers and a puffed white shirt, as a swordsman might.

"Sir, I would like to have a word with you," I say.

He stops, quizzical. "Yes?"

"Are these the rifles I have heard so much about?"

"Yes, Spencers and Henrys. Why do you ask?"

"Because I believe they will kill hundreds, if not thousands, of young men for no purpose at all."

"Thank you for telling me that, Miss Florence," he replies. "I will pass that on to the tens of thousands of Southern soldiers who have been killed by superior weaponry."

"My feelings are my feelings. Snideness does not become you, sir."

"I apologize," he says, bending at the stomach. "You and Miss Hannah mean the world to me."

I feel myself blushing, because I believe he is sincere. I also believe that the damage done to his face by the duel is leaking into his soul. "I want to take Hannah to Memphis and on to Shiloh."

"I fear that both of you will be taken by the law. Look around you, Miss Florence. Civilization follows the sun. Perhaps our time has come."

"That is the drivel of nihilists, sir."

"You have a remarkable vocabulary, Miss Florence. Will you make me a promise?"

"If I can."

"Don't hurt yourself or Miss Hannah. Tell me what you need and I will give it to you if I have it."

"I need enough money to get to Shiloh Church."

He has a tear in one eye. I do not know why. I know he is a good man. But one's goodness and one's moral compass do not always coincide. He squeezes my hand, then walks away, rabble of every kind churning in his wake, overjoyed with their new weapons.

35

PIERRE CAUCHON

I have a hard time deciphering Captain Endicott. I suspect he's a conflicted man who lets three-fourths of his character do the dirty work and leaves out one-fourth to take to church on Sunday. The only credit I can give him is his ability as a detective. Once the Suarez family realized the barrel of jewelry and gold and silver plates and candle holders and coinage had been pulled from the lake, they contacted Captain Endicott and gave him a list of those who might have known about the barrel's presence.

Guess whose name was at the top of the list? Not mine. I was second. Darla Babineaux was first.

I don't think he struck her. But other Africans said he yelled in her face and slammed his fist against the wall right next to her head and degraded and frightened her terribly. I swore I would fix his wagon. However, promises of revenge made inside oneself are poor fare for the victims of a bully. It took a week for him to track me down at my cabin behind The Shadows. I was looking forward to it. With thoughts about hanging his guts on a doorknob.

So that's where I am now, staring out my door at this hand-some, youthful fellow whose career spans from feeding the meat-grinder at Shiloh to confiscating cows and bullying colored women to intimidating widows and allowing his men to fire into the quarters at Lady of the Lake Plantation.

"What can I do for you, sir?" I say as cheerily as I can.

"For starters, how about getting your worthless ass out here."

"Since you put it in such a grand way, how could I refuse?"

I step into the morning light and the warm breeze blowing off the bayou, the Spanish moss swaying in the live oaks overhead. Six or seven of his men are dismounted down by the bank, playing mumblety-peg and rolling dice. I have the feeling the good captain does not want to share his conversation with them. A white canvas bag lies by his foot.

"You leave a singular track on a mudbank," he says. "A bit like a duck with half its foot cut off."

"Really?" I reply. "You're conducting an ornithological study of some kind? Maybe you should talk with Wade Lufkin. He's keen on that sort of thing."

Endicott widens the drawstring on the bag and removes several pieces of the barrel and drops them on the ground, then takes out the treble grappling hook I stole from the barn just one hundred feet away. "This pointy little fellow came from The Shadows," Endicott says. "I picked it up from where the duck print was. What do you have to say about that?"

"Are you trying to sell me one?" I ask. "You know, for an extra dollar or two? For whoring and things like that?"

He dips into the bag again and gently unwraps the remnants of the crawfish net. "How about this? The weight of the barrel ripped it pretty badly, but the grandson of The Shadows' owner has identified it as his. You seem to be setting new standards, Mr. Cauchon. I mean stealing in order to steal. Do you ever get tired of playing the role of the consummate fool?"

"I heard what you did to Darla Babineaux, Captain," I reply. "It takes a special kind of man to terrorize a woman, particularly one who was enslaved most of her life."

"If it were not for this uniform, I would call you out, sir. Then I would shoot you and plant a toadstool in your mouth and bury you in a dung heap."

"Say that again, please?"

"You're a cretin. I suspect your mother shit you in her chamber pot."

I slap him across the face, blistering and hard, something I have never done to anyone, although I did spit on Wade Lufkin, which I deeply regret.

Endicott presses his hand to his mouth, holding back the pain, his lip bleeding. His men are staring up the bank, dumbfounded. He takes his hand from his mouth. "You have one day," he says.

"To do what?"

"Use your imagination." He opens a gold watch and looks at it. "It's now nine forty-two. A raccoon will chew off its foot to get free from a trap. I hope you enjoy the experience."

I have underestimated Captain Endicott. He knows how to plant fear and uncertainty in his enemies. My mother said the trick was not to engage your adversary, and also to make a covenant with yourself, namely, that you will not change the person you are, no matter how much the world hurts you. "Grin when they throw their worst at you, and leave them with broken glass in their entrails," she said. "Because that's the only place they can put their vitriol. It's a fine way to be, son."

God, I loved my mother.

So rather than think about Endicott, I saddle up Varina and ride to St. Martinville and the quarters at Lady of the Lake. The plantation is not looking well. The windows broken by Endicott's soldiers have not been repaired but just boarded up. The gardens and walkways around the house are untended, the flowers in the hanging baskets unwatered and brown, and the trumpet vine and climbing roses on the trellises knocked to the ground. It's evening by the time I find the husband of the woman and infant who were killed when the blue-bellies unloaded on Wade Lufkin as he galloped past the slave cabins.

The husband's name is Joe Dupree. He's a big man, shirtless, shoeless, his trousers held up by a rope, his chest plated with muscle, his head as black and hard-looking as a cannonball. He's carpentering a birdhouse by the edge of the lake. I get down from Varina and introduce myself.

"I would like to offer my condolences," I say.

"Thank you, suh," he replies.

"I don't know Mr. Wade very well, but I suspect he's sorry for what happened."

"I know that, suh. Mr. Wade never meant no harm."

"I'm the man who fought the duel with him."

The black man nods, his eyes veiled.

"If I hadn't forced the duel on him, his features would not have been destroyed and maybe he would not have ended up in this kind of trouble."

"You ain't got to tell me, suh."

"You have other children, Joe?"

"Yes, suh. Six. That's why I'm fixing this birdhouse. Mr. Wade had all these bird books and used to show them to the children. He could make all kinds of bird calls."

"I have a hundred dollars in coin I'd like to give to you."

He looks into the distance. Either at the Lufkin house or at the reddish-purple sky in the west or at the beginnings of a turbulence out on the Gulf. "I ain't gonna borrow no trouble," he says. "No, suh. I done had enough of it."

"I'll explain to Miz Lufkin where the money came from, Joe."

"She already manumitted me. She said slavery done caused me enough grief. I just ax people to leave me and mine alone, suh."

"Well, all the best to you, Joe. You sound like a fine fellow."

He shows no acknowledgment of my words and begins tapping a nail into his birdhouse, a great green raincloud forming over the swamp, lightning leaping silently through the heavens, a salt spray blowing in the wind, both warm and cool at the same time. At the top of the slope I turn to wave goodbye to him, but his back is to me, and I'm sure it is not by accident.

Actually, my visit was self-serving, but that doesn't mean it was unvirtuous. I wanted to do a good deed for Wade Lufkin because I forced him into the duel that ruined his life. In some ways the widespread events that have occurred since the secession have been mirrored in our small communities in southern Louisiana. At first there was great celebration, with no thought about the penalties we would pay (the blockade, the scarcity of food, the cotton bales that could not be shipped to market); then the expectation that after a skirmish or two the Yankees would fold up, followed by Manassas and Shiloh; then the stories of heroic kindness in battle (the Angel of Marye's Heights), followed by atrocities and martial hangings and firing squads and prison camps that are hell on earth.

I have done my best with all of it. I am proud to have been a greyback, but it's time to think in a different way. The Stars and Bars will become a memory. Lunatics like Quantrill and Carleton Hayes will probably be marched off to asylums, and fantasizers like Jubal Early will be left to rant in empty assembly halls. The Earth will abide forever. That's the real lesson.

Unfortunately, centipedes like Captain Endicott are part of our burden, and they can either control us, lay the sting on our backs, or be expelled from the Earth. Which would you choose?

The contents of Minos Suarez's barrel are in a place where Endicott will never find them. But he has power over me because he has power over Darla Babineaux. How do I change that? Not by fighting the way we did at Corinth. We went at Rosecrans with twenty-two thousand men, in blistering heat, without water, and were decimated by their cannons. It's Jackson who knew how fight a war: "Mystify, mislead, and surprise."

How does that apply to Endicott? I am not sure. Also, I hurt Darla deeply when I asked if she had slept with him again. I wondered what General Jackson would say. He was certainly a homely man, by reputation an eccentric not given to romantic tales, galloping at the enemy's line with one arm propped at a forty-five-degree angle because he believed his vascular flow would remain balanced and not disturb his thinking processes.

It's late evening now. I took a walk and bought a dried apple from a street vendor, and now I'm cutting it up and feeding it to Varina on my palm. I stroke her between the ears and kiss her on the nose, which always causes her to look at me a little strangely.

"What do you think, old girl?" I say.

She nickers in response and moves her head up and down.

"I don't know what that means, Varina."

She leans her forehead against my chest and lets out her breath. It smells grassy and scented with the apple slices I have fed her. The placement of her head bothers me, though. Varina has always been able to read my moods. She only places her forehead on my chest when she senses death or loss. She did that when my mother died.

"I have no plan, old girl. Don't mourn. You and I have always gotten through bad times, haven't we? How about when the colonel was shooting at us?"

But her eyes are truly soulful. I try to convince myself it's the Morgan blood in her. Yes, that is what it is. The treefrogs are throbbing and the sun has turned to an orange smear on the edge of the Earth. It's just one of those moments when the brevity of life announces itself and takes hold of your heart and squeezes the light from your eyes. That's all it is. I pat her head again. But she will not let go of her stare.

Later I begin to put certain items on my bed. They do not indicate a particular plan, but they do reflect my immediate situation and the one I will have at 9:42 in the morning if Captain Endicott keeps his word, which in this case is causing pain to others, a job he seems to get better and better at.

I lay out some clothes, a blanket, a slicker, my best hat, my half-top boots, underwear, socks, wallet, penknife, a few silver dollars, a silver watch that is as fat as a biscuit, a bowie with a blood groove, a whetstone, the Bible given me by my mother, my cap-and-ball .36 caliber revolver, and my lever-action Henry rifle. I cannot overpraise the Henry, with its brass parts that look like old butter.

It holds sixteen rounds of .44 caliber ammunition and has a ladder sight that is deadly. I hear that out West the Indians will pay any price for them. God help the blue-belly cavalry who have to use single-shot Springfields against them.

What is the aggregate of these things piled on my bed? You've got me. Or maybe better said, I don't want to think about it.

I rise fresh in the morning and shave and eat a breakfast of eggs and ham, my silver-encased watch open on the table. Nine forty-two comes and goes, but I know one way or another Endicott's machinery has already clicked into gear. My guess is he wants to get me into an isolated situation, one where his lads can have a go at me. I also think the good captain has monetary motives and would love to dip his hands in the gold and silver I stole from under his nose (and which I buried under the livery stable of Willie Burke's mother without her knowledge), and I suspect Endicott would like to do something else with his hand, namely, with Darla. The thought of that makes me sick.

To hell with all this thinking. I need to see Darla and apologize for offending her, and get her away from Endicott and Suarez culture and all the people who have hurt her over the many years. The world is a big place. Why do we have to confine ourselves to a society that tells us whom we can marry or not marry? We can live in the Islands or in South America, or join up with the war that's brewing in Mexico. If you are determined to go to war, Hispanic and Italian ones are the best. The causes are irrelevant. Everyone has a fine time tearing things up, and changing sides whenever they feel like it.

I can hear Varina nickering and blowing in the railed lot by the barn, which is her way on a cool morning, although I do not know why. She is the only mare I ever saw pick her suitors, and just arbitrarily shut all of them down for no reason. That's just Varina. One day I want to introduce her to President Davis's wife.

I load my revolver and my Henry, swing my bag up on my shoulder, and go out to meet the day. Big storm clouds are gathering over the Gulf, but the sun is shining through the oak trees, the bayou wimpling in the breeze, a blue heron standing among the lily pads, as though it's painted on the air and God's handywork is still in the making.

I try to keep my mind empty as Varina and I approach the Suarez plantation. Smoke is coming from both chimneys in the main house; a fat black woman is shaking out a quilt on the second-story verandah as I enter the pecan orchard, her face stern, a look that usually means she accepted her lot long ago. She drops the quilt on the banister and goes back inside. Varina's ears are glued back, her gait unsteady on the soft sod under her hooves. But I attribute her caution to the wind kicking up and rattling in the trees, and the smell of electricity and distant rain.

I pet her on the neck. "Everything is fine, old girl," I say. "Don't be a scaredy-cat. That's not your way."

She rears and almost throws me. This is something Varina never does, unless we come up on a snake or a black bear that comes out of a thicket on the barrier islands down by the Gulf.

A sickening stench strikes my face, like a combination of entrails and feces and hair burning in a fire. Then I see curds of black smoke rising from the other side of Darla's cabin, and hear men laughing and a woman yelling incoherently. Varina begins fighting with the bit.

"Slow down, girl," I say. "Come on, you know better than that."

But she doesn't. She's genuinely frightened. Pieces of cloth are burning inside the smoke, bursting into tiny threads of fire, then floating as ash on top of the heat. I turn Varina around, pointing her away from the fire and stench, and slip loose my bag's drawstring from the pommel, then dismount and pull the Henry from the saddle scabbard and place it next to my bag.

"We have to be brave, Varina," I say. "Our only family is ourselves. Each of us goes where the other goes. Are you listening?"

Her rump is swaying back and forth, her head jerking. Now I hear someone sobbing where the smoke is. It is the kind of sobbing you only hear from a woman, because it comes from pain that men do not have to bear; it's the pain of labor; it's the pain of rejection and betrayal; it is a form of rage so great there is no receptacle big enough in which to confine it. And worst of all, it cannot be described or understood by those who have not experienced it themselves.

I lead Varina past the cabin. Captain Endicott and five of his men are mounted on their horses, watching a bonfire stacked with dresses, quilts, shirts, undergarments, watercolor paintings, clay dishes and bowls, wooden utensils, unsanded furniture, shoes, Mardi Gras beads, and Darla's beloved purple jacket. Two buckets of chitlins are boiling in the middle of the fire, and also a hogshead, the brains bubbling in a yellow froth from the nose and ears.

Darla Babineaux is sitting on the ground, weeping, her skirts spread around her. Captain Endicott raises his hand to get my attention. He's smiling. "Don't get the wrong notion about this, laddie," he says. "I have orders to remove her to New Orleans for a hearing about the title of the plantation and the possibility she murdered Mr. Suarez. I think she may be an innocent woman. I tried to explain that to her. But she has to act decently and do her job for her mistress, and not act like a temperamental whore."

"Would you mind saying all that again?" I ask.

"No, I don't mind at all. All she had to do was fry the chitlins. She chose otherwise. So we have an emotional mess on our hands. Clear enough, laddie?"

"Laddie? I love that. It has a lovely ring," I reply.

The wind is rippling in the willows on the lake. The five enlisted men are watching, leaning on their pommels, their saddles squeaking. Their faces are sun-browned and lean under the brims of their kepis.

"Nothing to say?" Endicott asks.

"You told her to cook chitlins while you burned her belongings?"

"No, the mistress of the house told her to fix the chitlins and to clean out the cabin because she would not have need of it anymore."

"Miz Suarez told her?"

"Yes," he says.

"Miz Suarez is in dementia," I reply. "She does not know if the sun rises in the east or the west."

"Darla scratched the face of one of my men, and tried to cut the dick off another."

"Did your men try to rape her?" I ask.

"They did not."

"Darla?" I say.

But she won't look at me.

A mounted corporal nods and points at a slash on his horse's neck. "That's what your crazy black bitch did," he says.

Endicott raises his hand for his enlisted man to be quiet, then looks at me. "Nothing to say about the return of some stolen property we discussed yesterday?" he says.

I have no weapon. My Henry lies across my bag inside the pecan grove. My revolver is inside the bag. I would love to blow him out of his socks. "I was just riding by. I don't know anything about stolen property."

His horse is shifting its feet. "No plans for the day?" the captain says.

"I might throw a fishing line in."

Darla's eyes lift to mine. She has a lavender kerchief tied on her head. Her skin is coated with dust.

"Want to say something to Miss Darla before you leave?" Endicott says.

"I just hope things work out for everyone," I reply.

"Well, you're quite a fellow," Endicott says. "Yes, a jolly fellow, all right. No risk-taker, you."

"I try to be a realist," I reply.

The captain gazes at his men, his eyes full of mirth, all of them sharing it with him. "Tell me, seriously," Endicott says, "were you actually in the army?"

"Briefly. I was never much of a scrapper."

They all laugh, and I laugh with them. Darla looks hollow-eyed into the fire.

"Well, you had better be on your way," Endicott says. "I'll be looking you up after I return from New Orleans. Take all the chitlins you want."

I get up on Varina and raise my hat to the captain. "Good day to you, sir."

"You'll be needing all the luck you can get, laddie," he says. "You went fishing in the wrong place."

"I'm sure you're correct, sir," I answer. "Just as sure as I am of the vows I took in this lovely paradise in which we find ourselves."

"Say again?"

I don't answer, but instead lean forward in the saddle and keep my eyes off Darla, lest the captain sense the moment of communication between her and me and the bond we made on the willow island that was a hunting camp for Minos Suarez. Varina goes into a trot, the saddle beating against my butt. In less than one minute I am inside the spangled shade of the pecan orchard, raindrops clicking on the leaves, the smoke from the fire hanging in the limbs, the stench still there.

I swing off the saddle and dig my revolver out of my bag and stick the barrel through the back of my belt, then pick up my Henry and lift the ladder sight into place and get down on one knee next to a thick-trunked pecan tree and steady the rifle against the bark and aim at Endicott's chest. Just as I pull the trigger and the recoil jerks into my shoulder, Endicott switches his position, and the .44 round rips the face off the corporal who claimed Darla stabbed his horse.

I start firing one round after another. In seconds all of them are in chaos, their horses rearing in the dust and raindrops, whinnying and snorting, colliding with each other. Every Yankee out there is a bully, and I say that because there is no such thing as a bully who is not a coward. I see one fall from the saddle and get up and run for the main house, holding the stub of his left forearm. Another runs into the shallows of the lake and hides behind a tupelo stump. I punch through the buttocks of a private trying to remount his horse. Varina never budges. Endicott has circled behind the cabin on foot and is firing at me with his sidearm. I fire a .44 round that blows his face full of splinters, but it does not put him out of the fray.

In the shooting I have lost sight of Darla. Oh, Lord, don't let me lose her now, I pray. I will do everything in my power to live a better life if you will spare us this bitter cup, you who know what it means to deal with evil men. Please, please, please do this and I will never again ask anything of you.

I swing up on the saddle, put the reins in my teeth, my revolver in my left hand, my Henry in my right, and give it to Varina and feel her power explode between my legs. With the reins in my mouth, I let out the Rebel yell, "*Woo! Woo! Woo!*" I may die on this morning, but what better way to go?

They didn't expect it, and now they don't know what to do. Varina is flying, hardly touching the ground. I let off with the pistol first, then the Henry. One Yankee trooper goes down, his boot caught in his stirrup, his head trapped and stomped by his horse's hooves. I catch another trooper in the throat with the Henry, and see the round exit his neck and splatter his horse's rump. A third bolts and runs, splashing through the shallows in the lake, a man who will never erase the mark of the coward.

I shove the Henry into the scabbard and reach down and pull Darla up on Varina's rump and feel her arms lock around my ribs and her thighs spread around the cantle, then I give it again to Varina, Darla and I both couched low, one body, one flesh, galloping up the slope just as the rain thunders down on the orchard and Varina's hooves pound on the soft, moldy carpet of pecan hulls, her lungs heaving.

Then we're out of the trees and into a clean-smelling, rain-scented stretch of green grass between a sugar-cane field and Bayou Teche, the rain stinging like chips of ice on our faces.

I have left my bag, but I can buy whatever we need down the road. In minutes we will be gone forever from the suffering that has been inflicted on Darla Babineaux, safe and unafraid and uncaring about the condemnation of others. I am only twenty-seven years old and she only twenty-three. This day will remain a special gift, and perhaps after it will come an unending journey across a wine-dark ocean beneath the Southern Cross, to a place that yearns for us as we yearn for it, perhaps an island where we can break coconuts on the coral and eat the meat with our fingers, and never be tainted by the world of vassalage again.

It's out there. It's not a myth. We just have to get there. Yes, yes, yes.

Varina, her mouth white with saliva, begins to slow as we enter a dirt road along the bayou. I pat her on the neck again and tell her what a wonderful girl she is. Then I realize that something is wrong. But not with her. Darla's thighs are still spread behind the cantle and her face still pressed sideways against my back, as warm as a shirt iron, but her hands are no longer locked on my stomach, her arms suddenly free of my ribs.

"Darla," I say.

There's no answer. "Darla," I say again.

I try to twist in the saddle and grab her before she falls. But I'm too late. She lands on her back in a bed of emerald-green grass dotted with buttercups. I swing off Varina, dropping the reins, and work my left hand behind Darla's head and try to push the grass away with my right hand to see where she is hurt. She puckers her mouth as though trying to regain her breath, or to cool a burn on her tongue.

"Where is it, Darla? Where did they hurt you?"

"Everywhere," she whispers.

I turn her on her side, her cheek trembling with pain, her blouse bleeding in at least four places, the blood thinning in the rain.

She knots my shirt and pulls me closer to her face. "I ain't afraid. I love you. You tried," she says.

"Don't talk like that, Darla. We'll go back. It's too far to town."

"No, they ain't ever gonna get their hands on me again. Tell Hannah I'm sorry I got her in trouble. It was me killed Minos Suarez."

"Fuck Minos Suarez. Fuck his family. Fuck the Yankees. You can't die."

She fumbles her hand on mine and pulls it to her mouth. I feel her breath on my skin, then it stops and her eyes close.

"God, don't let this be," I say to the sky. "I will do whatever you say. She's too good to die like this."

But I hear no answer and no sound except the wind and the rain drumming on the bayou and a slave bell clanging on the Suarez plantation. Then I lose my balance and stagger around like a drunk man, trying to hold Varina's reins, trying to remember who I am or to whom I'm praying. Then I hear myself, as though there is a piece of glass in my viscera, one that cuts through the chest and throat and leaves me on my knees, beating my fists on the ground, digging a grave with my fingernails, not for her but for me, a helpless fool who tries to blow his breath on his lover and unseal her eyes in order to drive the cold from her face, the blueness from her skin, and the stillness from her heart.

Then I see three Yankee soldiers on a roofed flatboat on the bayou, poling upstream, wearing slickers and flop hats, unshaved, strangely familiar. A cage full of oinking piglets is on the bow, a tarp draped over it, like a harbinger of death and cruelty. "Who are you, and what's your business?" the shortest of the three soldiers yells.

"Pierre Cauchon is the name! I need your help!"

"The fuck, you say," he replies.

"What?" I say.

"It must be the Good Lord at work. Stay there. We'll pull in."

I have no idea what he means.

They push with their poles into the reeds and cattails until the boat nudges onto the mudbank. "Remember me?" the same man says. "I hit you in the back with a pinecone when you were ordering up a breakfast in town. We made fun of you about Shiloh and Corinth. We were pretty much on the grog and regretted acting like assholes."

"I have a woman here. She's dead or dying."

"Say that again?"

I don't like trusting the Yankees. But I have no choice. "She's been shot. Punish me but not her. I will give you everything I have if you can save her life."

I can hear the thunder over the Gulf. The bayou is as yellow as clay and full of organic debris, the surface dancing with raindrops. "There's talk about you and Captain Endicott," the short man says. "Is the captain mixed up in this?"

"Draw your own conclusions. Will you help us or not?"

"What do you want us to do?" he replies.

"Take us to a doctor in St. Martinville."

"I got news for you, Reb. Every soldier in the Union Army hates Endicott's guts. He never heard a gun fired in anger, no matter what he says. Get your horse and your lady and your ass onboard. Anybody who was at Shiloh is our kind of fellow."

36

HANNAH LAVEAU

The colonel will not accept that God unlocked his eyes, rather than me, which means he thinks the power is mine, and if I own it, he can take it from me.

I am beginning to hate this man. Miss Florence is of the same mind. Wade Lufkin had promised to arrange boat passage for us to Shiloh, but we have had great difficulty finding a means to get us there. We actually got on the steamboat, with smokestacks and the big waterwheel in back, and got almost to Vicksburg. Cotton bales were stacked along the gunwales, with Yankee sharpshooters behind them. A deckhand with a Yankee accent said snipers sometimes fired from the banks, but I didn't see anything like that. What I did see were cannons in the woods along the shore. It was late in the afternoon, and the sun was red and wobbling on top of the water, and the woods were dry and the leaves were dropping, and I could see the wheels on the guns and heat waves rising off the gun barrels.

Somebody said that was Grant's artillery. Somebody else said, no, they were Rebs, and they were going to scatter grapeshot all over the decks just out of meanness because the people of Vicksburg had to live in caves and eat rats before the city finally surrendered. They said General Forrest was going to drive every Yankee soldier out of the state of Mississippi, and that he was a brilliant soldier who outthought and outfought the Yankees every time they went up against him. If he was so smart, why did he have to make a living selling colored families and li'l children and pregnant women and even feeble-minded people into the cane fields of Louisiana? I wish somebody would tell me that.

A gambler on the boat started following me around, with a funny look on his face, like a cat sniffing around a mice hole. He asked me if I was Miss Florence's slave, and I said no, there ain't any slaves anymore and if he thought different, he should talk to President Lincoln. What the gambler actually meant was if I didn't belong to Miss Florence, I was up for grabs. He tried to get close to me by the cotton bales after Miss Florence went to bed in our li'l cabin, so I took off my shoe and smacked him on the side of his head, not once but twice, and then for good measure on his nose hard enough to make him more cross-eyed than the colonel used to be. Except he was dumber than the colonel and wouldn't give up.

Early the next morning he came to our door with liquor on his breath and showed me a wanted poster with a sketch of Miss Florence and Mr. Wade and me he found on an announcement board by the wheelhouse. He said the boiler room was empty, and I could come down there with him or be turned over to either the Yankees or the Confederates at the next landing.

I didn't know what to do. I wanted to kill him, and was starting to worry about myself. I was becoming more like Darla Babineaux than like my own self, although I ain't blaming her for the times she had to defend herself.

"Make up your mind, girl," the gambler said.

The sun wasn't hardly over the horizon, the fog still clinging to the river's surface, a warning bell clanging where a Union prison boat blew up and lot of Confederate soldiers got scalded to death or drowned after they thought they were going home. I tole the gambler I would meet him below decks as soon as I got something to eat.

"Don't be late," he said, and touched me on the cheek.

I checked on Miss Florence, then went down the ladder to where the gambler was waiting for me. There was nothing but a few board planks to stand on, and bilge was sloshing under my feet and made me dizzy when I looked at it, and a big piston was going up and down, in and out, until my ears and heart were both hurting. He had already taken off his coat and unbuttoned his pants and was smiling at me. He had a small mustache and a tiny goatee. He was holding a rose that had a stem on it, a weak one, green and all bent over.

"You ain't given me your name," I said.

"Mine is not important. As long as I know yours."

"Give me the flower and close your eyes."

"That's part of a game?" he asked, still smiling.

"You'll find out. You ain't scared, are you? Nice-looking, strong man like you?"

He stuck the rose in my hair. I folded my hands in front of me while he shut his eyes. There was a wrench on a worktable not far from the piston that was pumping up and down, clanking louder and louder, a hissing sound leaking from the valves. But I didn't touch the wrench. I shoved him backwards off the planks. The bilge was as black as oil and deep enough that he went completely under, his eyes and mouth squeezed shut, his clothes loading up with every nasty thing in the bilge.

"Explain to people what you were doing down here," I said, and tossed him the rose. "By the way, there's a big, fat snake swimming right next to your face. He looks like he ain't had breakfast."

So we came back to our tent in the colonel's army. We had no other place to hide. The Yankees had warrants on us. And the Confederates sure weren't any help. Richard Taylor, the son of an American president, was sending colored troops back into slavery, right after the battle at Port Hudson. In fact, that's what they were all doing, including Lee and Stuart, at Chambersburg and outside Washington, D.C. I read it in the newspaper. I wonder how they would like that to happen to them.

Miss Florence's complexion is better than it was; it ain't gray like cardboard anymore. The problem is, she gets through the day on the spirit, not on food. She doesn't keep it down, or she gives it away to colored people begging by the road. I tell her that hurting herself ain't what Jesus taught. Jesus gave his listeners fish and loaves for a reason; he was a poor man and knew the needs of the poor, and he didn't try to sell them a lot of trash about beating yourself. Read Genesis 1:29–30. God gave us the green things of the Earth, and He didn't say we got the right to kill the animals or the birds. It ain't there. Anyone who says it is can kiss my bottom. God said the green things were made there for all of us. It's not hard to understand, no.

I'm worried about Mr. Wade, too. I like him. I always did, particularly for his kindness to me when he returned from Virginia and set aside his own wounds and worried about others. But he doesn't understand how suffering works. If you heap it on yourself, it gets to be a vanity. I think that's what the scarring of his face has become. He has put on sackcloth and ashes that nobody can scrub off.

Sergeant Langtree brought me a New Orleans newspaper. There was a story on the front page I couldn't believe. Pierre Cauchon and Darla Babineaux killed a bunch of Yankees on the Suarez plantation outside New Iberia, then stole a flatboat hauling confiscated hogs on Bayou Teche and disappeared around St. Martinville. The hogs got away and so did Mr. Pierre and Darla. Here, I'll read it to you. It seems like it was written by somebody who cain't think. I thought you had to go to school to work on a newspaper.

> It is thought that the servant Darla Babineaux may be part of an insurrectionist group of Negroes and one white man who were hanged in St Martinville in June of 1861. The detail of the white man is important because Pierre Cauchon, a constable in charge of Negro affairs in several parishes, may well be a northern infiltrator. He also may have injured himself with an ax to avoid honorable service in the army. It is also thought that the Babineaux woman may be a concubine who was shot several times by Union soldiers whom she compromised. The general feeling in the Red River parishes and the Acadian communities is one of shock and horror, and there is wide speculation that Cauchon and Babineaux are longtime confidence operatives. There is much talk about "severe correction."

"It is thought"? "Severe correction"?

Who had that thought? And what is the meaning of "severe correction"? I will tell you: Cutting off people's parts and then setting them on fire. I've seen it. It ain't human. And the person who says it is should have his face pushed in it.

* * *

The days and weeks go by. It's either late October or early November now. It's funny how time gets away. The days are short and hold no promise, and the glimmer in the sun is never more than that, a smudge on the rim of the Gulf. There's gray in my hair, and Miss Florence has a shine in her eyes, the kind that children with rickets get. It's like a single candle burning inside them, a teaspoon of hope leaving them every day. They burn from the inside out, and then they're gone and leave nothing behind. It makes me sad.

It's cold this morning, the tent stiff with frost, when I hear Mr. Wade's voice. "It's I, Miss Hannah. Would you walk with me, please?"

Miss Florence is sound asleep. I do not want to walk with Mr. Wade. I cannot fix him. I cannot console him. I cannot clear his mind. I don't know if God can. In his mind he has become a warrior. But of what kind? He seems to take pride in the battles he has fought. I don't think they are battles; they are raids. And raids are a way to steal everything people own. Yet Miss Florence and I would be dead or starving were it were not for the gentle and kind Mr. Wade I knew at Lady of the Lake Plantation.

"Yes, suh, I'll be right there," I reply.

When I step outside he's wearing a heavy, dark-red wool overcoat, the collar up to his ears, a gray flop hat pulled right on his head, a scarf covering most of his face except for a hole where his breath is smoking. A small fire is burning next to a log, with eggs and fatback and bread cooking in a skillet, a coffee can pushed into the ashes. There are no other tents around us. Mr. Wade took care of that, which bothers me a li'l.

"I may have information about your little boy, Samuel," he says.

My breath and heart stop. I cain't speak. I am afraid of what's coming next.

"He's alive," Mr. Wade says.

I feel the air come back into my lungs, like somebody pulling a knotted rag out of my throat.

"Where's he at, suh?"

"Will you stop calling me 'sir'?"

"Mr. Wade, stop talking to me like that," I say. "Where's my li'l boy at?"

"Maybe downriver from Natchez."

"I was on the steamboat and went right past him?"

"Don't think of it that way," he says. He picks up a plate and begins filling it for me. "Think of what you're gaining today."

I pull the plate out of his hands and throw it in the fire. "I ain't interested in your wisdom, Mr. Wade. He's at Natchez now? How do you know this?"

"Through Ira Jamison."

I have to think about the name. "The man Mr. Pierre was always talking about? The one who didn't show up at Shiloh?"

"He's a businessman, Hannah. Sometimes we have to make a deal with the devil."

"Like making a deal with yellow fever and pretending it's not a disease?"

"Well, I guess you've got me there. I also have news about other people we know."

"I ain't interested in news about other people, Mr. Wade. Please tell me how I can get my li'l boy back. If I got to work for Mr. Jamison, I'll do it. I ain't afraid. Do you understand me, suh?"

"Yes," he replies. "I will do everything I can. But I'm talking to you about another issue. I need your help."

"How?"

"I fear for my soul. Pierre Cauchon has made contact with me. He and the former enslaved woman Darla Babineaux are not far from us. They want refuge. But I have a hard time forgiving Cauchon."

"About the duel?"

"Yes, and also his locking you in jail."

"I take care of myself, Mr. Wade. Don't use me as an excuse. Your uncle called Mr. Pierre trash. That's what started all this. It's on your uncle, not Mr. Pierre."

"I wish I had your objectivity."

"Then go get some, suh."

He almost smiles, then lowers his eyes. "You're a grand woman, Hannah."

"I don't need that kind of talk, Mr. Wade. Don't be doing it. Not at all."

"Is it my face?"

"No, suh. It is not. It's what you do with it."

I shouldn't have said it. Saint Augustine said don't use the truth to injure. I just did it. Mr. Wade stares at the fire, his hands on his hips, sparks blowing in a cone around him, his face as dead as clay.

"I'm sorry, Mr. Wade," I say. "You been mighty good to us."

"Major Jamison will arrive in the next few days," he replies, his eyes wide open in the smoke and heat.

37

FLORENCE MILTON

Know what baptism is? I do. That's when you get stamped. I was fourteen years old and way up the Merrimack when I got dunked, right across from a textile mill that made a fortune on the labor of children and filled their little lungs with lint. It was also cold, in March, the wind blowing, and me in a white gown with sheer undergarments, when the parson held me in his arms and lowered me into the current.

The shock was electric. My teeth were chattering. I clung to the parson's black coat and wanted to crawl inside it. But I also wanted to get away from him. He was a young widower, a homely one, and known for his loneliness and temptations. The gown was not sufficient to hide my frailness, my adolescent changes, my vulnerability. "Take me out, Parson," I said.

"No, I must take both of us under," he said.

"I don't want this. Please. I'm cold."

But it was not the cold that terrified me.

Before I could speak again, he pulled me below the current. The coldness blinded me. It was like a hammer made of ice beating me between the eyes. I wanted to die.

I don't think he touched me improperly, but I can't be sure, even today. My skin was blue, my senses dead, my head splitting. Then something happened, and it had nothing to do with the homely parson.

While I was still underwater, a white light burst inside my head and created a sack of glowing warmth shaped like an embryo around my body. It was like a sea breeze in summer. I had never experienced anything like it. When he raised me from the water, I had already lost all awareness of him, as though he were an irrelevant adverb trying to modify a noun.

It was at that moment I knew my calling and knew I would adhere to it for the rest of my life. I would march with the women and children in front of the mills in Massachusetts and the sweat-shops in New York; I would learn to love the Irish who came over on the coffin ships, and strike with them on the railroads and in the coal mines; I would go into the Southland and help free the colored people; and lastly I would never fear man or ignorance or evil again.

Why am I telling you this? It's because baptism can come in different ways, and it doesn't have to happen waist-deep in a river or inside a church vessel. You'll see what I mean.

I knew Ira Jamison before the war, when he was an engineer in New Orleans; he built levees and the street car that runs downtown and on the neutral ground arched with live oaks in the Garden District, but I always had the feeling he was just warming up. He had a lean and hungry look, and it was not about the ladies. He worshiped money for what it could buy him and his family. He lived to entertain. There was no form of poverty or human suffering or social injustice that had any influence on him. I never knew a greedier man. Upon secession he acquired a major's rank and the friendship of General Beauregard, and I wondered at the time if the South had any chance at all. You probably know General Beauregard is another New Orleans product, one who has the singular distinction of firing the first shot at Fort Sumter, which has now resulted in the deaths of hundreds of thousands of human beings, and unknown numbers of animals, and undoubtedly many more to come. What a lovely tribute to chisel on one's tombstone.

Up the Mississippi River is a place called Angola. Its owner supposedly has amassed millions of dollars in the cotton market. Supposedly he is beloved by his enslaved workers. Tell me, how many people have you met who love being enslaved? How many medieval serfs enjoyed their iron collars?

Unfortunately for the owner of Angola Plantation, both the Confederates and the Federals have been raiding it, not on a lark or for a few drunken hours of theft (the sort of thing Colonel Hayes specializes in), but in earnest, with tens of thousands of dollars of cotton hauled off to New Orleans or up the river to Memphis.

I think there will be many opportunities for Major Jamison. His talent is not to strike while the iron is hot. Major Jamison's talent is to strike before the iron has even reached the smithy's forge.

A while back I mentioned the theories of Mr. Darwin. I wish to disagree with one of his conclusions. I do not believe we all, apes and humans, descend from a "common ancestor." The ancestors of men such as Jamison had their own tree.

*   *   *

I see him coming in a surrey, a colored man driving, Jamison in the back seat, his hand clamped on a black cane with a gold head. He's probably close to thirty but is barrel-chested and looks older and stouter and more confident than his age group, with a bit of gray in his hair and a bead in his eye. Colonel Hayes and Wade Lufkin come out of their command tent to greet their visitor. Surprisingly, after they shake hands with him, the second thing they do upon his arrival is motion me to join them.

I pretend not to see them.

"Miss Florence!" Young Wade shouts out. "We may have good tidings! Please bring Miss Hannah!"

I do as he asks. I even do it with my arm hooked in Hannah's. The uncouthness of Colonel Hayes is enough to affront any woman, but combining it with the cupidity and powdered porcine sleekness of Ira Jamison is probably more than any decent person's stomach can tolerate. Just the same, I take her by the arm and walk her to the colonel's half-open tent flap.

But both of us cannot enter at the same time. I let Hannah go first. Then a corporal stretches his arm across the entrance so I cannot enter.

Their rudeness is disgusting, but I can bear it. The issue is that Hannah is standing alone in front of three white men who are seated. This is why I spoke to you about the nature of baptism and the significance it can bestow upon us. The moment is here, and I am convinced that in the next few seconds every one of us, for good or bad, will never be the same.

Young Wade rises from his chair. It is hard to read his expression because of his facial disfigurement. The two other men do not move.

"Major, this is Miss Hannah," he says. "Miss Hannah, the major has made two visits to Natchez recently. A friend of his took photographs of the city and some of the servants and the Negro children who were driven from the Shiloh area."

Hannah nods. She has a plum-colored kerchief tied on her head, with red strings on it. The tips of her curls have been bleached by the sun. She looks beautiful. "Thank you, suh, for coming here," she says.

Jamison says nothing. His eyes go up and down her body. Young Wade is becoming more uncomfortable in the silence. He looks at me. "Why are you waiting out there, Miss Florence? Please come in."

The corporal does not remove his hand from the tent pole. Neither the colonel nor Jamison has moved from his chair. Young Wade's gaze goes from me to the colonel to Jamison. He blinks, then coughs slightly.

"Gentlemen, Miss Hannah is an extraordinary young lady," he says. "She helped me greatly with my recuperation and my painting when I returned from Virginia."

But they are sewn to their chairs. The colonel studies the tops of his buccaneer boots. He has already forgotten the woman who corrected his misaligned eyes. Young Wade is still standing. Jamison has not budged and seems to be growing irritable.

"Are you hearing me, sir?" Young Wade says.

"Let's get on with this, please," Jamison says.

"No, sir," Young Wade says. "We need to understand something. Our culture of manners and humanity is being destroyed. Our precursor is Thomas Jefferson. We have to be examples; otherwise, we will be no better than the likes of William Sherman. I'm sure you gentlemen concur with our mutual purpose. We must not emulate our Northern enemy, and I mean no offense to Miss Florence, who is admired by all those who know her."

Jamison takes his watch from his vest.

Innocent Young Wade. He understands nothing about these men. They are self-benighted and cannot undo what they have done to themselves; they live among toadstools; their minds are covered with warts. They measure themselves by the amount of power and misery they can impose on others.

However, maybe I have underestimated Young Wade's maturity. His consternation is visible, his control starting to slip. He picks up three photographs from a folding table. "Look at these, Miss Hannah," he says.

She takes them from his hand and looks at each of them slowly. Her feelings are masked. Then her eyes film.

"Is that Samuel?" I say through the flap.

"What color eyes does he have, suh?" she asks.

Jamison's hand is cupped on top of his gold-tipped, shiny black cane. He squeezes it, as he would a fig. "Maybe blue green. Like yours."

She puts her hand to her mouth and is about to cry.

Then Jamison says, "I don't want to get you excited. I'm not sure. The photographer would be a better source."

"You cain't think about it a li'l more? You didn't ask any questions? What's so hard about remembering a lost li'l boy? You see that happen all the time? That's what you do, suh? Taking pictures of children but not finding out if they have parents?"

Jamison blows out his breath and looks sideways. "I knew I got baited into this one."

"Stand up," Young Wade says.

"What?" Jamison says.

"I said get up from your chair before I rip you out of your shoes."

"Slow it down a little bit, here," the colonel says.

"You stay out of this, you miserable old man," Young Wade says to the colonel. Then he turns back to Jamison. "You, sir, are a disgrace to the Confederacy. Countless men and boys died because you left them enfiladed on the slope above Owl Creek at Shiloh. I would like to whip the skin off your back. Now you get the hell out of here, and if you come back, be assured I will saw off both your legs. Look into my eyes and tell me I am lying. Blink once and I will tear you apart, sir."

I think about the warm light that encapsulated me at age fourteen beneath the Merrimack River, and the lost children everywhere in the world, and the iconic thorns that seem unfairly imposed on the human heart, and the baptism that can come like a rainstorm of light outside a textile mill, and I know that somehow we rise above the woe and the sound and the fury and the mire of human veins that drag us back again and again into the maelstrom, bathed by a luminosity so intense that we can stand on a scaffold with John Brown at our side, unafraid, Golgotha nothing more than a vapor on the horizon.

Hooray and welcome to our club, Young Wade.

38

DARLA BABINEAUX

Pierre don't know how good a man he is. Just like he don't know how evil John Endicott is. From the first time I saw Pierre, I knew the kind of home he grew up in. A father who was gone and a mother who just got by and loved her child more than anyt'ing on earth and tole him that the world was a hard and scary place, so he had all these t'ings piled up on him before his first day in school when a bully probably pushed him down in the dirt.

I will never forget seeing him riding t'rough de pecan orchard, a pistol in one hand, a rifle in the other, the reins hanging from his teeth. One Yankee wet his pants, right there in the saddle. Wasn't just him that was scared, either. On his horse Varina, Pierre sailed right over the bonfire, shooting wit' bot' hands, and all the time I was saying inside myself, *He's my man, he's my man, he's my man.*

Because that's what he was. From that time unto the grave. When I got on Varina's rump I wasn't afraid no more. I held tight on Pierre and buried my face in the muscles of his back and the smell of his clothes and the cordite in the flashes of the guns, and I hooked my legs in his and squeezed his ribs and kissed his shoulder, then I wanted to lick his skin and taste the salt in it and bite his muscles and reach up and touch the sweat in the back of his hair, where it grows over the collar.

Then I heard the shotgun go off. It made a booming sound, not like the pistols that were like Chinese firecrackers. I felt the pellets cut through my blouse and enter my body, but they didn't hurt. I don't know why. I felt as though I wasn't human anymore. I was flying through the air, the whole earth between my legs, the Yankees scattering, Captain Endicott still shooting, his face full of wood splinters, like a porcupine's. But I knew I wasn't gonna die. At least not then. It's because of a story Pierre read to me. It's about King Arthur and a lady who lives inside a lake, and the sword he returns to her when he doesn't need it no more.

I remember axing him if that was the Lady of the Lake in St. Martin Parish, and he said, "It could be. Or it could be anywhere there are people like you, Darla."

And I said, "What you mean?"

And Pierre said, "You're special, Darla. People like you have magic in their eyes. You glow when you lie down with me. You're the sun rising in the morning and the smoke winking in the stars at night."

After he said that, I knew we would never be apart. If he died and I had another man, it wouldn't matter. He wouldn't be Pierre. He would just be another man, somebody, a person you talk wit' or let sweep up or let be a doorstop.

Captain Endicott was shouting from the corner of the barn, "Nigger! Nigger! Nigger!"

I didn't feel a t'ing.

We are hunted by both sides now. I don't care, though. They can kiss my foot. You can t'ink of people as groups or as individuals. The t'ree Yankees on the flatboat probably saved both Pierre's life and mine. The doctor who dug the pellets out of my back fought side by side wit' my man at Corinth. The colored man who sold us a stolen carriage had broke out of The Walls, a prison in Baton Rouge where the cells are so dark the rats turn white.

You know that feeling you have when you're li'l? You wake up in the morning and you know that this is gonna be a special day, full of good t'ings, no matter what happened yesterday. That's how I feel. Good t'ings are gonna happen.

We're just a mile from Colonel Carleton Hayes's bivouac. In the distance there's a lake, and beyond the lake the Mississippi River, and in the early light, fog rises from the fields, and in some places fires are burning, the smoke black, the ashes drifting like dirty snow on grass that is six feet high and full of gators, slapping their tails out there, wit' breat' that smells like sour mud.

We have two carriage horses, wit' Varina tied on back. It's the third week of her mont' and she has gone into season, which is causing a bit of commotion because she wants to be wit' the geldings, even though they cain't do what sometimes is still on their minds.

The bivouac must be stretched a half mile along a stream that people here call a coulee. A coulee ain't like most Louisiana waterways. The water is clean and clear and has a pebble or sandy bottom, and smaller and gentler animals come down to drink from it, because gators stay in the swamp, among dead t'ings that stink and stagnant water and quicksand and a blanket of green-white lichen that floats as thick as paint on the surface.

On the banks of the coulee cookfires are burning and soldiers are drilling and some officers are racing their horses. It looks like a peaceful place. But I know better. I ain't ever seen Carleton Hayes. I don't have to. Every colored woman knows that kind of white man. It ain't just himself he disrespects. The big victim is his family. He don't respect his own seed, his own wife, his own children. In his home he settles every problem wit' de razor strop. You can hear it sing.

The carriage is enclosed and comfortable, and I don't want to leave it. The seats are deep, the inside lined with felt. My bandages are stiff wit' medicine and need changing. I wish we had stopped earlier. I know the looks that we'll soon be getting. Other than the men who raped me, the worst people in my life have been the white trash who stare at me, when I cain't do anyt'ing about it, their eyes going under my clothes, crawling all over my skin, just like they were touching me. I want to kill them. And I want to hurt them really bad before I kill them. And it ain't just me who feels that way.

"Are you feeling all right?" Pierre says.

"Sho'. How much money we got left?"

"Enough."

"What's enough?"

"To buy you whatever you want," he says.

He has hard money, heavy coins that rattle in his pocket. But he ain't tole me where he put Old Man Suarez's treasure away. I ain't axed him, either. Because if I know where it's at and white people gets me in their hands, I won't never be the same. Don't tell me different, either. The 1811 Rebellion taught us there's people who ain't human. They look like it, but they ain't. My grandmother worked on a plantation outside New Orleans and saw it. She said for thirty miles there were heads stuck on poles along the levee. And even worse t'ings happened. But I ain't gonna talk about it no more.

"Where we gonna go, Pierre?" I ax.

"I had a dream last night," he says. "About a place I saw when I worked on a boat. I think that might be our new home."

He looks like a li'l boy when he grins. I love my darling Pierre. I pick up his hand and put his thumb in my mouth and bite it. He laughs, his face full of sunshine. "Why do you do crazy things like that?"

"Mine to know."

Then I see a man walking toward the carriage. His face looks like a mask, one that has swirls of bone in it. I know him. He visited the Suarez plantation once or twice. He is the one who makes my man feel so guilty about the duel, when it was his family that called my man white trash. My man is the best man on earth, and I feel like taking Mr. Horror Face and stuffing his head in a pickle barrel.

I put my hand on Pierre's arm. It feels like a smoked ham. "We ain't got to stay here, no."

"I need to tell him I'm sorry," Pierre says.

"You t'ink he's gonna do the same? Rich people ain't ever sorry. You t'ink they gonna apologize for slavery? They're just getting started."

Pierre looks at me for a long time. "How did the likes of me find a beautiful thing like you?"

39

COLONEL CARLETON HAYES

I don't like the way things are looking here. I have nine hundred irregulars in those tents, men I brought together. No one else has done that. What did Napoleon say? An army crawls on its stomach? Or something like that. I fed them. I gave them respect. I also gave them power. They can go without liquor; they can go without food and womanly delights. But they cannot go without power. Or at least its appearance.

Our first serious liberation of a village occurred on the Sabine River, on the Texas border, an odd place that voted against secession and had a woman schoolteacher as a mayor. It was evening tide, the sun sliding down in a red ball on the edge of a swamp filled with miles of skeletal trees, all of them looking as if they were about to burst into flame. We walked our horses into town, our faces down, wore-out, little more than shadows creeping down the street, harmless and quit for the day, uninterested in the surroundings, the cannon at the rear of our column an out-of-date brass artifact that we might leave as a souvenir.

Children looked from the windows. A woman crossed in front of us, followed by a three-legged dog. The wind puffed, then blew dust in the air; both the woman and the dog ran for no reason I can explain. There was a freshly painted church on the street, and a saloon with a solitary lamp burning, and a drunk man in a three-piece suit and a crushed stove-pipe hat standing on a boardwalk yelling jolly remarks at us, then pissing into the street while he went on babbling, obviously a happy town character.

An old wood building with a second-story balcony next to the saloon had all the aspects of a straddle house: a lively girl or two stepping out onto the balcony, a rustle of their dresses and petticoats, then disappearing, a few giggles leaking from a half-open window. This was at the beginning of the war, when few people knew about the diseases east Europeans were spreading across the country.

There were no more than thirty of us. You'd think a town in wartime would invite us into an eating-house or just offer us a drink or a bath or just a kind word. Silence always makes people think the worst. The wind started gusting again, cool and smelling of dust, the sun a red diamond splitting apart and flattening through the swamp. Then a drop of rain hit my forehead. I wiped it with my finger and licked it, although I don't know why. At the same time I saw one of my men stop in the lee of the straddle house and touch his face, just as I had. Except he looked up at the balcony where a girl was standing, her dress blowing to the knees.

"You spat on the wrong fella, you Irish whore," he said, and pulled his pistol and shot her dead.

Then we were all shooting, and the townspeople were doing the same, don't claim otherwise, no, sir. They were out to kill us. I was proud of my boys. Maybe we started it, maybe not. Let the historians sort it out. I will tell you one thing, though. Casting blame does no good. No matter how a war or battle starts, you have to finish it. The sooner you end it, the sooner you have peace again. My boys spread through the town, yelling like Indians and shooting through windows and curtains and at balconies and rooftops and even at the people trying to hide behind the tombstones in the town cemetery. I never ciphered out why they thought that was the place to go.

Then there was a calm, and one final shot at a man hiding in a cistern, and it was over. We did a summary trial in the saloon, and by dawn the whole matter was adjudicated. A couple of iron-ball rounds were fired from our cannon, several houses and businesses got splashed with kerosene and burned, and a couple of bad deeds were done to the schoolteacher and the drunk pissing in the street, but I have pretty much shut these things out of my mind, war being what it is.

Now look at what I got on my hands and tell me if it's fair. A voodoo colored woman cured my eyes but refuses to cure my face. Half of it looks like melted candle wax. Each morning I have the pleasure of watching the infection crawl across my nose, turning it into a shell, shrinking the eye above it. Have you ever seen the features on an Egyptian mummy?

An abolitionist woman poured out my whiskey in my own tent and treats me like the stink on cat shit. To be honest, I do not know which way to turn. Wade Lufkin has used his education and his knowledge of Lee's and Jackson's tactics in the Shenandoah Campaign to outwit a bumbler such as Nathaniel Banks and transfer the loyalty of my boys from me to him. This hurts me dearly. I didn't take them simply from the life of medieval serfs but from one that was lower. Yes, that is not exaggeration. They lived the lives of

Southern white trash, just like a bunch of peasants working with grubhoes outside the castle wall. An enslaved darkie was worth a large amount of gold. The white trash have no value at all, except as cannon fodder and I suspect down the line as terrorists to get the emancipated blacks back in chains.

Coincidentally, guess who just walked in.

"What can I do for you, Sergeant Langtree?" I ask.

He salutes and stays at attention. He's not wearing his kepi. His two revolvers are stuffed in his belt. "There's a white man and a colored woman coming in a carriage, sir."

"At ease. Why are you not wearing your hat?"

"I was trying to show respect for the colonel, sir."

"If a soldier is armed, he leaves his hat on in a building or tent. If he is unarmed, he removes it. Do you know why that is?"

"No, sir."

"Keep thinking about it. I am sure you will figure it out."

His face is as inflexible as stone, his eyes fastened on the canvas behind my head. "Mr. Lufkin was walking toward the people in the carriage. I thought the colonel would want to know."

"Why would I care about Mr. Lufkin's doings, Sergeant?"

"I do not know, sir."

"You are telling me you do not know why you bring me information?"

"I reckon I am confused, sir."

I let my eyes slide off his face. My irritability is growing, but I don't know its source. I would like to hit this boy with a quirt, then hit him again and break things inside him. I am opening and closing my hands under my table. "Who's your family?"

"Folks that just get by, sir."

"I know you from somewhere else," I say. "You put me in mind of a boy who took a mean licking from his father night and day, and never did anything right, at least according to his father."

"My father wasn't like that, sir."

"Don't lie to me, boy. He waled you until you wet your pants and hugged his legs and begged him to stop."

His eyes are half lidded, his jaw clenched.

"You remember it now, don't you?" I say.

"Yes, sir."

"He told you the best part of you ran down his leg, didn't he?"

He's sniffling now. "Yes, sir. It was just like you say."

"Here's a handkerchief. Wipe yourself off."

"I don't need no handkerchief, sir. I've been a good soldier."

"Then get the frog out of your throat."

"Yes, sir."

"Good! Now drag your ass out of here."

He salutes me, but I don't return it. After he's gone, I step out into the sunshine and the glory of the day. I'm shaking all over. Why did I do that? Out in the trees I see Wade Lufkin talking to a man who almost killed me on a Sunday morning on Bayou Teche, and I experience a strange sensation. I feel I am inside a book that is about to close its cover. I can see the pages flipping, my face inside them at age nineteen, climbing up a hill toward a Spanish mission where Mexicans are firing at us over a stucco wall, the sky blue, the white puffs of their rifles dissolving in the wind, my heart thudding not with fear but with the assurance that I am as loved by the Creator as the knights of old.

I have no doubt I am standing on the edge of mortality. But for some reason I do not fear it. Perhaps the greatest loss in my life is not what I did but what I did not do. I hear a rumble of thunder in the distance, and I wonder if a great army has been sent to drive me from the Earth. However, I know better. War is a confession of failure, and its perpetrators are the merchants of death, not because they are killers but because they never had the courage to live a decent life.

40

WADE LUFKIN

I remove my hat when I reach the carriage, perhaps to let Pierre Cauchon see the disfigurement of my face rather than as a courtesy. "I figured you would be along," I say.

"Why would you think that, sir?"

"Unfinished things, I suspect. Or perhaps you have no other place to go."

"You're half correct, Mr. Lufkin. May I introduce my friend, Darla Babineaux?"

"I have met Miss Darla on one or two occasions at the Suarez plantation," I reply, bowing slightly. "It is very nice to see you again, Miss Darla."

She puts her hand on Cauchon's forearm and looks straight ahead and does not reply. I keep hearing thunder in the distance, or better said, a rumbling sound, like bowling pins clattering. The sky is yellow, swirling with dust, and smells like sulfur. There is a large green cloud over the Gulf, lightning flicking inside it. I can feel Cauchon's eyes on my face.

"May I be of service to you, sir?" I ask.

"I came here to apologize," he says. "You tried to prevent the duel. You did so not in fear but in conscience. I am the one who forced a heinous act to go forward. I will never forgive myself, sir, but I hope you will forgive me."

I let my eyes go flat and stare into the distance. The wind is cool on my face, or the parts of it that still have feeling. I think of the Union soldier reading the poems of Robert Browning on a boulder next to a creek in Virginia, and the bayonet-fixed rifle I drove through his lung. Suddenly I cannot keep places and dates and events in order. The life I lived before the war seems to have never existed. Everything that has occurred since April of '61 seems like stained church glass shattered on a flagstone. I feel the sod shift under my feet. What is the day of the week? The Sabbath?

"Are you all right, suh?" the colored woman says.

I touch my forehead before I answer. "Yes," I say. "I'm fine."

But no words follow, as though I have forgotten how to speak. Cauchon gets down from the carriage and walks toward me. "Why don't we go over to the shade?" he says. "We have the makings of a picnic, if you like."

"What did you say?" I ask.

"Sir?"

"Those words, 'the makings of a picnic.' I said something similar to a young Union officer in Virginia."

"Well, good for you," he replies.

"You don't understand. I killed him. I drove a bayonet through his chest and held him down on the ice and snow. I still see him there. By a creek. His book of poems where he dropped it."

Cauchon and his lady look away from me, unable to hide the lights of pity and embarrassment in their eyes. I hear the rumbling sound again and want to believe that elves are playing ninepins on a town green close by, but the magical legends of Washington Irving have faded from our era and have been replaced by the four horsemen in the Book of Revelation. I wonder if the horsemen bear the same scars as I. Perhaps I have finally discovered the role I have earned.

Oh, enough with self-flagellation. The pillory is for fools and for those who enjoy their own torment.

"You owe me no apology, Mr. Cauchon. You were treated shabbily by my uncle. I brokered the duel. It was not your doing. Miss Hannah and Miss Florence are here. I am sure they will be happy to see you."

"There's something else," he says. "Do you know this Endicott character?"

"He tore my uncle and aunt's home apart and opened fire on me and killed a mother and child in the quarters."

"I hear he's headed this way," he says. "In large numbers. I think he may have followed us."

"Really? I don't quite know what to say." I feel like wringing Cauchon's neck.

"You're not a bad fellow, Mr. Lufkin," he says.

"Please call me Wade."

I arrange a tent and cots for them, and Miss Hannah and Miss Florence change the bandages on Miss Darla's back and bring them a large ration of food. The Yankees have made a big tactical jump forward with the use of hot-air balloons. They have launched them from the east side of the swamp and run telegraph lines from the baskets down to the ground, and they have spotted our moves with deadly results, particularly in terms of morale. I think the legitimate Confederate Army is not entirely unpleased. A howitzer round arching out of nowhere into the midst of one's breakfast table can certainly dampen one's day.

Worse, we don't know if the howitzer crew is just having a little fun or if Sherman has shifted his emphasis and decided to cross the Mississippi and blow us to mincemeat, because that is the rumor we have heard. More succinctly, we are considered a nuisance by both the blue-bellies and the greybacks. It is not easy to command irregulars. Imagine this situation: the sun is going down in the west; our cookfires have been buried with wet dirt hauled from the coulee bank; then in the twilight a few fellows on the grog start popping at observation balloons and howitzers almost one mile away, giving up our position and ensuring a sleepless night. Have you ever wanted to declare war on your own troops?

It's afternoon now and I feel no different than I did in the morning. I feel that the earth is shifting under us, that the greenness in the sky and the smell of the salt and the distant rain are signs not to be dismissed. The natural world is a cathedral. The canopy above the heads of primitive people was the skein between Heaven and a church pew made of stone and cushioned with lichen. The industrial surge of the nineteenth century has cost us our cathedral.

I think the deciding battles will take place next year, in '64. Sherman will have Tennessee locked down, then he will move through Georgia and into South Carolina and turn the South into a charnel house. That is not a metaphor. I think Sherman will make a weapon of hunger and destitution.

Nonetheless, honor is honor, and duty is duty. I see Sergeant Shaye Langtree, his skinny frame bent low on his horse, flying up the long slope toward the woods, his hat blown back on his shoulders. I do not understand why that boy has stayed with a man like Carleton Hayes. The colonel seems to have a poisonous attitude toward him and never misses a chance to humiliate him. I think the colonel sees himself in this poor boy.

He's out of the saddle and on the ground, with the horse still in motion.

"Hold on, soldier!" I say. "You're about to run us both down!"

"There's blue-belly infantry about two miles away, Mr. Lufkin."

"How many?"

"I couldn't tell, sir. They were putting up a skirmish line on the edge of a woods. That ain't what scares me. They got cavalry on both flanks and at least six cannon up on the levee. What do you call that?"

"Pinchers?"

"Yes, sir. What's-his-name, the Confederate general, he used that in Virginia."

"I think you're talking about General Jackson," I say. "Let's leave him out of the discussion. I think you need to slow down and quiet your nerves a little bit."

"Colonel Hayes is gonna get us all killed, Mr. Lufkin. I didn't sign up for this. I don't like being no messenger boy, either, sir."

Looking into his face is like staring at the sharpened edge of a hatchet blade. "What are you talking about, Sergeant?"

"I saw the blue-bellies in the woods through my telescope. Then I took off, lickety-split-and-gone, and about five minutes later I was going hell-for-breakfast across a creek and a bunch of Yankee cavalry strung a rope between some trees and liked to rip my head off."

His eyes go out of focus with his own words, reminiscent of the colonel. He's wearing two .36 revolvers, both snugged in their holsters with leather thongs.

"The Yanks didn't disarm you?"

He wets his lips before he speaks. "No, sir. I didn't try to draw. I didn't have no choice. They would have blown me out of the saddle. Their officer said to give you this message."

He takes a folded piece of paper out of his shirt pocket and hands it to me. His wisp of a beard is rising and falling with his breath. He cannot look me in the face. He obviously fears I will accuse him of cowardice.

"You did a good job, Sergeant. Did the officer give you his name?"

He takes a deep breath. "No, sir, he didn't. He was a handsome fella, but his face looked like he'd run through a rose bush. He had an accent like Miss Florence's."

"A Boston accent?"

"I wouldn't know, sir. He wrote out his message on his saddle. It looked like he brought his pen and paper with him." He starts to speak again, then looks into space.

I unfold the two sheets of paper. The handwriting is in a flowing calligraphy, the capital letters in swirls, the tall letters like little knives. It reads:

Dear Mr. Lufkin,

   I hope you and your family are recovering from the personal losses you have had to endure—the three Lufkin brothers who were killed at Chickamauga. It is a shame that we are on opposite sides of war, because I believe we have a common bloodline, a British one, and in a better time would have been close friends.

Sir, I need to correct an injustice, punish a villain, and see that a Negro child is returned to its mother. Can you help me do this? By this time you probably know the events and the people about whom I am writing. The constable Pierre Cauchon murdered and wounded several Union soldiers under my command. He is now travelling with Darla Babineaux and has sought refuge with Carleton Hayes' brigands.

I am not interested in other parties. The war will probably not last much longer. When it ends, a general amnesty will probably be granted to those who used poor judgement. That's fine. But Cauchon should not be allowed in this group.

I know the story of Hannah Laveau and her child. The child is in an orphanage on the west side of the Mississippi, not far from here. I can lift the child with my own hands and place it in the mother's arms. But first she must surrender herself and the fugitive negress Darla Babineaux and the murderer Pierre Cauchon.

I am sure Babineaux and Laveau will be released. Cauchon will be taken to a prison, where he will remain until he is hanged. If you wish proof about the child, I will let his mother view him under a white flag. At three tomorrow you can send a contingent to the place where I now stand.

Sir, you are a gentleman. The men around you are not gentlemen. Don't let them be your albatross.

Sincerely,
Captain John Endicott

I fold the sheets of paper and put them in my shirt. Sergeant Langtree is chewing on a long piece of grass. "Is there something I can do, Mr. Lufkin?" he says.

"How far can you hit a pie plate with a rifle, Sergeant?"

"I ain't that good at it, sir. Can I say something personal?"

"Please do."

"I think that officer is sniffy and toplofty. When he finished writing the message, he gave it to his sergeant to hand it to me. Like I'm dirty."

"You're a good young fellow," I reply. "In Texas there's a name for a man like the captain. I think it's 'sidewinder.'"

"Yes, sir, it is," he says, smiling.

As I walk back to the encampment, I can feel the barometer dropping, the electricity in the clouds ginning up, the salt in the air intensifying, like a wave full of kelp curling on the sand. The presence of Pierre Cauchon has complicated things, although I do not blame him, nor do I wish him to feel he is a burden. Hannah Laveau is washing clothes in a tub in front of her tent. She looks up at me and smiles as I approach.

"Captain John Endicott claims he knows where your son is, Miss Hannah. He also says he will allow you to see him. I think this is a treacherous man, and I am not sure how to proceed. But I will do everything in my power to have your son returned to you, so help me, God."

She drops her wash and wipes her hands on her apron; her hands are scarred from shucking oysters, the top of her shirt unbuttoned, her breasts visible. "You don't got to swear to God, Mr. Wade," she replies. "He knows His children and which are good and which ain't. Don't be afraid, suh. He ain't gonna let us down."

We're the superior race? What a joke.

41

DARLA BABINEAUX

I knew Endicott was gonna get to us, and try to divide us up and use what is best in us against ourself. He's a master at it and mean from his hairline to his socks, and he knows how to hurt people from afar. He's a small man who is only big when his anger swells him up, like a sore with pus in it.

Troot' is I'm scared. Pierre stole the barrel of gold plates and silverware and jewelry from the Suarez family, and Endicott is gonna dig up half of Louisiana to find it. It ain't just the money. He used to tell me his family came to New England on the *Mayflower* and his ancestor was the first governor of the colony, but an enlisted soldier tole me Captain Endicott's parents were indentured servants and maybe were mixed up wit' the Salem witch trials and saved themself by giving evidence against their neighbors.

I already knew he wasn't no kind of royalty, though. Know how? He has these gaps in his teet'. People wit' gaps in their teet' are never royalty. Also, in his saddle bag he has a book on manners

280 JAMES LEE BURKE

and a book on proper speech. I've seen him practice at night in the corner of the room, making round sounds in his mout'.

Oh, Lordy, I know I'm filling up my head with all dese t'ings for only one reason. I'm afraid somet'ing awful is about to happen. It's like the Eart' is pulling on me. It's like ain't no power in the world is gonna let me be wit' my man, like it ain't just society against us, it's nature itself, like all the promises in the Bible ain't gonna happen and we ain't gonna get a chance at bringing Eden back.

I've heard crazy white people singing in their churches, "God give Noe the rainbow sign, it ain't by water, it's the fire next time." They're looking forward to it. Why is that? Other people got more money than they do.

I got news for them. It's coming. But not like they t'ink. Smell the salt in the air? It's the same smell that rises from a fresh grave, one that's in wet ground and full of white slugs, wit'out no coffin. Or the smell of quicksand in a swamp when it's full of dead animals and gator eggs.

It's all around me. Pierre cain't smell it. That's because he believes we're going to the South Seas, to an island below the Southern Cross, where the ocean looks like burgundy under the stars. That's how he describes it. He believes in the Eart' and what he calls the curative power of the seasons and the blessing that can be cupped from a spring pooling among rocks. Those are the t'ings he says. That's one of the reasons I love him.

I don't argue wit' him, because I don't believe words are gonna get rid of John Endicott. He's here to destroy Mr. Wade, Hannah, Miss Florence, Pierre, me, and even the li'l boy Samuel. If he could get rid of God, he would do that, too.

I t'ink this can end in only one way. Men did t'ings to me I will never talk about. They did t'ings to me as long as I would let them. When they were dead, they didn't do it no more.

I would like to get close to Captain Gap-Teet' and see what he t'inks about it.

Here comes Pierre now, carrying some food for me and some medicine to rub on my back.

"Why are you crying, girl?" he says.

"I wasn't crying. I was just t'inking about all the good t'ings we got."

He kisses me on top of my head. Some white trash a few tents away look at us, then look away. They scowled yesterday. I talked to them, though. I have a knife that is so sharp it can cut paper right down the middle wit'out no effort. I showed them how I peel potatoes. They was real attentive and said t'ank-you for showing them that.

It's the next morning now. The sun is warm, much warmer than is usual this time of year, red-colored, the grass pale green in the field, smoke rising like steam in the swamps and coulees, purple ink spreading across the clouds above the Gulf, the way it does when it's fixing to rain.

I feel sticky all over and can smell myself inside my blouse. Pierre didn't sleep all night. That's because Mr. Wade said he had to be honest and tell us everyt'ing John Endicott tole him, meaning Hannah and me and Pierre got to turn ourself over to Endicott, but Miss Florence gets a free pass and Mr. Wade doesn't need to worry about crunching a man's head off his shoulders in New Orleans.

That's what I mean when I say John Endicott knows how to situate himself on the hilltop while the li'l people down below choke each other to death.

Mr. Wade said he ain't taking no deal wit' Endicott, and Miss Florence said the same t'ing. Hannah didn't say anyt'ing. All she knows is her son is close by. She's lit up like a candle. I t'ink she's getting too happy too fast.

But somet'ing else is going on, too. People say Gen'l Forrest has been made the commanding officer of the entire state of Mississippi, and he's running every Yankee out of the state. That don't sound right. Grant took Vicksburg by cutting the railroad and starving out the city. That means the Yankees own the whole river. Nobody cares who occupies farmland with not'ing on it except a burned chimney sticking out of the weeds. Maybe Gen'l Forrest will figure that out, since he's so smart.

The one who seems left out of everyt'ing is the one who is supposed to be in charge. Right now he's walking around mumbling to himself. Half his face looks like a strawberry cake somebody stepped on. He axed me twice who I was. I said I was the friend of Pierre and Hannah, and I appreciated him letting us stay wit' him. He bowed and swung his hat in front of himself and said he would like to have us all for dinner, but would I mind axing Hannah to fix his face so people don't get sick at the table. I'd hate to tell him this, but there ain't no way to fix that face unless he wants to saw off his head and float it down the coulee.

It's afternoon now, almost t'ree o'clock, as all of us take a position in the place where we are supposed to meet John Endicott—Mr. Wade, Pierre, me, Hannah, and Miss Florence. The wind is straight off the Gulf and smells like tiny fish trapped in pools of water and warm sand. I t'ink today is Friday. I don't know why I just thought that. My heart is thumping, like it doesn't have space to breathe.

The funny t'ing is, the person I trust most is Mr. Wade. He ain't taken in by bad men. I love my Pierre, but his goodness is his weakness; he'll let the Romans stretch him out on a cross and watch while they hammer nails in his hands and feet. Miss Florence, too. She ain't ever married or had children, so she t'inks the only gift she has is her life. It ain't a good way to t'ink.

Hannah's mind is in the next world. This ain't the time for the next world. This is the time to deal with *now* and *here*. John Endicott is coming out of the trees wit' eight other men on horseback. A sergeant is holding a stick wit' a white rag tied on it. Ain't one of those soldiers look worth their dirty undershirts, and believe me, they are dirty.

Pierre and I and Miss Florence are in the carriage. Hannah is sitting behind Mr. Wade. But I don't see no li'l boy. *John Endicott is a liar,* I say to myself. *Cain't these people understand that?* And that ain't all that's happening. John Endicott has taken on a change, like an actor taking a new role. He's wearing a dark hat, a sky-blue cotton shirt, a yellow kerchief around his neck, a buckskin coat, rowelled spurs, and pirate boots like the colonel's.

"Where is the child?" Mr. Wade says.

"In time," Endicott says.

"You'd bloody well better get him out here, Captain," Mr. Wade says.

"Do you agree to turn over Babineaux, Laveau, and Cauchon?"

"I did not say that," Mr. Wade says. Then he lifts a hand. Thirty or forty mounted men ease out of a sugar-cane field that is purple and gold in the sunlight. Their long hair is hanging out of their kepis, their pistols strung from their pommels. Their faces are in shadow, their backs straight.

"What a grand group of lads, Mr. Lufkin. It looks like you have found your level," John Endicott says. "But let's stick with the issue. You will not surrender your charges?"

"That is correct. But I will accept your surrender."

John Endicott turns his horses in a circle. "I'm afraid you underestimate me, sir. When I set a goal, I let nothing get in the way."

More Yankees come out of the trees, some on horseback, some on foot. The backs of my legs are quivering. A wagon emerges from the shade. It's pulled by a single horse. A white woman on the seat holds a child in her lap. The child is wrapped in a shawl to keep the mosquitoes off.

"Recognize the horse?" Endicott says.

It's Varina. Pierre straightens up next to me. I put my hand on Pierre's arm.

"We stole her from under your nose, Mr. Cauchon," John Endicott says. "What do you have to say now, you dumb fuck? The woman on the wagon seat is a lunatic from the jail in Baton Rouge. She strangled her own child. The little boy is Samuel Laveau. A cautionary word: Be very careful what you say or do now. I have no mercy. Or would you like a demonstration?"

Endicott's horse is dancing under him, so tense and scared that Endicott has to keep jerking his head. Hannah is already fighting to get down from behind Mr. Wade's saddle. The blood has drained from Pierre's face. His pistol is on the floor of the carriage, but he knows John Endicott well enough not to give him provocation.

I want to kill John Endicott. I'm the one who can do it, the one who knows the dark creatures he releases in a bedroom, the pain you don't see coming. I take my knife from inside my jacket and hold it behind my hip and get down from the carriage and walk toward the Yankees.

I have no expression in my face or eyes. I can already tell what Endicott plans for me. It will be hard and long, and when he finishes there will nothing left of me except rags and pieces of things nobody will recognize.

"I surrender, Captain John," I say. "You ain't got to hurt nobody. I'm gonna do whatever you want. Suh, please don't hurt Pierre's horse."

I'm looking up into his face now. Then I say what may be the last prayer I ever send Upstairs:

It's Friday and t'ree o'clock, Lord. I know no matter what I do, You ain't gonna put me in hell. Like Hannah says, we're already inside the kingdom. I just want to protect my man and that li'l boy yonder in the arms of a crazy woman. Thank you, Suh, for helping me do what I need to do. It might get kind of rough. Amen.

42

COLONEL CARLETON HAYES

What in the goddamn hell is going on? I can hear shooting in the wind, small-arms fire undoubtedly, then cannon booming way off in the distance, followed by the snapping of airbursts, which means the cannoneers have snipped the fuse on the balls too short and are wasting their ammunition and probably raining shrapnel on the frogs. My boys are creating a pandemonium, asking me what to do, yelling, carrying on like I haven't trained them. I told them to form up. Soon as I said that, a cannonball landed in the middle of a tent and blew a cook and a cauldron of pinto beans all over the tree trunks. Evidently my junior officers are not rising to the occasion. I cannot find my sword, either. How am I supposed to lead a charge without a sword? Jesus Christ, this may be my chance to walk into the history books.

That's what George Pickett did at Cemetery Ridge. I knew him at Chapultepec in '47. I think he's the kind of twerp you don't give power to. I think down the road y'all will see him for the mean-spirited bastard he is. I love the army. I spent most of my life loving it. I just wish the army had loved me more.

I can smell a battlefield. I'm not talking about cordite, either. Battlefields don't have birthdays. Past, present, or future, they swallow their dead the way the ocean swallows water. Except the ocean cleanses itself and lends its purity to heal the wounded and appoints porpoises to escort the dead. The ocean is our mother, and she takes the worst of us to her breast and re-creates us in her womb and later lets us play in the sand at the bottom of the sea. I learned that at age sixteen after a wreck on a clipper ship. A battlefield is a mortician's delight, a tool used to reduce the herd, and every poppy on it is nursed by a corpse.

The antebellum world of ladies and knights has fallen asunder, like a brick house on shaking ground. I believe the Grim Reaper is real and now in our midst. I cannot say I am undaunted. I have seen the Reaper cross a battlefield or sometimes stop and rest in a Mexican village that has turned to ash. Oh, he was an ugly fellow, a troll with a gleam in his eye. Those who felt his touch said he had a sharpened fingernail and a breath like ice water and a stench that would rattle your bones.

I saw many die, all around me, in ditches and surgical tents, begging for their mothers, but Death showed no interest in me, as though he could take me anytime he wanted. In my vanity I was actually affronted. I sat on a brick fence and ate my lunch while three blue-bellies popped at me for almost twenty minutes. When they ran out of ammunition, I pulled down my britches and pointed my rear in their direction and did my daily constitutional.

Has my hour come round, that moment that is like a hush in the ear, a feather on the cheek? I do not know. I'd like to ask my boys, but they're shooting into the trees and fixing bayonets on their muskets because we didn't have enough ammunition for our repeaters, and some are caving over when they catch a Minie dipped in garlic or shit.

I go to my tent and unfold my battle flag and tie it to a tent pole and march into the fray, but nobody pays me much mind. My boys are dropping around me like fruit from the trees. The smoke is so thick my eyes are burning and my lungs are full of glass. My flagpole jumps in my hands each time a bullet strikes the cloth. I can hear bullets whining away in the woods, sometimes thudding into a hard surface, sometimes coaxing a grunt from a boy who is already curled in a ball, waiting for his turn to cross the Styx.

Ahead, I can see mules and horses with empty saddles running wild-eyed in a field, their hides splattered, stirrups flying, some disemboweled, their hooves tangled in their entrails. But Mr. Death does not acknowledge me, and leaves me as the contemptable man I am, an object of pity and ridicule, rejected even by the grave.

43

FLORENCE MILTON

I do not know where all the soldiers came from. The smoke is yellow and smells like sulfur in an incinerator behind a military hospital. The events that are taking place before my eyes seem out of perspective, without cause or origin or consent, as though the rules of nature and human behavior have been abandoned.

I feel like I am inside a dream. Darla and Hannah were both heading toward John Endicott when he fired his pistol through the ear of Mr. Cauchon's mare, causing her to rear and try to tear loose from the harness and poles and straps binding her to the wagon. Cannon on a levee were firing sequentially, each barrel and set of wheels rising from the ground, the gun crews turning their faces away, sticking their fingers in their ears, squinting like monkeys.

I got down from the carriage also, backwards, unsteady, like an old woman. Hannah was climbing onto the wagon box where the crazy woman from the Baton Rouge asylum had put the black child. The lunatic was trying to whip the horse out of the trees, her face affrighted, her eyes the innocent pale blue you see only in the genuinely insane. I wondered if she thought the child was hers, and in her desperation would end up killing both the child and herself. Then I saw Mr. Lufkin get down from his horse and drop a tethering weight on the ground, the reins tied to it. The weight was shaped like an elephant's head. Mr. Cauchon was trying to stop Darla from attacking Captain Endicott.

All sound and movement stopped. I opened and closed my mouth and breathed as deeply as I could, but it did no good. The wind blowing in the gum trees and water oaks was frozen in time as though an artist had painted it on a canvas. I felt I had gone to Hell. Or I was in a place between Heaven and Hell, the place we actually live in, one filled with dissonance and cacophony and ruinous choices.

Then the artillery roared again, and I saw everyone around me resume whatever they were doing, and now I am back in the present.

I have never seen so many soldiers, except at Corinth. Colonel Hayes's irregulars are taking a beating on the edge of the sugar-cane field. They have no shelter and are firing on one knee, and one by one toppling on their sides, as though they were tired and wished to take a nap. In the distance I can see more Union soldiers trotting in formation, bayonets fixed, their ambulances already set up in the rear. In the south, down toward the Gulf, I can see Confederates in gray uniforms, a rarity after the first year of the war. I do not know who they are or how they got there. Perhaps General Forrest has crossed the river in hopes of thwarting Sherman's attempt to move the war into Georgia and South Carolina, although there is a rumor he has leukemia and has started to waste in the saddle.

May I say this to you? I think we may be watching a prelude to our nation's ultimate fate. Civilization follows the sun. We have scorched our way to the other end of the continent. No matter how much we took, no matter how many living things we killed, there was never enough. The molten ball descending into the Pacific has overtones that make me shudder.

Something has just occurred that has dampened the intensity of the gunfire. At first I thought the pause was to allow a wounded and exceptionally brave soldier to be taken off the field. That has happened many times in our war against ourselves. But that's not it. Colonel Carleton Hayes has somehow gotten on a sickly mule and is riding into the field between his men in the sugar-cane rows and the Union infantry who are smothered by the smoke from their own weapons. He looks drunk or badly wounded and is waving Lee's battle flag over his head. It has literally been shot to pieces. Sergeant Langtree is trying to grab the mule's bridle. A shell bursts directly over the Colonel's head, and in his typical irrational manner he rages and curses at the smoke of the exploded round and the damage done to his flag.

I guess I feel sorry for the colonel and the abused boy Shaye Langtree, who is still trying to win the approval of a man whose brain glows with the venereal consequences of a profligate life. The irony is that my Puritan ancestors bred many a woods colt like Carleton Hayes. They hid their anger and their lust, and groped the innocent and killed the Indians so they did not have to kill themselves.

As I walk toward my friends and the situational choices they have made, I am possessed by a terrible fear. Maybe this is because of the penalty I will have to pay for taking human life. But please do not misinterpret me. I am not judging myself. I did not intend to harm others. I was forced to kill. But the content of your dreams does not take orders, and a stone bruise on the soul can be forever.

I wonder sometimes if the people who died in front of the gun I held will gather around my deathbed, perhaps to forgive me, perhaps to walk with me to the place dead people go. But I know this about the dead. They are not gone. They turn into a vapor and slip through the stones we pile on them and suddenly appear like elves in the trees at twilight. I do not want this to happen to my friends. They are very good people and have made my life worth living.

Oh, good heavens, what is that old man doing now? Does not the world have enough trouble already without the presence of Colonel Carleton Hayes? Why did Our Lord put such a creature in our midst, unless it was to show us there are worse things than Original Sin.

44

DARLA BABINEAUX

Captain John Endicott knocks me to the ground. He has hit me so hard that my eyes feel detached from my skull. I have never been hit that hard. Out of the corner of my eye I can see the crazy white woman, on the ground also, and Hannah driving the wagon back into the trees and taking Pierre's horse Varina wit' her. I don't know how far she's gonna get. Endicott's men are holding guns on us. I don't t'ink we are gonna get t'rew this day. This has been a terrible mistake. They ain't gonna take us to the rear. They're gonna kill us. I have my knife in the sleeve of my jacket. If I can get close to John Endicott, he's gonna die the most painful deat' he ever had.

I try to stand up, but he pushes me down wit' his boot. "Stay where you are, girl. You can have a totally new life. Just don't give me trouble."

I know what kind of life he has in mind. He'll execute Pierre and install me in a bordello in New Orleans.

"Pick me up," I say. "I won't fight wit' you no more."

"You don't think I know what you're doing? You'll have a dirk in me before you're off the ground."

Then something changes. No one is looking at me anymore. Some of John Endicott's soldiers are laughing. Colonel Hayes is riding into the clearing on a mule wit' ribs like barrel slats, his hand clenching a flagstaff flying the Stars and Bars, although it makes me t'ink of cheesecloth that rats have been chewing on. This white-trash boy who is always following him around is trying to help him down from the mule, while the old man keeps slapping at him. The Yankees are all laughing now.

The colonel crashes on the ground, then gets up and starts swaying around. I'm sure he's drunk. He's got a smell like vomit and another smell in his pants, too.

"Who the fuck are you?" Endicott axes him.

"Colonel Carleton Hayes at your service, sir."

"What happened to your face?"

"I can't remember. I think I spent some time in Galveston."

"Well, get out of here. Take your sergeant with you."

The colonel waves his hand at the fields and clumps of trees. "I own this. From Baton Rouge to the Gulf. What are you doing on my land, you goddamn Yankee?"

"Get out of here, old man."

"I'm Colonel Carleton Hayes, you cocksucker. Straighten up yourself."

"What did you call me?"

"Colonel, we need to leave," the sergeant says.

"Oh, hi there, Long Tree, or whatever your name is," the colonel says.

"Did you hear me?" Endicott says. "What was that name you called me?"

"Fuck if I remember," the colonel says. "But I know you well. You round up milk cows and chickens and hogs and do other scut work for that shit-ass William Sherman."

"Get down on your knees," Endicott says.

"Why would I do that?" the colonel says.

Endicott cocks his pistol and fires a round through the top of the colonel's foot.

The colonel's boot jumps. A bubble of blood rises from the bullet hole in the leather. But the old man keeps his balance, his eyes hazy with pain, the diseased side of his face dripping on his neck. "Why did you do that?" he axes. "I did you no harm."

"What's your name, Sergeant?" Endicott axes.

"Sergeant Shaye Langtree, sir," the boy answers.

"This man stinks of urine and God only knows what else. Now get him out of my sight."

"What's gonna happen to these people, Captain?"

"That is not your concern. Go or be summarily executed."

"Sir," says the boy, "Miss Hannah has got her little boy and is done gone. Cain't we call it quits, sir? Ain't no point in hurting the other people here, is there?"

"You're quite a diplomat," Endicott says. "We just call it quits? That man over there, the one named Pierre Cauchon, who murdered my men, should receive a pardon issued by yourself?"

I start to get up again. I recognize the tone in John Endicott's voice. I remember the sounds he made on top of me in the dark. I remember him curling my hair on his finger, then jerking it. When I am almost up from the ground, he shoves me down again. He stiffens his finger at me, the tip trembling. "Next time, I'm going to hurt you, woman."

Then my man steps forward, his palms held up in front of him, like he's shoving back the world. "I am going of my own volition, Captain Endicott. I possess some objects that were taken from the Suarez plantation. I will turn them over to you. I think you know what I am talking about."

"You're going to turn these 'objects' over to me no matter what happens here?" John Endicott says. "Do I understand you correctly?"

"Yes," my man answers.

"You're offering me some kind of bribe?"

The sky is dimming, the rain beginning to patter on the trees, the air filling with a smell like salt spray and tarnished brass in the sun.

"You confiscate hogs. What do you call that?" Pierre says.

Oh, Pierre, Pierre, Pierre, why did you have to say that? My beautiful, brave man, what have you done?

"Tell me what you think of this?" Endicott says. He lifts his revolver and fires a ball pointblank through Shaye Langtree's left temple. It pops a black hole in his skin and comes out the other side, so fast the boy is smiling like somebody played a joke on him. He goes straight down, his eyes sightless before his knees thud on the grass. The grass is eight inches high and covers the wounds on each side of his forehead so he looks like he's quit the war and fallen asleep.

"What did you do?" I hear the colonel say. "You cannot have done this. He's only a boy. What have you done?"

There is blood splatter on his shirt, and pieces of brain. He presses both hands to his ears, as though he is drowning in sound no one else can hear.

45

HANNAH LAVEAU

I whip the reins down on Mr. Pierre's horse as we come out of the woods and up the slope of the levee where the Yankees have their cannons, the barrels blowing clouds of black smoke in the rain and wind, and the lightning flashing in the sky. I've got Li'l Samuel between my thighs, his face pressed into my belly, his arms wrapped around me, bouncing up and down when I hit a bump. But he ain't afraid, even when the cannoneer jerks the lanyard and the cannon jumps in the air.

They're looking at me now, maybe because they're bored. They're killing people almost one mile away but seem to get no thrill out of it. One man takes out his private part and urinates at me. An officer walks over and says something to him, then makes a hand signal for me to stop. I do as he says because I ain't done anything wrong. Also, I know God has given me back my child, and He ain't gonna let anybody take him from me. That ain't going to happen.

"You shouldn't be out here, Missy," the officer says. He cain't be more than twenty-five and has a neat haircut and no sign of a beard. He wears a kepi instead of a wide-brim hat, and his uniform looks like it was tailored for his small body. "There're Reb snipers down by the river. They're a desperate bunch and not choicy about their targets," he says. "What are you doing in the midst of a battlefield?"

"Taking my son to a safe place, suh," I say.

"You won't find it here." He looks away at the rain front moving from the Gulf, as though he's studying something inside his head. "I think I have seen a drawing of you on a poster, Missy."

"There are lots of those."

"These had to do with a killing or two."

The rain is falling on Samuel's head. I put the crazy woman's shawl over him. "Suh, we've had a mighty hard time. My boy and me don't mean you no grief. Let us go, suh."

He takes off his kepi, then puts it on again. "What happened to your horse's ear?"

"A Yankee officer shot it."

"What's his name?"

"Captain John Endicott."

"What's your name, Missy?"

"Hannah Laveau."

"Miss Hannah, John Endicott is not representative of the Union Army. Do you have money?"

"No, suh."

He takes three coins from his pocket and puts them in my hand. "Go a half mile, then turn toward the river. You'll find a village there. It's burned, but you can buy food and maybe find lodging."

"Suh, I have friends on the other side of those woods. Your shells are exploding right over their heads. You got to show some mercy."

"Take care of your son, Miss Hannah. I can't change the place your friends have chosen to be. Your friends will have to depend on the angels."

I pick up the reins from my lap. "I hope you have a good life, suh. I hope you have children and they grow up strong and healthy and take care of you when you're old. I hope they don't see the world my li'l boy has seen."

I flick the reins on the rump of Mr. Pierre's horse, the one he calls Varina, the one he obviously loves, the one that carried Darla Babineaux away from John Endicott. What am I going to do? My stomach feels sick. I'm deserting my friends, and in so doing I am deserting God, who ain't ever let me down.

I follow the young officer's direction for about ten minutes, then cain't go any farther. God gave me back my li'l boy because he ain't just an ordinary li'l boy. He comes right out of the story in the Bible. He wasn't born just for me; he was born for the world. He walked out of the smoke at Shiloh Church, and that wasn't by accident. That li'l child has the word of God written on his soul, just like it was glowing on stone tablets on the side of a mountain. How can I believe all these things, then run and hide with Samuel and leave our friends to die?

That ain't what God's children do. We ain't afraid of anybody. I pull the left rein and turn the wagon around. Samuel has gone to sleep under my dress, even in the rain. The cannon are still roaring, like a row of doors slamming. The sky is gray, the fields green. The tops of my hands are slick with rainwater, the scars on my skin like pink worms, the same kind my mother had. I saw her body after she was taken to the guillotine. The only thing I looked at was the scars on her hands. I never forgot them. But I don't know why I am thinking about this now. I never know. No matter what I do, I never know.

46

FLORENCE MILTON

I long for my small house on Bayou Teche in New Iberia. Yankee-bred girl that I was, I never thought I would fall in love with the tropics and a Caribbean way of life that was like the influence of a narcotic on the soul when waking to robins on Christmas or listening to the rain ticking on the banana fronds outside the window or watching a paddle wheeler puffing with fire on a foggy morning.

If *they*, meaning my fellow human beings, had not cursed themselves with the enslavement of their fellow man, they would have lived in a near-perfect society. Oh, well, I did what I could and have taken a page from Mr. Whitman, who never judged, who loved his country dearly, who volunteered as a nurse in hospitals and battalion aid stations, and never gave up hope for a better world.

So that is the way I think today as the rain spins in the sky and the fog blows through the woods and meadows and covers the humped bodies of Union infantry and Jayhawkers and greybacks who signed their enlistment papers with an *X*.

I feel a sense of peace that scares me, the kind that entails flirting with the edge of a cliff. Or rather flirting with death itself, which is probably the most egregious and vain expression of the vanities. What do I mean? You can become part of the Milky Way just by looking at it. Do you want to throw that away?

The colonel is obviously insane with either grief he cannot explain or the diseases and alcohol that have ruined his brain. Hannah has just come back through the woods with her son and Mr. Cauchon's horse, Varina. She has offered no explanation. But I don't have to ask for one. I think she is one of those who open the door through the dimensions for the rest of us. She's a cathedral in herself. I suspect her son is exactly who she says he is. And if he isn't, I don't care. Holy people have an aura about them, often a flicker when all light seems to have been sucked from the world. Who cares where they get it? They're the light-bearers. They go down with the ship, the decks awash, guns blazing. How can you not love them? Or not accept their love?

My gift to the world will be small. I genuinely feel sorry for the colonel. He's weeping and holding his head in his hands. For some reason he seems to think he can talk John Endicott into undoing the heinous deed he has committed.

"You must do something," he says. "You have surgeons and field hospitals and ambulance wagons at your beck and call."

"Shut up, you nasty thing," Endicott says.

"You crippled my foot, you hurt Cauchon's mare, you drove a mother and child from our midst. What kind of man are you?"

"You don't seem to have a good memory about your own deeds, you smelly old sot. Now begone."

"I told my father I was sorry," the colonel says. "I told him over and over. He never forgave. So I killed him."

"What does that have to do with us?" Endicott asks.

"I was going to make it up to the boy. To Langtree. But you shot him. He can't come back."

Endicott motions to his men. "Put him in handcuffs and stick a rag in his mouth."

"What about the others, Captain?" a sergeant says.

Endicott looks back at him without reply. The sergeant tries to hide his expression from the rest of us. I have no doubt about our fate.

I lean over as though I need to tie my shoe, then pick up the lead bookend that Mr. Lufkin is using as a tethering weight, one shaped like an elephant's head. I smash it into Endicott's face. Then I hit him again. And again. I see and feel the cartilage and bone break, an eye pop like a grape, his lips burst on his teeth. I cannot stop hitting the captain, even though guns are firing around me, guns in the hands of Mr. Lufkin and Mr. Cauchon.

Suddenly Darla pushes me aside and drives a knife into Endicott's throat, all the way to the hilt, twisting the blade, his carotid artery spurting like a hose.

"You shouldn't be doing this kind of t'ing, Miss Florence," she says. "You'll get yourself all dirty."

Hannah gets down from the wagon box with her boy in her arms. She puts the shawl over his head so he cannot see the world he is inheriting. The sky has darkened and the rain has increased, and we are left with soldiers whose days we have ended, our clothes and bodies flecked with their blood. I look for the sun but see only a silvery glint in the west. Then a strange phenomenon takes place, one I have seen only twice in my life. Small fish trapped inside a thundercloud have burst from the heavens and are raining down on our heads and shoulders, at first one or two, then steadily, striking the quick and the dead indifferently, flipping iridescently on the grass, their mouths and gills laboring for air, hoping to find their way back home.

I walk over to Hannah and stroke her little boy's head. I start to compliment her on her beautiful child, but instead I look at the glow in both their faces and say nothing.

EPILOGUE

In the year 1893, a self-exiled French painter stumbled onto a peculiar colony of Americans on a small island not far from Tahiti. The colony's inhabitants farmed and lived in harmony with one another on a plantation built by a Parisian aristocrat who was shot by his mistress, a black woman, who then shot herself and her children.

Many thought the house was haunted. It was made of white stucco, two-stories high, with a tile roof and ceiling-high windows and ventilated storm shutters and a view at night of both the ocean and the Southern Cross. The wind was warm and cold at the same time, and the ocean wine-dark at night and reminiscent of Ithacan legends or, in many ways, of an antebellum society far to the north. None of the community members used a last name. None spoke of their past lives.

The painter was intrigued by the mysterious nature of the group, because he had never seen one quite like it, and after asking permission of the parents he began to paint the children. The painter was afflicted with alcoholism and syphilis and an affinity for young girls, and he painted the members of the colony as much for his spiritual well-being as for his art and his finances, which were never good.

Most of his canvases were concerned with the natives on the islands, whose world was portrayed in brilliant, even jarring colors that would dominate the Impressionist movement and later open doors for artists like Picasso. But the strange group of Americans on the tiny island was different, primarily because they seemed more like wraiths than flesh and blood.

Some of them had jet black hair and gold skin, eyes the color of violets, and white teeth that never corroded. They slew no animals and grew and sold pineapples and broke coconuts on coral reefs and slept in the sun on table-flat rocks next to the ocean. The children were an amalgam of their parents, a strange, antithetical mixture whose commonality was the shared conviction that the Earth abideth forever and that Heaven was not a reward but the place in which we already live.

The artist not only painted but wrote about the colony on the island, and was obviously perturbed by the influence it had upon him. He was deeply committed to a sybaritic way of life, one that the cobblestone back streets of Arles had provided him, but the colony took away his desires and sometimes left him seated behind his easel in an aesthetic stupor. He was once quoted as saying, "My canvas is empty, my brushes dead in my hand, while the sun drums on the dark blue of the ocean. How can this place and these Occidental and African people be so beautiful and yet be so difficult to capture? The mountains are covered with green lichen, like velvet, the rocks atop wind-carved into gray obelisks, the disparate members of the colony a mystery. Why did I waste so much of my youth?"

The initial colony on the tiny island was one the Polynesians at first left alone, then grew to like. One man's face was terribly disfigured, but he seemed indifferent to the cruel joke fate had played on him. A woman who would probably scold John Calvin ran a school and taught the works of Charles Darwin and Emily Dickinson and Harriet Beecher Stowe. The leader of the colony, although he would not consider himself such, was a self-educated yeoman who seemed incredibly brave but humble among the simplest of his fellow human beings. His wife was a woman of color named Darla whom the artist would have liked to paint, but he did not trust his own desires and did not want to lose a hand.

The woman named Hannah was the one who seemed to have the greatest faith, although the painter did not think the term adequately described her view of the world. She did not *believe*. She simply *knew*. God was simply *there*, wherever *there* was.

Her son, Samuel, was a minister, but certainly not an ordinary one. He claimed his earliest memory was a roar of cannon fired by the devil himself, not because it killed men but because men enjoyed killing and made every excuse possible to do it over and over again, no matter what they said. In his view, they were the acolytes of Moloch and had no place inside a Christian church. His lungs had the thundering resonance of Quasimodo swinging on the bells of Notre Dame. His homily was seldom met with wild applause, although his words certainly got the attention of his congregation.

The one figure in the colony the artist could not tolerate was a red-bearded buccaneer who looked like he had slept with half his face on a hot stove and who wandered the cliffs railing at the seagulls until he fell seventy feet into a pool and was swatted out of it by the tail of a baby orca. From that point on the buccaneer considered himself an important Biblical character who deserved a place in the Louvre. The artist responded by saying his closest friend cut off his ear and gave it as a present to a prostitute in a brothel, but he, the one-eared artist, was a study in rationality compared to the madman buccaneer.

The artist fell on bad days and died in 1903. Most of the paintings from the colony disappeared inside the homes of wealthy collectors during the first quarter of the twentieth century. Then they appeared briefly in a showing by Hermann Goering in 1942 but were never seen again. They may be in a vault in Austria or a cave in Switzerland. Or maybe they were burned to ash in the firebombing of Dresden.

A cynic could conclude that evil had its way and took from us a pictorial record of Eden regained. But those of us who consider ourselves wayfaring strangers know better. We do not give credence to the dying of the light or the sorrow that can drive us to madness or the wickedness that thrives in the benighted. For us, vespers is the entryway into sunrise, the crossing of the Jordan no more consequential than sliding your bare foot into the foam rolling up a beach. It's that easy.

ACKNOWLEDGMENTS

I consider *Flags on the Bayou* my best work. But as every writer knows, the success of a book involves many people whose names are not on the book jacket. I'm fortunate to have an extraordinary group of people upon whom I depend almost daily. Some of them are old friends, some new. But without them, I would probably not have the career I have enjoyed for so many years, nor would I continue to have it. Better said, it's a great honor to be among them.

I would like to thank my editor and publisher at Grove Atlantic, Morgan Entrekin, and Zoe Harris and the team, Deb Seager, Natalie Church, Ian Dreiblatt, and Judy Hottensen; the people at the Spitzer Agency, Anne-Lise Spitzer, Mary Spitzer, Lukas Ortiz, and Kim Lombardini; Erin Mitchell, who was Pamala's best friend and knows how to fix every problem on earth; my film representative and legal adviser Penelope Glass; my children Jim and Andree and Alafair; and my wife Pearl, who has been my co-pilot for sixty-three years.

Lastly, I want to express my gratitude to the readers of my books. An author could not have greater support or readers with more humanity than the people who write to us in large numbers by email and on our Facebook page. The warmth and good will, the decency, the kindness toward me and among themselves is like none I have ever seen anywhere. It's a special club, one that has no equal, at least not that I have seen.

Put it this way, when you have friends like these, you lose consciousness of the inning because the scoreboard takes care of itself. I think it's a pretty good way to be.

One Big Union,
JLB